Written by my cousin

GH00983951

SEVEN GRIM
Love Stories

JACK DRUMGOLD

BALBOA
PRESS

A DIVISION OF HAY HOUSE

Copyright © 2016 Jack Drumgold.

All rights reserved. No part of this book may be used or reproduced by
any means, graphic, electronic, or mechanical, including photocopying,
recording, taping or by any information storage retrieval system
without the written permission of the author except in the case of
brief quotations embodied in critical articles and reviews.

Balboa Press books may be ordered through booksellers or by contacting:

Balboa Press
A Division of Hay House
1663 Liberty Drive
Bloomington, IN 47403
www.balboapress.com.au
1 (877) 407-4847

Because of the dynamic nature of the Internet, any web addresses or
links contained in this book may have changed since publication and
may no longer be valid. The views expressed in this work are solely those
of the author and do not necessarily reflect the views of the publisher,
and the publisher hereby disclaims any responsibility for them.

The author of this book does not dispense medical advice or prescribe the use
of any technique as a form of treatment for physical, emotional, or medical
problems without the advice of a physician, either directly or indirectly. The
intent of the author is only to offer information of a general nature to help
you in your quest for emotional and spiritual well-being. In the event you use
any of the information in this book for yourself, which is your constitutional
right, the author and the publisher assume no responsibility for your actions.

Any people depicted in stock imagery provided by Thinkstock are models,
and such images are being used for illustrative purposes only.
Certain stock imagery © Thinkstock.

Print information available on the last page.

ISBN: 978-1-5043-0283-8 (sc)
ISBN: 978-1-5043-0284-5 (e)

Balboa Press rev. date: 06/16/2016

INTRODUCTION

The most noble emotion, love, is biological in the living world. Maternal love is instinctive in both man and animals and ensures the survival of species. Love in the higher human sense has been the main concern of humans since long before the creation of the Venus of Willendorf and the trials of Psyche and Cupid. No doubt the supposedly knuckle dragging ancestors of the Neanderthals loved their wives and families as much as modern humans.

Even in those early years the record of the bones indicates that love sometimes had its grim side. From those ancient times down to Hank Williams 'Midnight Train' the story of man has been suffused with the emotion of love. No doubt religion emerged from conflicting fears, superstitions, love and the baser emotions.

In this small group of stories I try to portray the beauty and nobility of love in its various manifestations, from the basic urge to procreate to the maternal and paternal bonds that make us what we are. Love has been the concern of the greatest artists and writers in the world. The most iconic love stories by the world's greatest writers are always fraught with difficulty, even tragedy, before love prevails, if at all. The great tragedies, like Othello and Anna Karenina are love stories gone wrong.

My grim love stories are not very high on the scale of tragedy. But that aspect does help create the scene and paint the love in brighter colours, as it does so often.

Chapter One

THEO AND THE DANCING QUEEN

Clean, bright wheat straw in the calving pen lay as deep as the green rubber boots worn by the Acadian farmer, Roland Boudreau. He was solicitous of the comfort of his cows, especially at calving time and this particular cow, which had been born on the same day, almost to the hour, as his seven year old daughter Rosie. His brown, long face had a concerned expression as the cow struggled with a difficult calving. The calf was presenting with its head turned back, with potentially fatal consequences for both cow and calf. Roland regretted his large size and great thick arms and banana fingered hands, as he muttered inaudibly in French. Sunday was French day in the Boudreau family, mainly in honour of Roland, usually they conversed in English but Roland thought in French.

He looked anxiously out through the barn door and down the hill to the road, hoping to see the return of his seventeen year old son Marcus from school. The boy was also a big fellow but he retained the slim waist and limbs of youth. He had been helping with calving since he was twelve years old. Roland was just about to ask his wife Janice to come out to help when he saw Marcus running up the road in a T shirt and blue track pants. He was driving himself hard on the last eight hundred yards uphill, after running the five miles from school. He did this every Wednesday and Friday, training for an athletics carnival in the distant next spring.

Marcus burst into the kitchen of the old, shingled farmhouse, the sweat around his neck whipped into a white foam, like that seen on racehorses in the winners circle. His mother watched in deep admiration as he recovered his breath. Then she took a hand towel and soaked it under the cold tap and tenderly cleaned his face and neck with the refreshing cool cloth.

"I hate to tell you this dear, while you are so puffed out, your father is in a fit about Rosita, she's having trouble calving. I was just about to call the vet as you came in."

Marcus recovered quickly from his exertion. He nodded and drank a glass of water as he rinsed off his arms and hands in the kitchen sink. "Thanks mum, I'll hop out and see what I can do. I'm getting better, that's the third time I beat the school bus home." The school bus followed a circuitous route dropping off students but it had become his performance benchmark.

He grinned and kissed her and went out to the barn straight away. As he stripped off his wet shirt and slipped on a clean pair of rubber boots from the boot rack he glanced at his father and said "Head?" He knew what to do and was pleased to see the cow had not been long in labour.

Normally, when delving inside a cow he would put on a plastic sleeve but this time he washed his arm with soap and disinfectant and a cotton calving rope with a noose that he slipped over his hand. Between contractions he was able to reach along the neck of the calf, but then she heaved another great contraction and squashed his arm against her pelvis. As she relaxed he was just able to slip the noose over the top jaw of the calf and nod to his father to pull it firm. Then he partially withdrew his arm and at the next relaxation he was able to push on the chest of the calf, back into the cow, using a grip on her tail with his left hand for purchase. Soon it was deep enough that his father was able to gently pull the head around into alignment with the birth canal, in the proper position on top of the forelegs.

"Great dad! That was easy. It's a good thing I'm getting faster by the day and got here just in time."

"Yeah thanks son. Another hour and we could have been in trouble. You go take a shower now and rest up. I don't know why you are killing yourself with all this runnin'. Are you gonna win a prize or something?"

"Sure dad. Greg Harboard told mum if I run in two races next spring, even if I come last, he'll give me an A on my year twelve report for Physical Education. If I have all A s I might get a scholarship."

Roland wasn't sure how important that was; he didn't concern himself with his children's education. Neither did Janice. She was just happy to see good report cards and did not get involved in dealing with teachers or school politics. She had been angry when the phys/ed teacher gave Marcus a C minus for the subject and when invited to an evening of parent and teacher interviews she made an unusual visit to the school. All the teachers were delighted to meet her and congratulate her on the fine performance of Marcus in their subjects. She steeled herself for the interview with Greg Harboard and hoped she could avoid displaying her emotion.

"I'm so glad to meet you Mrs Boudreau. I'm sure you have enjoyed meeting the staff. Everyone adores Marcus," he said.

"Apparently so Mr Harboard, yourself excepted. How come you gave him a C minus or failed mark for physical education last year?"

"Please call me Greg, Mrs Boudreau. I too admire Marcus but I have to be truthful in my marking. A math teacher can't give a basketball star an A if he can't do math. The boy made no serious effort in my subject. He laughs all the way through wrestling class, he can't hit the backboard in basketball and he didn't even put his name down for hockey trials.

'I have played shinny with the kids on Fishers Pond in the winter and I know Marcus is a fine skater and loves to play hockey. He is indifferent to physical education as a subject. It's all a bit of a lark to him. I'm disappointed by that"

"Greg he is a farm boy. This summer he made thirty thousand bales of hay and ran the crew that loaded them on wagons and stacked them in the barn. Some of your champion sports boys came to help but quit after the first day, because their fingers were sore. Take a look at his hands. They show how physical he is. He doesn't care about pitching a ball through a hoop like some bored kid in a ghetto with nothing else to do."

"I take your point Mrs Boudreau. There are other children like Marcus who work very hard on the farm. It concerns me a bit. I feel there is an element of exploitation of children. They need a chance to be kids, not workers, at such a young age. I hope you aren't offended by that."

Janice thought about the comment and put herself in his position. He did have to do his work honestly and her children did work hard at home, even little Rosie feeding the calves and Simon doing morning milking till the hired man arrived.

"Yes Greg, call me Janice if you like, you must be honest in your marking and my kids do work. But they get wages into their bank account every month and I'll bet there's not a boy in the school with a better bank account than Marcus.

'I'll tell him he must have a go at something in year twelve. He certainly can't meet the training for hockey but I'll urge him to be more serious about your subject and try to get his only C up to a B."

"Splendid Janice! He has the potential of an athlete about him, more than most boys, I'm sure he can do something. There is a track and field carnival in the spring term and if Marcus can enter a couple of races I'll guarantee him an A even if he comes last. He is such a fine student I don't want to be responsible for a blemish on his year twelve report."

"Well Greg you know what he's like; he won't enter if he might come second. If you guarantee him an A he'll start training tomorrow."

They had a little more conversation about her younger son, Simon. He was doing well in sports and would be unlikely to have the same problem as Marcus, at least for awhile. But Marcus had other problems.

A host of concerns were bothering Marcus Boudreau. Most of them related to sex.

He was seventeen years old and stood six feet two inches and weighed one hundred and eighty pounds. Surging through his strapping young frame were hormones that caused him to get spontaneous erections that he feared others might notice. Sometimes he would wake up with his pyjama pants flooded with sticky semen. Not from erotic dreams that he might have enjoyed but just for the devil of it. He was embarrassed one morning when Janice found him washings his PJs in the laundry and he had to explain how this phenomenon sometimes caught him by surprise. She smiled and gave her son a reassuring cuddle.

"Marcus, all my brothers had the same problem. It's a boy thing. At least you're not making smutty jokes about it. Your hormones are trying too hard. Don't worry about it, just pitch your pyjamas in the laundry basket and get a clean set. It could be worse you know; imagine if you were a girl?"

"If I were a girl I'd want to be just like you and Rosie. Thanks mum, it is a bit embarrassing."

His problems didn't end there. The whole subject of girls consumed him. Because he was such a math nerd and scholar he was not regarded as one of the cool guys. Nor was he a sports star or a party goer or drinker. He heard other guys telling stories about this or that girl and the things they did in the back seat of the family car. He believed them too. Sometimes he couldn't open the door of his locker because some couple were necking furiously against it and he was too shy to ask them to move over and endure the hateful look on their flushed, hot faces.

The most graphic tales concerned Linda Kennedy who lived on the farm next door. Linda had been promiscuous since she was fifteen years old and although they had known each other since infancy she was almost a total stranger socially, even though she had been great help last summer getting the hay under cover. She was built like a movie star and he had heard guys tell about her exploits in cabins in the woods and by the lake. Apparently she could hook her big toes in the waist band of a guy's jeans and yank them down as soon as he released his belt buckle.

With scenes like this in his mind he could hardly say hello to her on the school bus in the mornings. Linda remained cheerful and blissfully ignorant of her reputation and the indiscreet gossip of her boyfriends. She just accepted his geaky persona.

Marcus felt as helpless as the character in "The Catcher In The Rye", Holden Caulfield. He wanted to warn Linda that her boyfriends were indiscreet but she might indignantly demand details of what he had heard.

The other people on the school bus were from a farm a mile down the road, the Degraffe girls, the five daughters of Peter

Degraffe and his wife Caroline. All were beautiful fair haired girls ranging downward from seventeen year old Gracie to Jetka who was the best friend of Rosie. Gracie had loved Marcus since she was five years old and no one else dared try to sit next to him on the yellow bus. They were calm quiet girls and Gracie was as much a scholar as Marcus. The only boy in the family was Theo, who had suffered brain damage at birth and didn't go to school.

All the families were close and Marcus was often at the Degraffe house, especially in the winter months when the snow was flying. Since infancy he had played with Theo and like his sisters, Theo's retardation was accepted as part of life.

Peter had three TV sets in his den and a great black stove. Other farmers were often there, watching the ice hockey games and drinking and smoking pipes and cigars. Peter was of the hearty drinking, smoking and cussing variety of Dutchman but had good friendships with the God fearing, clean living type who wouldn't even haul hay on a Sunday, even if wet weather was likely. On 'Hockey Night In Canada' Theo would lie on his father's chest and punch the air with joy when the game caller yelled "He shoots, he scores" in a rising cadence.

Marcus loved those evenings and Sundays playing hockey on Fisher's Pond with Peter and his girls and other neighbours. They could play for hours until darkness fell at around four and he would go home to do chores and give his father a spell from evening milking. Peter had always been the fun dad for local children.

One day, in a fit of erotic imagination, Marcus went to town and bought a Chev Bel Air sedan with a capacious back seat in blue leather, but he had yet to get a girl into that thing, except for Rosie and the Degraffe girls. On a weekend he took his brother and sister and three of the girls to a movie over in Peterthorpe. It was a scary movie about a shark so they didn't take Theo;

he had a tendency to pee his pants when upset or frightened. "Jaws" was indeed a horror movie and Rosie buried her face in Gracie's jacket whenever it was too horrifying. The other little one's handled it better. Simon said he didn't even want to go in the lake next summer.

All the best laid plans for seduction that Marcus came up with ended up in trips like that, with family and not a siren in sight. The night of the shark movie Rosie had nightmares and ran out of her room across the hall into Marcus bedroom. Her parent's room was at the end of a long, dark hallway. Under the thick carpet, boards creaked and groaned and outside in the wind, things went flap and bumped in the night; Marcus was safe and closer. As she crept in beside him shivering she whispered

"Marcus I'm scared."

This was not an unusual situation. Simon crept in with Marcus sometimes when he was a little one with disturbing dreams; so he just cuddled her and they went back to sleep.

The spring and summer months were over and still the back seat of the Chev remained unchristened. The annual Thanksgiving Ball was coming up at the village hall and his imagination turned, like birds in spring, to thoughts of love. He drove his car down to the village and in silvery moonlight parked in a shadowy spot along the river bank, his imagination going at fever pitch. As he approached the lighted hall and heard the fiddle and banjo of the Benoit family playing country music he was reminded of Robbie Burn's poem about Mary Morison being the fairest of them all. He enjoyed English Literature at school and felt a kindred spirit in Burns preoccupation with love.

In his best blue jeans and new, red cambric shirt he strolled into the hall. The Degraffe girls were standing with their brother Theo, nodding and bobbing to the music. He looked frantically around for other girls on whom to make an impression. His spirit drooped as there were none he felt confident in approaching. As if by a miracle Linda Kennedy drifted up beside him and smiled mockingly over her shoulder. "Hi Marcus. Have you taken up dancing then, after all these years?"

"I was thinking of something a little more exciting Linda" he said flirtatiously.

Her burst of laughter shook his attempt at small talk back into its shell and he could venture nothing further. Linda also bobbed to the music, her fair curls bouncing and her round young breasts heaving under her blue cashmere sweater, like kittens under a bed sheet. Marcus felt a choking desire to try again and blew it immediately.

"Linda, why don't you have a dance with poor Theo? You've known him all your life, not like these other girls who just see a stumbling idiot."

"Are you kidding Marcus? People would laugh like hell at me. I would at a party but not here."

Marcus felt a burst of anger and frustration, mostly with his social awkwardness.

"Fuck you Linda, I always took you for a kind hearted person."

She was astonished to hear Marcus swear. Everyone did, but not Marcus.

"Ok neighbour I'll do it for you. Is there anything else you'd like?" she said, with a knowing sneer. She could tell what he was thinking and knew about his big fancy car, but she had all the boys she could handle without a lanky nerd like him.

Linda marched across to Theo and was about to sweep him out onto the dance floor when the band announced they were taking a break and would put on an Abba record.

The first song was 'The Dancing Queen', her favourite, so she grabbed Theo and led him unsteadily out onto the floor. She held him close to stop him from falling and swept around

9

in circles with her breasts squeezed up close to Theo. He was smiling giddily, overwhelmed by the whirling motion, the music, the perfume on her neck, her warm body and the confusing arousal in his jeans, that she soon became aware of and pushed against as they turned. Round and round they went as his sisters clapped and others stopped to admire. Linda became aware that she had become a star from dancing with Theo. His face was red and sweating and he was squeezing himself up to Linda like an amorous puppy. She realised that he was tremendously turned on and was glad when the song ended and she could release him to his sisters. As Linda broke free from Theo's clinging embrace Gracie realised that her brother was in a little trouble with his emotions. She tried to coax him to a seat and told one of the girls to get him a can of pop. Theo was struggling to break free and looking frantically around for Linda but she had seen her boyfriend and was in his pickup already, heading for his cabin.

Marcus saw the girls leave with Theo but didn't realise how upset the boy was.

Later on his brother Simon showed up with his scrawny buddies, with their caps on backwards and the tongues of their unlaced yellow boots hanging out, like thirsty hounds They were soon in conversation with girls two grades below Marcus. He turned back to watch the dancers, feeling like a total misfit and wondering why he was so gauche. He felt someone grab his elbow and turned to see Simon with a grin on his face that looked as though it might have had some alcoholic supplement.

"Marcus, have a look at old Lorimer Clements dancing around with his wife. He's got his hand up like a goddamned mailbox flag."

It was true. Lorimer was a little apple grower with a big wife. He had his right hand on her ample haunches and she had her left on his back. With her right hand she hung onto Lorimer's thumb and his palm was up and rigid, like a lollipop lady stopping traffic at a school crossing. They were a picture of total concentration.

The analogy dispelled the sombre mood of Marcus and he enjoyed the rest of the evening but drove home alone. His father wasn't well that winter and with the extra farm work, study and training for his A in phys/ed he had no social life and the Chev stayed in the shed, covered in snow that blew under the eaves and door. On in late January on a bitter cold day, with snow swirling he walked down to visit the Degraffe family. Gracie had begged him to come by for a break.

Everyone was pleased to see him. Gracie brought him a mug of coffee with a shot of rum in it and a couple of prickly Dutch donuts rolled in castor sugar. The stove was glowing and a couple of other guys came in for a visit. Outside in the gathering dusk Theo was propped against an empty apple bin with his Christmas binoculars stuck to his face as he peered up the hill at something. When it was too dark to see he came in shivering and covered in snow. He kicked off his felt lined boots and Gracie hung his parka on a hook with his mitts and tuque, then he went over to his father and climbed on his lap like a three year old. Peter cuddled him as he shivered and Marcus asked quietly, "What was he looking at out there in the snow?"

"Ever since the Thanksgiving Ball he has been looking up the hill to catch a glimpse of Linda as she does the chores around the calf hutches. That's why I bought him the binoculars for Christmas." As she said it Gracie was rubbing the frozen hands of her brother and Peter was gently stroking his son's neck and ears.

In a voice choked with emotion Peter suddenly said, "Wouldn't that be something, if he's fallen in love?"

Marcus saw tears streaming down Peter's face and felt a frightening sense of guilt that he had encouraged Linda to dance with Theo and she had made such a joke of arousing him. She still thought it was funny. He resolved to tell her how serious it was for Theo's family, but it wasn't her fault. Gracie whispered that since that night he wanted a turntable and an ABBA record and he drove the family crazy by playing it all the time in his room and turning up the volume when Dancing Queen came round.

Marcus stayed for an hour and then went home in the dark, leaning into the wind and driving snow, glad of the yard light by the dairy to keep him on track. He hardly noticed the weather, his mind was so full of regret for his stupidity in urging Linda on to Theo. With a troubled heart he wondered if Theo felt the same silly urges that had prompted him to buy the second hand Chev. As he recalled the years he had spent growing up with Theo he became emotional and his salty tears were diluted by the snow melting on his face. He recalled the many times that Theo had shown his capacity for love and delight as he played with puppies and piglets and when he was brought to tears of joy by the feel of a new duckling in his gentle hands. Peter DeGraffe's grief for his son's future weighed on the troubled mind of Marcus Boudreau and he was still upset when he arrived home. Rosie and Simon were out in the barn. Janice could see that her son was unhappy. Without any reserve he told her how bad he felt for Peter and Theo and his sense of guilt for urging Linda to dance with Theo. "Peter is so sad mum; I cried all the way home. You know what Peter's like, always the happiest man you could meet. It broke my heart to see him cry."

Janice hugged him and loved him for his tender feelings. "I'm sure Linda will break a lot more hearts than poor Theo's darling. Time heals all so don't blame yourself or Linda for an act of kindness. Theo will be ok and so will Peter."

As the spring crept in reluctantly through March Roland recovered and Marcus was able to devote his time to study and training for the races he had vowed to enter. Gracie Degraffe was doing just as well in her studies and was captain of the girl's basketball team. Both were the top students and had been for a long time. They were interviewed by the Principal who told them they had been invited to McGill University to check out the campus and the courses available. The best students from other schools had also been invited and contingent upon top grade twelve results some scholarships might be available.

One sunny spring day, with the grainy snow under the nearby spruce trees dripping into the ground, they found themselves alone by the running track and were talking about the exciting prospects of university and how they might do in the track meet. Suddenly Gracie turned resolutely to Marcus, her fair complexion blushing a deep pink, even to the roots of her silky fair hair.

"Marcus, have you ever had sex with a girl?" she asked directly.

The question took him by surprise. He had known her so long they were almost like siblings. He wasn't bothered by it as much as she was in asking it. He grinned, looked down into her radiant blue eyes and said, "No, but I've been thinking about it for a hell of a long time."

Gracie burst into laughter, her embarrassment gone. "Me too! How dopey we are Marcus. I've been having ideas about this trip to McGill. Why don't we do it right when we go to Montreal? I don't want this fumbling about with rubbers in the back seats of cars or ants up my bum in the woods. I want to go on the pill and do it in a warm bed, behind a locked door far from home with someone I love. That's what keeps me awake at night."

Marcus raised his big hand for her to slap. "It's a deal Gracie. Why I've got a hard on just thinking about it." She grabbed the collar of his parka and pulled him down to a spine tingling first kiss as she groped his jeans with her right hand to verify his statement. Marcus was indeed as thick as a brick and she jumped back in mock alarm.

"You have so, you great lump. It's gonna be hard to wait Marcus. Do you think we should?"

"Sure, you always have the best ideas. We've known each other since we were babies Gracie. What's a few more weeks?"

That evening Rosie whispered in her mother's ear that Gracie had kissed Marcus on the school bus. Janice felt her heart skip a beat and a tear of joy welled up at what might be in God's plan. She cuddled her little one and whispered, "Thank you for the secret Rosie."

Marcus ran in all the races from the one hundred to the fifteen and he won the four hundred and eight hundred and got his straight A s. Gracie won the long jump and like Johnny Cash in his song about school days, they graduated with straight A s in love, on the trip to Montreal.

Chapter Two

SIASSI STANLEY BITES THE APPLE OF TEMPTATION

I first met Siassi Stanley when his business career was just beginning. He had left his home village on the far west coast of New Britain and found employment with a logging contractor who was cutting great hardwood trees for sale to the Japanese. He was a hard worker and was soon a foreman with a crew of men to supervise. They cut and hauled through the muddy jungle tracks, huge logs which they stacked up on the beach until a ship stopped by to hoist them aboard, when they had been floated out alongside with floats to prevent them sinking.

The Japanese were difficult to deal with, as sugar growers, pork producers and other suppliers had found in many countries. A contract was honoured only when it was agreeable to the Japanese. If prices changed in their favour they would want to renegotiate the contract. When they saw the huge pile of logs stacked up on the beach they knew the logger had spent a lot of money on labour and machinery and urgently needed to be paid to meet his mounting debt at the development bank. The Australian logger refused to accept less than the price on his contract. The ship left and the logger went under. He didn't care.

His loan was on the basis of a signed contract. He had done what he said he would do and he told the bank they now owned the logs and they 'could deal with the Jap's if they wanted to.'

By that time Stanley, or as the natives called him, Senlee, had learned the lay of the land. He knew the kind of goods and services people needed in the isolated villages and missions and on the scattered plantations, which often had large numbers of native workers with wages they wanted to spend. He started trading along the coast of the Bismarck Sea with an outrigger canoe and sourcing his goods from a lonely Chinese trade store. His orders for lanterns and kerosene and drums of petrol grew, along with coloured cloth and cheap clothing, footballs, razor blades, tobacco, mirrors and talcum powder.

His supplier began to trust him and in return he bought from Stanley the bags of cocoa and copra and shell that he picked up. Gradually his canoes grew bigger until he had a sixty foot dug out with a decked outrigger and a fifty horsepower Johnson outboard motor.

In other, more prosperous and fertile areas a fleet of small coastal ships serviced the outstations, but along the north coast of New Britain there was insufficient trade at the time to make it worth their while. Stanley's little operation thrived because it was simple and cheap and reliable. I had increasing reason to be along that coast doing my duty as an agricultural extension worker helping to build fermenteries and cocoa driers and introducing little groves of robusta coffee. The department was pushing coffee but the villagers liked cocoa. Some had worked on plantations and were familiar with the crop. Gradually the output grew and increasing cash flow raised the demand for all the basics that Stanley supplied via his Chinese mate.

Government staff from health and native affairs as well as people like me and forest surveyors were regular customers of Stan. Instead of slogging along on foot through the mud and creeks and steep forests along the coast we could travel in comfort on his big canoe with all our gear and staff. Mission stations, mostly Catholic or Lutheran, used him all the time and his canoe was loaded at school holidays with kids going back to their village for the break. There was a major cocoa project to be set up for a village with a progressive chief and Stanley came way out of his range to pick us up off the beach to take us there.

In that camp we were a half mile from a saw mill, on the beach of a sheltered bay. At night canoes with lanterns on the prow used to drift in the bay fishing. In the still, humid air you could hear people talking and occasionally plucking a ukulele, even from a mile out. It was the only recreation available and I mentioned it to Menias; the leading man and cook in my crew. He agreed it would be nice to have some fresh fish and promised to talk to the locals about a small canoe. The following evening, in my habitual routine, I was smoking my pipe after another boring supper of bully beef curry and rice. Menias slid into view with a benzene lantern, pumped up and casting a wide pool of white light.

"Canoe he stap" he said, with a grin, as he handed me a reel of line and a tin of beach worms he had skillfully dug up. There was no doubt about old Menias, he personified the saying *No sooner said than done*. I had on just a pair of football shorts and was ready to get wet if necessary. The sea was as warm as the air anyway and the air seemed as humid as the sea. I followed Menias down to the beach in my shorts with a belt carrying a bamboo sheath for my bush knife. I could have done without the shorts but would have felt naked without the knife.

There in the water was a good sized canoe, about twelve feet long with a split bamboo deck on the outrigger. A woman stood in the water holding it steady while Menias tied the lamp to a stick lashed to the outrigger and propped up at about forty five degrees above the prow. The lamp cast a wide pool of light around the canoe and revealed a young girl, sitting amidships holding a paddle. She looked like one of the kids from the mission across the bay. Her big hair was coral bleached to a gingery blond and she wore a red laplap round her waist. She gave a beaming white smile as I stepped into the stern of the canoe, facing her with the outrigger on my left in the usual way. As Menias pushed us off the beach she turned her back to me and we both began to paddle out into the bay. I wanted to find a deep hole to drop my line with its stone weight, in the hope I could haul up some red emperor, as I used to do in Blanche Bay when I was at home near Rabaul.

As a rule local children from a very early age became expert at fishing so I had full confidence in the girl up front. I asked her if she knew where the deep part of the bay was, "Maria you savvy long wonem hap solwara, im go down below tru."

"Nawonem" she said, confirming that she knew where to find the deeps. We paddled on for a considerable time until she shipped her paddle and stood up, with a thin bamboo spear in her hand which had a fan of wire points on the end. I held up my paddle as the canoe glided silently. I watched the graceful girl as she stood with her left foot up on the edge of the hull and her spear held ready to strike, her right hand near the end while her left hand supported and aimed the centre toward the target.

Some spotted mackerel swam into the pool of light and lingered, as if astonished to find such a phenomenon. The girl struck with power and accuracy and then nearly tumbled into the water as she reached over the side to grab the pole with a briefly struggling fish jammed in the wire prongs. A good fish, about a foot and a half long was scraped off on one of the thwarts and lay flapping on the bottom of the canoe. I clapped her success. She had struck the fish with supreme accuracy, an inch or two behind the gills. "Im nau Maria, you one true" I yelled. She was wet and laughing as she started paddling again and now looking closely at the pool of light for more success. She speared two more fish before we stopped to try my deep line, baited with sand worms.

We sat silently on the glass smooth water in the moonlight. The pressure in the lantern was dropping but the pool of light revealed a huge hammer head shark circling us on the edge of the light. She could tell I was a little worried and as the shark sank away into the deep blue she smiled and said, "Him too painim kaikai." He too was looking for food. I hoped it wouldn't be my fish, if I caught any. Soon I felt a tug on my line and I tossed Maria the reel to wind in while I hauled up as fast as I could, for fear of losing the fish. Soon the wriggling stopped and the fish became a dead weight. As I hauled it over the side it was clear that the rapid decompression from depth had killed the fish. Its eyes were popped right out and a sort of bladder protruded from its mouth. "You one masta" yelled Maria, mimicking my congratulations on her first fish. We hauled up another four within the hour and decided to head back.

Black clouds were forming and lightening was flashing out at sea, behind the mission lights on the point. We made it back to shore before the rain started. As we hauled up the canoe I thought we would divide up the fish and go our separate ways. My men were ecstatic about a feed of fish. They stoked up the fire on the cook house floor and started scraping the scales off the red emperor with an empty bully beef tin. The fish were quickly wrapped in leaves and covered in hot coals. Heavy rain pounded on the palm leaf thatch and fell in a curtain around us. Maria and her mother had invited themselves to supper and soon we were all squatting close round the fish, laid out on a couple of banana leaves. We used our hands to help ourselves.

Followed by a mug of black tea and a pipe I was content. Bully beef curry with fresh fish for dessert was about as good as it gets in my line of work. Before I went to bed Maria's mum cadged a pinch of my Erinmore Mixture for her pipe and I left them to it. The next morning, over breakfast I thanked Menias for organising the fishing.

"That little Maria is a smart kid Menias. She can chuck a fish spear as well as old Isidore, the Arawe boat skipper." Menias gave a big grin and said "Yes, tasol im mary pamuk true." This was a bit of a shock. She looked about fifteen years old. He went on to explain that she was a habitual prostitute and her mother was her pimp and manager. He said that she serviced the whole area for everyone. "Mipella too" he grinned. They had all had a turn with her after supper and paid her mother. All the guys at the sawmill were her regular clients on pay days and plantation workers too, who had to save up several of theirs; apparently she wasn't cheap. They could have the mother cheaper but Maria was in demand.

Later, on a courtesy visit to the Catholic Mission the priest told me about her activities. I kept quiet about fishing and my blokes. He probably knew anyway, they don't miss much gossip, not to mention what they pick up in the confessional booth.

A few days later we hired Siassi Stanley to shift us along to the next project along the Bismarck shore. He showed up without his usual crewman but he had Maria on board. She greeted us like old friends before racing into the creek for a freshwater wash, like a grade three kid dashing out of school into the sea at recess time. She was quite handy on the canoe and as we sped west a hundred yards from shore she stood in the prow like a little brown goddess, with the wind flapping the red laplap round her waist. Siassi Stanley, on the tiller, watched her with a dreamy smile of contentment on his face. Suddenly she raised her arm in the air and turned around with her finger to her lips.

Up ahead she had spotted a turtle on the surface. Stanley cut the motor and we drifted silently forward as he grabbed a strong pig spear with a coil of line attached. He crept carefully forward in bare feet, over our boxes and equipment. He poised himself like Queequeg, Moby Dick's harpooner. His tall, lithe body was like a coiled spring as he turned to me and indicated that he wanted me to paddle quietly to maintain way on the canoe. We glided up almost onto the turtle until he thrust down with tremendous force with the steel tipped spear. The point pierced the shell of the animal with a sharp crack. A mighty threshing ensued as the turtle tried to dive, while all hands clung to the stout nylon cord. Stanley sprang overboard and a rope noose was secured to the turtle and we headed for the shore to load it onto the outrigger platform. The struggle and the swell almost upset the canoe and Maria fell backwards into the hull, momentarily losing her red laplap in the fall. Her legs flew apart in front of everyone, before she recovered herself by hooking her ankles on the sides of the canoe and springing back up with athletic grace to recover her scanty garment.

Menias heaved with laughter at the mishap and shouted in bawdy delight, "Im nau, kaikai melon." The other guys in my crew roared with laughter, slapping their thighs at his comment. Maria too screamed with laughter, completely unabashed by her brief loss of dignity. I was about to grin myself when, to my surprise, I saw that Stanley's expression was as dark as thunder and a shadow of fear had erased the pratfall joke from Menias's face.

By the time we reached the shore, things had calmed down. The other men realised how cross Stanley was and they fell silent. They were as surprised as I was; surely Stanley could not be upset at the incident? Maria paddled nonchalantly up to the beach and jumped overboard as we nosed up onto the sand. Here we hauled the turtle ashore and then crowded around to lift and lash it, on its back, to the outrigger deck. At sea again with the motor running we continued our voyage, but in a subdued and quiet mood, with a dour looking Stanley at his post on the tiller.

After we disembarked I paid him and asked to be picked up again in ten days time and taken back up the coast to Kilinwata Bay where a government workboat would take us back to Rabaul. As the canoe headed back up the coast the girl stood in the bow waving to us and the unfortunate turtle did the same, waving his great yellow flippers in an instinctive and futile attempt to swim. The animal would no doubt wind up in the freezer at the Chinese trade store and maybe later in turtle soup at the ChungChing Restaurant in Chinatown.

Stanley had not recovered his carefree nature, even ten days later when he had collected us and brought us alongside the *Tilburra* to go back to Rabaul. I paid him and told him I would be back along the coast in December and would send a radio message to the mission about when I would need him again. Maria waved to us as they sped away but Menias didn't wave back. Stanley had his eye on him until they were well away. Menias looked at me with troubled eyes.

"Man here, him he long long true" he said sadly. I could see his point, there is indeed something sad and mad about a jealous man.

It would be the last time I saw Siassi Stanley.

That night I was glad to be clean, dry, shaven and enjoying a few beers in the bar of the RSL Club in Rabaul with some old friends. When they left I was thinking about the events of the trip and what Menias meant when he said Siassi Stanley was crazy.

He had fallen hopelessly in love with the whore of the Bismarck Sea.

Sitting alone at the bar thinking over the past few days I suddenly realised I had been the victim of a subtle trick. Menias had probably arranged the canoe and sand worms and fishing line and the dalliance of himself and his friends with Maria, all in the one package, paid for out of the generous expense allowance I gave him to run my house and camps. I started to giggle, knowing I had been deceived by a clever plot. The barman, aware that I'd only had three schooners of beer, grinned and said "What's the joke mate?"

One can't admit to being dopey, enough people know it already, so I just said,

"I think I have met a promising politician."

A couple of months later I got on the radio sched' and asked the clerk at the Catholic Mission if he could contact Stanley to pick me up at Kilinwata Bay the next Monday. I had scheduled time for our follow up work along that coast.

"Sorry too much" he said, "Stanley him die finish. He hangimup with his own leather belt, two weeks ago."

It was dreadfully sad news. When I told my guys a few minutes later they were shaken to the core. Almost as much as the time when I told them President Kennedy had been shot. On that occasion they had all burst into tears of anxiety and grief. It was unbelievable that someone would shoot 'Number One blong America'. It had seemed like the beginning of the end to them; me too, in my heart.

Menias dropped his head sadly and groaned, "Him fashion blong ol Siassi man." He went on to explain that it was not unusual for men of Stanley's tribe to commit suicide in moments of stress. The crew declined to come with me and I had to pick different men to accompany me to that area. I don't know if it was grief, or fear that Stanley's spirit was still angry with them for laughing at Maria's embarrassing tumble or because he found out they had all copulated voluptuously with his beloved.

Sometimes people make too many connections. She wasn't involved with Stan when they met her but still they felt bad about his suicidal misery. "Maybe she told him about us," said Menias; tortured by shame that he may have contributed to the despair of Stanley.

She was still there, doing the rounds with her mother on pay days but she avoided us this time. I asked the headman of the village nearby if he knew what had happened to leave Siassi so distraught that he would hang himself. He told me that Maria had grown tired of riding around on his canoe and went ashore to join her mother. She had missed her valuable daughter and promptly arranged assignations for Maria with anyone with money to pay. Stanley, insanely jealous, followed her everywhere and neglected his business. He became derisively know as a "Dog man." One who wanders in the shadow of his wife, like a faithful dog. Increasingly angry with his presence and restrictions Maria had turned to him in a fury one day when she was trying to creep into the forest to meet some men.

"Bihainim me long wonem, you like kaikai pekpek blong me?"

Why do you follow me? She had said. Do you want to eat my shit?

Her customers, from the sawmill, were hiding in the bushes and had heard her scream the insult. They had trouble suppressing their laughter but they too were afraid of Stanley's jealousy, though he wasn't a violent man. He left her immediately and went back to his house on the beach and promptly hung himself with his wide black belt from the round beam over the entrance.

Such is the power of love, jealousy, obsession and shame. A good man was lost. Some societies would blame the intrinsic evil of women. Others would say she was a free spirit and he was dangerous and over possessive. Maybe there is a degree of truth in all comments but the most awful truth is that such situations are often with us. Possibly if Stanley had not been such a kind and honourable man he would have been able to cut her loose and not look back. Or he could have paid the mother until they both got used to him and had formed a more solid relationship. Some might even say he had an inflated ego which couldn't survive being punctured.

My feeling was that he paid the price for isolation from his own people at the western end of the island. If he had been working for a white man he would have been sent home for a minimum of three months every two years. This was one of the important laws relating to native labour which ensured that workers maintained their kinship obligations, land rights entitlements and marriage prospects. As a self employed entrepreneur he had neglected the bedrock of his mental health.

At least he only harmed himself.

Maria refused to accept any responsibility for his death.

"Asua blong im," she said. "Mi no boatscrew blong im."

It was his decision, I wasn't his boat's crew.

Chapter Three

THE UNINVITED GUEST

After the second world war as part of the United Nations Mandate, Australia was charged with the responsibility to prepare Papua New Guinea for Independence from colonial administration. This required development of all the trappings of a western capitalist economy to make it a brown copy of the western governments that drew up the mandate. The indigenous strengths of village level democracy, land use, food self sufficiency and matrilineal inheritance were not regarded as valuable basic building blocks of a modern nation. The push was for business and cash economy.

Universal education was a requirement as well as agricultural and industrial development to accompany the rule of law and the early stages of western style democracy based on the concept of one man one vote. The heavy lifting of evolution from savagery and sorcery to civilization had largely been done by brave Christian missionaries by nineteen ten. Often these missionaries were local or other South Pacific people.

Australia began the task with vigour and foresight. The Australian School of Pacific Administration (ASOPA) was set up in Australia to train a civil service. A crash course for educators was also established to flood the country with school teachers so that every child could go to school up to grade six, by which time high schools would be up and running followed by agricultural colleges and universities.

Hundreds of Australians with a minimum grade twelve education were recruited and trained for six months to deliver the E course to Primary T Schools. The whole plan was very well done by Australia and all deadlines were met.

The agricultural development proceeded along similar lines and an army of men fanned out across the country setting up agricultural extension stations charged with introducing a cash crop economy and training people to grow the crops appropriate for the area to which they were assigned. I was one of the people who concentrated on the development of cocoa, coffee and rubber as well as some livestock production. In high, mountain regions trials were done to develop tea and cool climate vegetables and huge areas of empty land were set aside for the development of oil palm; a crop that was rapidly taking over from rubber in other countries as synthetic rubber depressed natural rubber prices. The natural competence of New Guineans as horticulturists and subsistence farmers inspired optimism for cash cropping.

On one occasion I had a memorable encounter with an American from the New Tribes Mission. We were travelling on a copra boat from Rabaul to Kavieng at the top of New Ireland. He asked me what my job entailed. He shook his head sadly when I explained that my task was to help people develop cash crops to improve their standard of living.

"These people don't need cash," he said. "What they need is peace of mind, and that's what we're here to give them."

I proffered no reply. He would have disagreed if I told him the native people I knew were already the most contented and happy folk I had ever met. The guy saw a giant cockroach dash across the galley table and his peace of mind was shot for the rest of the trip.

Later, it was no surprise when I was instructed to survey a large tract of land inland from the north coast of New Britain and make a soil and topography map of the area. It was a daunting task as the wettest part of the year had just begun and the whole area was under untouched rain forest. Progress was required and with three unfortunate native workers to help I was dispatched by government workboat to the north coast with boxes of supplies and equipment and some mildewed maps from which to take my bearings. Arrangements had been made with a plantation manager in that area to supply me with accommodation plus any other assistance required, for which he would bill the department. My boss gave me a few tips on how to proceed and warned me to be ready if I couldn't stand my host.

"He claims he was one of the Hitler 'yoof' John, I'm told he is a tiresome arsehole and those who know him wish they didn't."

Thus I embarked in better heart. Optimistic that despite my host, at least I would not be sleeping in a mosquito infested bush hut of bamboo and sago thatch, eating brown rice and bully beef curry for weeks at a time, as leaches and tinea corroded my body in the daily torrential rain.

The outward passage from Rabaul, against the swells of the north west monsoon and the endless rain, proceeded with barely a glimpse of the sun between noon and dusk. When at last we pulled up alongside the plantation jetty I anticipated a warm welcome as we had hauled on board several great Spanish mackerel on the troll lines deployed behind the *Tilburra;* until sharks arrived and chomped every fish as soon as it hooked on.

Alas there was no one there as we stepped onto the jetty late in the afternoon.

The rain began to fall again. Quickly we unloaded our gear into a silver painted, corrugated iron copra shed, from which bagged copra was loaded on ships via a little railway line trolley which ran from the shed along to the end of the jetty. We also unloaded a couple of crates of supplies for the planter and stowed them in the shed. I looked around and was glad we had a kerosene stove and some lanterns. At least we could sleep out of the rain on a pile of copra sacks and cook some more fish for supper. The dismal, narrow beach was ugly and covered down to the waters edge by thick mangroves. The place looked like a sand fly and mosquito heaven.

I left the men, to make themselves comfortable in the shed while I walked up to the plantation to locate our host. At that moment a couple of young boys, around sixteen years of age, came into the shed, with beer bottles wrapped with fishing line, to do a little fishing from the jetty. There were no customary smiles and handshakes as they engaged in a whispered conversation with my blokes. I had a sinking feeling at this unusual taciturnity but hoisted my umbrella and stepped out into the rain to climb up the hill to the plantation house. One of the newcomers shouted after me "Karim stick masta, big fella dog, savvy kaikai man istap." I wasn't surprised at his warning, many timorous planters kept vicious dogs to deter native people from approaching the house.

Our cook, Menias, promptly ran over to the mangroves along the shore and with his machete lopped me off and trimmed a stout stick to defend myself. "Solapim good masta" he said, with a broad grin, the silver rain drops clinging precariously to his woolly hair and dripping from his long, tattooed nose. His cheeky grin cheered me up no end. "Solapim" is a delightful pidgin word which means to "make him swell up," like a boxer's face on the end of some good shots. I hoped it would not come to that, though there was a strong possibility as it was coming on dusk, when both men and guard dogs become a little more nervous.

At the top of a steep hill I emerged from a tunnel of dripping hibiscus bushes and approached the dimly lit, corrugated iron house, so far unmolested by dogs. Possibly the thunder of rain on the roof and the overflowing tanks muffled my approach, but as I ascended the wooden steps, under a cascading overhanging eave, the vibration of my booted foot triggered a terrifying, deep bass explosion of canine rage that would have been a perfect sound effect for a film of "The Hound of the Baskervilles."

A massive red dog skidded to a halt before it could crash through the flimsy, mosquito screened door. I was so terrified that I'm sure the adrenalin in my system would have given my mangrove club enough power to kill the dog with one blow, had it broken through. It was clear that the dog had been soundly beaten in the past for smashing the screen door and I almost grinned as it gave a whimper and a look over its shoulder before resuming the blood curdling racket. A woman appeared with a lantern that silhouetted her figure, beneath a thin cotton dress. She gave the dog a barefoot kick in the belly and said in pidgin, in an angry tone, "Whosat i stap?"

"Good evening Mrs Lau. I believe you are expecting me. I'm from the Dept of Agriculture in Rabaul."

She opened the door and looked coldly at my dripping, forlorn figure. The dog came out and sniffed around my feet, with no apparent evil intent, although it looked with suspicion at my heavy stick.

"Wolfgang" she shouted, "The government bloke is here." Then she said in a sneering tone, "Why do you come creeping around here at this hour? If Cannibal had been outside you would have needed that bloody stick."

As if to confirm her notion, Cannibal gave a low growl, probably in response to her hostile tone. Heavy bare feet stomped through the house, which shook visibly on its wooden stumps. A big, burly man in shorts and a singlet appeared and dwarfed the woman as he stood beside her, looking down at me. His face was in shadow but his expression seemed decidedly unfriendly.

"Vhy you are so late? You were to be here by three o clock."

I refused to return his comment immediately, to let him know that I knew he was well aware of the heavy seas and poor visibility we had encountered all day. Finally I put out my hand and introduced myself while murmuring about head seas and storm rain.

He did not take my hand. He just turned and went back inside and commanded

"Kom" over his shoulder.

We sat down at a round, timber table with a lamp hanging over it and a timid little native entered, like a nervous brown mouse and plonked down a large blue teapot and a bowl of damp sugar, beside a can of Sunshine milk powder.

"For dinner you are too late, but help yourself to tea" said Mr Lau, pouring a cup for himself, ignoring his wife and pushing a cracked yellow mug towards me. It was clear that he wished to appear truculent. Having eaten plenty of fish on board there was nothing I desired more than a big, cracked, yellow mug of hot sweet tea. I thought of my help, shivering down in the copra shed and felt sorry for them. It was our evening ritual to share a billy of tea when out in the bush. Sometimes after a very tiring march across mountains in the rain we would make a billy of thick, hot cocoa with a can of sweetened condensed milk poured in to revive our tired bones.

Wolfgang Lau did not look like a bloke who would give a native a cup of tea.

31

I thanked him for offering me a place to stay while I did the survey on forest land behind the plantation and explained how I would sign the expense log so that the department could pay him for his trouble. I asked about where my workers could billet themselves and cook their meals, as well as access to the back of the property.

Lau ignored my questions and sneered at the stupidity of the department for sending me out to survey flooded forests at this time of year. Inwardly I agreed with him but could not give him the impression that I was anything other than a loyal public servant. He showed me a space on an open verandah where an iron cot with a mouldy looking mattress lay, just out of range of the water pouring over the gutters. There was no sign of a mosquito net or bedding. I told him I would walk back down the hill to get my kit. He flicked his hand dismissively and walked away. A few seconds later the little house servant appeared at my side with a lantern to help me. This was most reassuring, if only to protect me from the affection of Cannibal on my return. My companion said nothing as we set off back down the hill in the rain. Within twenty yards of the house however, the rain stopped abruptly and the roar of rain on the roof and bushes was replaced with what seemed like utter silence. Then, the music of the night emerged as frogs croaked in delight in the wet, crickets started up and drips and gurgles of water joined in the chorus, with occasional eerie calls of night birds and owls and the flapping and squeaking of fruit bats in the crowns of coconut palms.

We took a slightly different route down to the jetty and came to a long steel building with smoke rising from chimneys at each end into the growing moonlight.

The rich, sweet smell of drying coconuts announced the copra drier and as we came alongside I saw my men in the red glow of the fire pit, warming themselves in front of the furnace.

A great brick and earth pile covered the fireplace at each end of the building and the hot air travelled along a pipe of welded oil drums to the chimney at the other end. Every now and then the fireman tossed a few coconut husks in to keep the fire glowing. It was a cosy place on a wet night and there were numbers of men squatting in range of the warmth, smoking sticky trade tobacco rolled in newspaper or native grown tobacco, called 'brus', in pipes and untidy looking cigars. It was awful rank stuff but the men claimed it gave them strength. "Bone blong mifella" they said.

I asked my men to help me carry my gear up to the house. They had already set up for the night in the store, where the copra was placed to cool after being unloaded from the wire decks of the drier, before being rammed into sacks. Menias pulled me aside and whispered in English. "All these boys say the masta here is man no good. He savvy fight, all a time. They are afraid of him."

I told Menias not to worry, if he gave us any trouble we would build a camp up in the bush and stay out of his way. We had enough rice and canned beef and there was a Chinese trade store back up the coast, where the *Tilburra* had dropped off supplies on the way in. I believed what he said and resolved not to make the gift of fresh fish to my host.

"You better share the fish with all your mates at the drier Menias, I'm sure they'd like a present."

He grinned and understood that I had been unimpressed by Lau. In pidgin he said,

"Ol man here, him he no one talk blong me. Him ol manki blong Sepik."

They weren't his tribe, just a mob of boys from Sepik.

I knew he would share the fish and I too had noticed that the men around the drier were all young lads; "manki" was the term for them, with no pejorative intent. Menias was a nice bloke and popular wherever we went. The fish would make him new friends. We sorted out some overnight stuff and they helped carry it back up to the house. The plantation manager and his wife had gone to bed early but they would be up before dawn to send the labour force off to work.

It was customary for me when working away from base to sleep on a canvas tube stretched over a couple of poles, like an army stretcher and secured to a cross of poles at each end. I rolled the canvas out on the mouldy bed and located a rafter above it to which I tied my mosquito net. With a sheet and a small kapok filled pillow I was set for the night and slept well, with the now friendly Cannibal snoring and dreaming beside me and occasionally thumping the wood floor with his leg as he scratched furiously at a flea, or dreamed he was chasing some miscreant native dog or human.

The clamouring of a bell woke me before dawn as someone down at the labour compound bashed a hanging piece of steel girder with a hammer. Wolfgang Lau was already gone when I came out to the kitchen. The smouldering butt of a Camel cigarette sat in the full ash tray, a battered South African peach tin. I brushed my teeth outside, next to a water tank and went down the hill to the labour compound where the workers would soon be lined up and assigned their daily tasks.

As the sun came up the shivering men shuffled over to the mess shed to dip out a mug of black tea from a copper laundry boiler that the cooks had prepared an hour before dawn. Soon they were all in line in their work groups. Copra cutters had their numbered sacks before them with an axe, machete and copra knife lying on the sacks. Drainers and road repair crew lined up with long handled spades, cocoa harvesters with cocoa hooks on long poles and the 'big line' with machete and sarif.

The latter being a sharpened piece of hoop iron, shaped like a cutlass to cut down weeds and grass. They sharpened this tool stone age fashion, by laying the edge on a rock and pounding it with another.

Lau walked menacingly up and down the lines, glowering at the little brown men. They kept their eyes down. The men were frightened of him and he was indeed a fearsome sight, like a child's image of an ogre. He stood well over six feet tall and must have weighed sixteen stone, probably double the average of his workforce. His visage was pink to red and his fat legs were decorated with dabs of purple gentian violet where he had dabbed nicks and scratches to prevent infection. His starched white shirt was already going limp from sweat and his scowling face seemed a personification of hatred and contempt.

Woe betide any man with betel nut or a smoke in his mouth. Such offenses copped an explosive slap across the face; rare now because they all knew the rules. One careless youth ducked into the fibro dormitory to get something he had forgotten. As he came out Lau punched his face with a closed fist, so hard that the boy staggered back and smashed through the fibro wall and lay senseless on the floor. As he came to the foreman of his crew helped him to his feet and picked up his tools, then they followed the rest to work, leaving a trail of blood drops on the grass. Apparently it was forbidden to re-enter the barracks after work had been assigned.

Wolfgang Lau offered no comment, nor did he acknowledge my presence as he walked across to inspect the cocoa drier and the copra drier. He cuffed a couple of other blokes and sent them to turn the cocoa and copra to help it dry. As it was a fine morning the roof of the cocoa drier was rolled back to expose the beans to the sun before the next downpour arrived. He looked angry to see my laundry hanging above the fireplace to dry, but made no comment other than to scowl at me. It crossed my mind that he might bill me for clothes drying expenses. I felt a surge of appreciation for Menias, who had taken the time the night before to wash my clothes in a bucket and hang them under the roof of the copra drier fire pit.

I was motioned into a Landrover and driven out along the neatly trimmed plantation roads while men on the way to work stepped aside with their tools to allow us to pass. When we got to the boundary he told me that was where I would have to proceed alone, to do my job in the forest. An old woman emerged from the jungle, bent over with a large coconut palm woven basket on her back, held there by a tump strap around her forehead. The basket was full of taro and must have weighed about eighty pounds. Behind her waddled a pet brown duck.

"The woman is long long (mad)" growled Lau, "everyday she brings down taro for the cooks."

At the Saturday market in Rabaul she could have sold her taro at two for a shilling. I didn't ask him what he paid her. The answer would probably have made me even more unhappy than I was already.

We walked into the forest for fifty yards as he sneered about the mighty oil palm estates I would develop and how many millions of dollars would be wasted.

The guy was indeed becoming tiresome.

The job didn't look too bad with the sun shining but as we got back in the vehicle the sky darkened and heavy rain began to fall. Soon we overtook the old woman, tottering along on the single lane track with deep ditches on each side. She tried to get to the edge of the road, with her load hanging over the rapidly filling drain. She was looking around for her duck, which stood in the middle of the road wondering what to do. Lau stopped the vehicle and roared out of the window, "Rausim patau" in a fierce tone. "Move your duck" was what he had said.

She tried desperately to bend over and scoop up her duck but her load and the strain on her neck was too much and her eyes were filled with fear and rainwater. I was afraid she would tumble into the drains. Lau got out of the Landrover and I thought he would pick up the duck, or put her load in the back of the truck to complete her journey.

He did not. He kicked that duck high in the air amid a puff of feathers and then got back in the vehicle and drove on. My stomach churned with revulsion. The muscles on my right arm went into spasm in my effort to avoid smashing him across the face. Somehow I kept control and consoled myself that I would immediately request his dismissal as soon as I met the manager of the company that owned the plantation. I knew that fellow and he was, as far as I knew, a decent chap.

It was clear that I could not live with this oaf for the duration of the survey. We drove up through the hibiscus tunnel for breakfast on a little verandah with a view along the drab, grey coast and leaden sea. My mind was churning with plans, to distance myself from this house, but it would have to wait until I had built a camp for us in the forest. We had often done this and my three men were capable of building a waterproof house in a couple of days, from materials growing in the jungle.

Mrs Lau sat silently on the verandah and didn't blink or nod as I said "Good morning." The tiny house servant smiled shyly and came in with tea and wholemeal pancakes made from the flour issued as a standard ration issue to the workers. This and a thick slice of tinned ham and some tinned beetroot constituted the Lau breakfast. I asked Wolfgang if I could borrow a tractor and trailer to take my gear out to the site. He nodded with his mouth full; his great fat jowls reminding me of a snuffling pig.

His small blue eyes watched me closely and his wife did the same, like a couple of pythons watching a rodent.

She might have been a beautiful woman if she could manage a hint of a smile. He was big and thick with thin sandy hair, on his arms as on his head. I knew he never socialized with the few other planters along the coast and it was clear his dour, uncommunicative style had isolated them, on one of the ugliest coastlines I had seen.

No wonder they seemed half mad. I told them I would be gone all day and would be back before dark. Again, there was no response. Cannibal licked my hand as I left so at least I'd made one friend. He enjoyed the feel of my hand about his silky ears. Once again the rain had eased off briefly while we bounced along on the tray of a trailer behind a blue tractor. All the steel patrol boxes and a folding canvas chair were there, with a wooden box of tools and a couple of others for core samples to be taken back. We passed the old lady and her limping duck, on their way home to a tiny hamlet in the forest. It wasn't possible to get much further than I had been with Lau but the loading crew of the trailer helped us carry our equipment up onto a ridge. On the other side lay a swamp where saksak palm grew and some massive ficus trees formed a tunnel over the river that ran out of the swamp. Here were building materials in abundance. The men knew we must build a house big enough for all of us and a cooking shelter where we could have a fire. I didn't make any comments about our host, no doubt they knew all they needed to know. We rigged up a small tarp to trees to cover our gear then everyone got to work digging holes for house posts and cutting down small trees. Menias took a machete to cut ropes, from the ficus trees, which were adventitious roots, dangling down into the river. "Lookout long puk puk" shouted one of the plantation men. They said a very large croc lived in the area, so I went with him to be a lookout. Menias ran out along great branches and lopped the ropes hanging down from them. These were what was called 'positively geotropic' because when they were a few feet from the ground they sprouted roots. If they hit the ground they would grow into pillars to support the outward spread of the tree. Here they dangled into the river and were swayed downstream by the current. One could not imagine more useful stuff for building a bush house, even in a hardware store.

By noon the frame of a house had been built and lashed with ficus ropes and split green "kunda", a vine that could be split into string or used whole to make furniture and fish traps. The rest of the construction was out of my skill level so I left the men to cut saksak palm fronds for thatching and set off on a compass bearing through the forest, which I marked as a datum point on the map. I walked until two o clock, by then the rain was almost solid so I retraced my steps, sloshing through hollows and sliding down slopes and stopping now and then to scrape black leaches off my arms with my machete. My legs and feet were clad in army surplus gear for protection against vines, thorns and leaches. Wet, wounded legs in this country were an invitation to tropical ulcer infection.

The men had done a magnificent job of thatching the dead straight ficus poles they had used for rafters. It was dry under that roof of green sak sak palm fronds but another day would be needed to make a floor of split limbom palm and to thatch the walls. In six months the whole structure would be destroyed by white ants and borers but it would answer our purpose and was therefore a quality product. The men decided to stay where they were as they had food and kerosene to cook with and could soon rig up some sleeping platforms till the hut was finished.

I set off down the ridge, in sunshine again but it was overcast before I reached the house and raining soon after. It was too much to expect a hot shower but an overflowing rain water tank would be no hardship. Cannibal came up to me all smiles and waving tail. How pleasant that was. No wonder dogs are called man's best friend.

The little house man also greeted me warmly and told me 'haus wash wash' was ready. He quickly carried a big kettle of boiling water into the shower and filled a bucket of water on a rope and tipped in the hot water before he hoisted it up on a pulley. Voila! A hot shower on the instant, through the watering can rose soldered on the base. Things were looking up.

Clean, dry and shaved and fragrant from a generous sprinkle of Johnsons Baby Powder, I responded to the tinkle of a bell and marched in to the round table room where the Laus were already seated. "Thank you for the hot shower" I said warmly, sure that the house servant had been instructed by them.

Neither of them responded. A white cloth covered the rough table and I began to feel quite the honoured guest. Now a large covered bowl was brought from the kitchen and then a heaped basin of steaming white rice. Wolfgang lifted the lid on the bowl, revealing aromatic curried chicken, which he ladled out onto his pile of rice and began to shovel into his mouth. Mrs Lau gestured to me to precede her. I guessed to take a little under half of what remained and then she took a small helping herself.

We ate in silence for awhile until Wolfgang said harshly, "I suppose you are an expert, Mr Agriculture?"

"Yes" I said, ageeably.

"In vot are you expert?" he said, with a full mouth of chicken curry.

"Agriculture" I replied promptly.

He almost choked in indignation as he exploded "Pah" and waved his great fists dismissively. His wife watched me without expression, so I winked mischievously at her, hoping for the trace of a smile. Her serpentine stare remained, unblinking.

It was going to be a long night.

He raved on for awhile about the world being full of 'so called, experts' but I didn't take the bait and gave my attention to the excellent chicken curry. It was quite hot so I filled a glass with iced water from a jug on the table.

"You don't like the curry?" he growled as I swallowed the water.

"Excellent curry sir, but I havn't had a drink all day" I said, hoping he would do what every other host in Papua New Guinea would do and offer me a cold beer, like the dewy can of Fosters he had before him. Of course he had no such intention. I looked at his wife and turned my eye to his beer but she remained unmoved. In spite of the hot shower and nice food I was beginning to feel grumpy. Above us, around the lamp, moths and insects were flitting around in increasing numbers and falling onto the table as they hit the hot glass.

Lau pounced on one specimen and handed it to me with an 'I've got yuh' leer.

"Vos ist das, Mr Agriculture expert?" he growled.

I had no idea and admitted I was unfamiliar with that specimen.

"Pah! Expert for Got's sake" he sneered.

Righto mate, I thought, *I'm sure that as your youth was spent doing push ups for der Fuehrer you are probably as thick as pig shit; let's play this game.* I always carried a little brass hand lens in a pouch on my belt, mainly to identify bugs that were eating crops or to get a better view of splinters in fingers or identify botanical features of collected specimens. I'd had one since I was sixteen. I pulled out my hand lens and had a close look at the crumpled moth on the table.

I looked up at his astonished face and said. "This is not a cocoa moth but it's very similar. Have you had any problems with maggots in your stored cocoa?"

"No, no problems." He sounded a little apprehensive.

"Well Mr Lau you should check your cocoa store. I noticed it's a bit untidy. If you have any dust or cocoa debris under the storage deck, cocoa moths can breed very fast in it. Before you know it maggots have hatched and entered your sacks and you have a ruined sample from cocoa borers. If crop inspectors find any they condemn the whole batch, be it ten bags or ten tons."

He hated to be in a defensive position and dismissed my truthful observation.

Then he decided to blunder along with his attempt to humiliate me. Now he grabbed another swirling insect and thrust it at me, "Vos ist das?" again. This time I was ready. I examined the fly with my hand lens while muttering nonsense. "Four legs, hirsute sillyoptrix and segmented thorax. Yes, this is definitely dytiscus marginalis. Would you believe that this bug is common in Europe?"

I remembered doing field studies at school and dytiscus marginalis was also known as the Great Diving Beetle. You can see them on still ponds, floating on little rafts on the end of their legs. I was one hundred per cent sure that he had never heard of it. The Latin name did the trick.

He didn't argue, he just grunted and handed me a little black beetle. I didn't bother with the hand lens.

"Oh, this one's easy, Ranunculus Bulbosa. It's one of the ranunculus group, but see the bulging abdomen? Hence, Ranunculus Bulbosa."

Of course ranunculus is the buttercup family, r.acris, r.repens etc. I had him by the balls now and could have rattled off Latin names of everything from pigs to elephants to common or garden weeds. He blundered along for awhile until I thought I would have to laugh or piss my pants as I made up names off the top of my head, from Roman emperors to planets.

Finally in disgust he could take no more and stumbled off to bed. Mrs Lau looked at me with that cold stare and I thought I had her fooled as well. I said to myself,

There you sit you silly mare, trying to make a fool of me and you're both a couple of galahs.'

"I suppose you think you are pretty bloody smart, Mr Expert. I used to be a school science teacher so you don't fool me with your Latin mumbo jumbo."

I was stunned and felt a strong surge of fear. I wished she would lower her voice and despite myself I looked nervously toward the direction of their bedroom. She continued to stare me down. She was onto me. I grinned ingratiatingly at her, hoping to coax a smile. At least she was good sport enough to keep her mouth shut while Wolfgang was in the room.

"Well Mrs Lau, you must admit I did quite well. It was nice of you to sit still without bursting out laughing. There's a lot more to you than you reveal. What the hell is a school science teacher doing in such a drab, isolated place?"

Suddenly she looked desperately lonely, I felt bad for despising her.

She looked at me with that same blank, heartless expression and said.

"My husband ran off with my sister a month after our wedding. I took up with the first man that crossed my path. It was Wolfgang, on leave in Sydney at an Octoberfest booze up. So here I am two months later, far from the wagging tongues of Sydney.

'Are you married John?"

How nice it was to have her use my name; I didn't know her's.

I was crushed by the desolation of this woman. She looked like a candidate for suicide. I returned her same intense stare and blurted out the first thing that came into my head. At that moment I felt ashamed to be a man.

"Heavens no Mrs Lau, I don't even have a girlfriend for God's sake."

As if the sun had returned she gave a most beautiful smile and her body shook with silent laughter. The change in her was as good as seeing a blind man's sight restored. When she recovered she reached out and grabbed my hand, squeezed it and said. "You're still pulling my leg, you cheeky little bastard."

Then she got up, went to the kitchen and came back with an ice cold Fosters.

She sat down again, still laughing quietly, tears streaming down her face, I hoped from the humour. We didn't say much more for awhile, she just watched me drink the beer with a smile on her face as the odd bout of giggling erupted from her, like gas bubbles rising from the bottom of a long stagnant pond.

Then in a hushed voice that, indicated she had not confided in Wolfgang, she told me about her bitter and brief marriage. I could almost see her shoulders rising as the weight of her humiliation was shared with a complete stranger, whose only quality was to have slightly restored her sense of humour.

"I worked as a colleague of my husband for five years without any romantic engagements between us. We began to work closely together on a few students who were falling behind a little and we shared an after work drink or two. Then we were part of a team that took a group of kids on field trip to a Barrier Reef island.

'Somehow we wound up in bed together and soon after we were married. It all seemed rather natural without all the fanfare of more traditional weddings. I loved it, being a wife. I never thought I would marry. Then my young sister came to stay with us when she started university. Soon my sex life ended as he put all his energy into her and then it was over, 'tout finis'.

'I'm so glad I told you John. It's a relief to share it with someone, though I can see you are upset. Don't be. I believe God sent you to hear my confession, and I'm not religious at all."

I was young and unable to think of any suitable response other than to mutter that I was glad she felt better and if she ever wanted a break in town she was welcome to stay at my place and could contact me at the town office. She nodded thoughtfully but looked a healthier woman than earlier in the evening.

"Thanks for the beer Mrs Lau, and for being a good sport about my silly games."

I went to my soggy bed that night with a huge sense of accomplishment that I had brought a smile to that woman's face. I didn't see her the next morning when I left for our new camp. We did the job and eventually it all came to nothing as the big development went much further west and all I did was fill in some gaps on the map.

When I got back to Rabaul I sought out Alastair Cox the director of that plantation company and warned him that Wolfgang Lau would bring discredit to his firm. He protested. "He's the best man we've got. The only manager we have who can handle these fucking big heads we are getting as labour from Chimbu and Wabag,"

"Well maybe so Al but I saw him bashing sixteen year old Sepiks. Poor harmless little buggers half his size. He will hurt you mate, I would sack him right now."

They didn't sack him and a couple of years later he was smashed to pulp with coconut stripping irons by a gang of Wabag labourers over on Kar Kar Island. He never returned from hospital in Australia and was lucky to recover from his smashed arms and legs without amputation. Thus his destiny was ordained, by the delusions of power he had imbibed as a boy.

From my point of view it couldn't have happened to a nicer bloke.

I don't know what happened to his woman, Mrs or otherwise. Apparently she stuck with him and maybe she is still. I hope she was ok. She deserved more from life than barely one brief love story.

Chapter Four

THE ANTHROPOLOGIST
AND THE WELSHMAN

Many people are under the weather on Monday mornings. It's not so much the prospect of another week at work, unless they have a really nasty job or an awful boss. Mostly Mondayitis is self induced by the stupid things people do on the weekend. You might take the kids to the beach and wind up with sunburn, or get stuck in traffic and have a row with everyone and go home in a grumpy mood to get scolded by your wife; or worse still, your mother in law. Sometimes it's too much food, beer or sex or a bad day at the races. Mondays can be awful.

It was a Monday morning when Brynne Lewis got the message on the morning radio 'sched' that his boss wanted to see him in the Rabaul office. Brynne worked as a field officer in the Papua New Guinea Department of Agriculture, Stock and Fisheries and he loved the job. His boss was a keen type who felt that every member of the department had to project a professional and disciplined image, befitting a public servant. Brynne admired him and tried to live up to his standards, but as a keen sportsman he often had a few problems on the first day of the week, such as a swollen hand from a cricket game, a limp from a sore ankle or heaven forbid, a bruised face or black eye from Sunday afternoon football. On that particular Monday he was in bad shape after being dragooned into a boxing match on Saturday evening followed by a hard game of football on Sunday.

Wearily he swung his leg over his old AJS motorbike and headed down the mountain to the district office. The front forks of the bike had worn out shock absorbers so it was a painful journey over the corrugated dirt roads. He was still impatiently waiting after three months, for new parts and this increased his gloom. He began to mutter about selling the damn bike and getting a cheap car. The roads around Rabaul are just graded grey pumice, which washes out fast in heavy rain and forms clouds of dust and corrugations when dry. It's not good motorbike country. That day was dry and he was well coated with dust when he pulled up outside the office.

He quickly washed his face in the washroom and was dismayed at the swollen cheek bones and fat lip he saw in the mirror.

That's another thing I need, he thought and he resolved to buy a mirror as soon as he was done in the office. He felt a trifle nervous when he tapped on Bob Gifford's office door, especially after the Chinese typist, Rosemarie, giggled at his untidy appearance.

"Enter" roared Gifford, in his usual attempt to appear authoritarian. He wasn't, but everyone humoured him.

"Jesus! Brynne, why do you always look like something the cat dragged in? Did you fall off your bike again or is it the usual result of playing bloody football with your hooligan mates?"

Brynne did feel a bit ashamed of his dusty and battered appearance and he knew Bob was genuinely upset. He had a mischievous sense of humour though and thought it a good time to wind Bob up a little more.

"Well Bob I got through the footy ok but I had a bit of trouble with a copper on Saturday night and he touched me up a bit."

"What! Bloody hell! Has it come down to fighting with policeman now? You piss me off Brynne. You know how I feel about the image we present to the public. I suppose you'll be in the paper after a disorderly conduct fine in court. Mate I'm serious here; you have to shape up a bit."

Brynne grinned, which made his boss even more furious. "It's not that serious Bob. I went with a couple of Papuan mates to a boxing tournament sponsored by the Apex Club and the Police Citizens Youth Club at the basketball courts. The referee was that great big South African copper, Kees Peeters. All of the bouts were between native lads and so was the crowd. Everyone was yelling and after the last match there was an outcry from the crowd for someone to fight the referee. Kees is about six foot eight and has hands like a couple of coal shovels.

'The next thing I know Les and Lahui grab me and hustle me up to the ring and the boys roar their encouragement, yelling at me to 'Swellupim number one Kiap.'

'One would be a lousy sport to back down with that much support. Kees was laughing his head off and already stripping off his shirt and shadow boxing to the crowd. I was trapped. Lahui volunteered to be the ref and Les was to be my corner man, ready to throw in the towel as soon as I got in trouble.

'We agreed to avoid belly shots and bloody Kees hit me in the guts with his first punch. That made me mad and I went after him to get one back. That's when I got all these bruises. Kees could hardly fight for laughing and I made a right galah of myself in front of about two hundred young fellers. They loved it though and at the end of the three rounds Kees raised my hand and then picked me up and sat me on his shoulder.

'I've never seen people laugh as much in my life, I felt like Charlie Chaplin.

'So before you get out of your pram to pick up your dummy, just think of the public relations value of a didiman fighting a giant policeman. I've done more for the Department of Agriculture than you have with all your posh knee socks and spit and polish."

Bob Gifford leaned back in his chair with a grin a mile wide.

"Your mum told me what a cheeky little bugger you were as a kid. You're still at it. I guess it's in your genes. I got a letter from her a couple off weeks back thanking me for being so helpful while she was here for the annual choir festival. I must have a bit of Welsh in me too because I love a choir as much as Gwen.

'Now, seriously Brynne, I want you to ditch that bloody worn out motorbike. The last thing I want is the job of writing to Gwen to tell her you've been ironed out by a native truck in a cloud of dust. You've done a great job this year guiding visiting scientists and government people and I have another such assignment for you. I took the opportunity to requisition a vehicle for your full time use and the Director approved it without a blink.

'Canberra leaned on him to go out of his way to help a woman who has just done a Masters at ANU and she wants to do a PHD in Anthropology and needs to come here for her research. It seems her old man is in the House of Lords and her uncle has been nominated for governor of New South Wales. Pretty heavy connections don't you think? Apparently she will arrive here on Friday and you are to pick her up at the airport. Evelyn Pemberton Davies is her name. That's all I know about her.

'No doubt she will have a plan about how she wants to proceed but it occurred to me that she could accompany you on your patrol through the Bainings. I believe you plan to do that in two weeks time. There aren't many more primitive groups that I can think of so they might be just what she's looking for."

Brynne was glad he was off the hook regarding his dishevelled appearance and he was still absorbing the rest of Bob's proposals.

Nice to have a government vehicle at last; he had already decided to give the bike to Les. He was a mechanic at the Public Works motor pool and would soon make improvements to it. As he pondered the task of escorting a woman across the Bainings he began to feel a bit uneasy.

On those patrols he was usually out for at least a month in tough conditions. The mountains were steep and wet, often cold and the bridges across numerous raging creeks were just a slippery, moss covered log, thirty feet above rocks. He had taken a film crew into the mountains the year before and had to carry an overweight and sick man out on a litter that needed six strong men and frequent stops. The fellow had ignored Brynne's constant warnings to treat scratches on his legs and had quickly succumbed to a tropical ulcer infection. He had responded to treatment but the glandular swellings in his groin were so painful he couldn't walk. On another trip one of the carriers slipped and injured his back and he too had to be carried for ten hours to the mission at Raunsepna. It took Brynne's shoulder a month to grow back the skin rubbed off by the carrying pole.

He kept quiet about his reservations. Bob Gifford had been wonderful to his mother and he knew that despite complaints about his appearance Bob was genuinely fond of him. He would have to manage the situation as best he could. She might turn out to be one of those women who have more toughness and endurance than men. As a PHD candidate she would be intelligent company and with her distinguished pedigree she probably had impeccable manners. Resolved to look on the bright side he looked into Bob's penetrating eyes.

"Sounds like a great job Bob, I'll have to pack the family silver and an extra bottle or rum."

He felt quite the grandee when he collected the new Holden ute from PNG Motors. The first thing he did was pick up Les

Gorore from work and hand over the motor bike before he changed his mind. Then he bought some items from the Burns-Philp store, including a new briar pipe, a bottle of scotch and a large shaving mirror for his bathroom. It seemed a bit ostentatious to hang that thing on the wall. His shower was a red ship's fire bucket on a rope pulley which had spent most of its life filled with sand and cigarette butts. It had a tap and a watering can rose soldered on the base and he always had enough water for his shower. The toilet had no water or cistern, just a rotating steel plate over a pit which was turned by a crank handle. He kept a bucket of water beside it to rinse off what the scraper had missed. With a little more effort the person who built it could have installed a septic tank. It had been there for years and was probably built by some cack handed Anglican Missionary. He rented the cottage from the Anglicans for five dollars a week. It had no power but he was comfortable with kerosene lanterns, stove and fridge and a million dollar view of Blanche Bay.

As he drove home up Burma Road his imagination formed pictures of the movie star anthropologist. Images of Susan Hayward on safari in Africa came to mind. Bulging breasts in tight cotton drill shirts and shorts held up with a leopard skin belt. He grinned and shook his head as if to clear his mind. *'She'll probably be as big and shrill as Hatty Jaques in the Carry On movies'* he thought.

His cook, Albert, was mighty impressed with his new car and wanted to go for a ride immediately. He sat in front breathing in the new smell and running his hands over the seats and dash, winding the windows up and down and looking in the rear view mirror, with a smile like an open piano.

Brynne couldn't resist teasing him. "You'll have to keep it clean Albert. These dusty roads will make it dirty all the time."

Then he felt ashamed when the look of delight lit up Albert's face. He knew straightaway that no speck of dust would be allowed on that ute. They passed Albert's niece on the way back and stopped to let her and her mother climb in the back with their baskets of sweet potato and taro. By the time they got home Brynne had come up with the notion that the girl, Iambata, might be a big help on the Bainings patrol. No doubt the anthropologist would want to talk to village women and Iambata could not only relieve him of translation and security duties but may well form a strong friendship with her; like his relationship with Albert.

She was a lovely happy kid, about sixteen years old with quite good English as she had completed grade six and she was strong and agile. As Albert's niece her parents would raise no objection and he could put her on the payroll as well as advise Evelyn Pemberton Davies to also pay her as a personal assistant. It would probably be the first time Iambata had ever earned her own money, other than her sales of garden produce.

Brynne felt proud of his brilliant notion and straight away put the proposition to Albert and the two women. Iambata jumped for joy, spinning around and slapping her thighs. She had never been further than Rabaul on the Saturday market truck and this was an adventure she could not have imagined. Her joy was so appealing that Brynne said a silent prayer to the Gods of good humour that Evelyn Pemberton Davies would be a kind and gentle person.

Gifford had suggested that Evelyn stay with him for the week before the patrol to become accustomed to roughing it a little and absorbing all the information she would need to make her six months study a success. Brynne didn't mention that she might have a completely different notion of how she would deal with the task before her. He had no other plan though so he hired a couple of men from the village to give the fibro walls and cement floors of the cottage a fresh coat of paint in a combination of maroon and creamy yellow. He bought a new mattress and mosquito net for his bedroom and moved his old one out to the spare bed on the verandah.

Iambata came by with a mob of kids and they cleaned up the garden and mowed the grass with their hoop iron sarifs. They slashed so close to each other's feet that Brynne could not watch them. Then Albert and his mates built a 'haus wind', a little gazebo, out by the Poinceana tree, with a superb view of Blanche Bay. His brother, Alphonse knocked up some cane chairs to put in it. By Thursday the place was so spic and span they could have played host to the Queen. The whole village was excited about the arrival of a 'young pela missus blong Masta Breen.' He didn't try to explain the true situation. There wasn't any way to explain it in pidgin. If he had said she was just his friend they would roll their eyes and hoot the equivalent of 'ooh la la.' A friend in pidgin can be a lover and if you say you will play with your friend it can mean you will have sex with her.

Brynne left the village to its fun. He was the only white man in it and the people found him a bit of a novelty. Like them, he never locked a door and the house was often full of kids looking at pictures in his magazines or asking questions or bringing him little presents like a fresh egg or a basket of tomatoes. The only thing that was ever stolen was a packet of shortbread biscuits and everyone was eager to dob in the poor little guy who took it. Every time Brynne stroked his curly head the boy, Steven, would cry with shame. At times he felt a bit like Gulliver in Lilliput and was quite humbled by their affection.

He had the sinking feeling that if his potential guest preferred to live in town the whole village would be disappointed. Whenever he had a party or a barbeque with his team mates the people would surround the place, at a respectable distance and be entertained by the antics of his boisterous friends. When the village had a wedding or ceremony or even just the Thursday night pow wow to air their grievances with each other; he was expected to be there. If the people had a word for privacy it would probably be a phrase like 'samting blong mi tasol'; my own business.

The lumbering DC3 aircraft from Port Moresby was due to land just before noon so at eleven a.m Brynne Lewis was ready to leave. His blue, Welsh chin was shaven, even to the bottom of the dimple in the centre. His black curly hair began to spring back out of his vigorous brushing, even as he watched it in his new mirror. The swellings and scuffs on his face were gone and he tried a smile to himself. He was disappointed with the result so to even things up a bit he dabbed some Old Spice after shave on his cheeks. It was a present from his mum on her visit a few months back. He would have to mention it in his next letter, she would be glad he had tried it eventually. The ute was gleaming from Albert's keen polishing and people waved gaily to him as he drove by the village.

Chapter Five

Moderation is a fatal thing. Nothing
Succeeds like excess.

Oscar Wilde

There weren't many people at the airstrip to meet the plane, just a
few husbands and wives and a couple of children. A few scruffy
Datsun taxis were in line and a small courtesy bus from the new
Wandlyn Motel sat beside a row of dusty Holden and Volkswagen
cars. Brynne's ute was the cleanest car there.

Soon the old aeroplane appeared in a wide arc and straightened
up to land, as gracefully as a seagull, in an incredibly short distance.
Brynne had flown often and was always impressed with the DC3.
It was an aerial version of a Holden ute, cheap, practical and
versatile. As he edged forward with the other people he realised
he was excited and on edge, like the kids eagerly waving to the
people walking down the mobile stairway. *This is inappropriate,* he
thought, so he turned and walked ten paces back before turning
to look at the passengers walking toward the terminal. There
were four women who might be Evelyn. Three wore floral print
cotton dresses and medium heel shoes and carried handbags. The
fourth wore a figure hugging grey dress, which looked expensive
and she had on light leather sandals and a floppy white tennis hat.

Over her shoulder, by one strap she carried an army surplus knapsack.

That could be my bird, he thought, hopefully. He stayed where he was as people embraced their relatives and several shook hands with native people who had come to collect them. Evelyn was not looking around with any urgency as she strolled over to the baggage collection booth and leaned on the rail, doing a few stretches to relieve the kinks of a long slow flight. The other women had all met the people waiting for them so Brynne casually moved toward his guest. He was pipped at the post by one of the sweating pilots, who had almost run in his eagerness to speak to her.

Brynne stood back while the jaunty pilot, with his gold braid cap and epaulettes helped her lift her suitcase off the trolley and asked her if she would like a ride into town. She smiled at the pilot and fixed him in her radiant blue eyes so that his heart skipped a beat.

"Thank you so much" she said, warmly, "but I believe I am being met."

She was so lovely and her voice and British accent so clear and polished that Brynne too was a little overwhelmed for a second.

"Indeed you are Miss Davies, I'm here for that very purpose. I'm Brynne Lewis from D.A.S.F."

The pilot looked a bit deflated but brightened up a little when she looked Brynne up and down in cold appraisal and said, "The name is Pemberton-Davies; Mr Lewis."

Suddenly Brynne felt irritated, by the pilot's lofty glare and her toffy nosed condescension. He met her assertive stare full on and paused before he said,

"So! What will it be my lady? Pemberton or Davies, both are honourable Welsh names, like mine?"

She sensed his irritation and regretted her attempt to impose on someone who, though unattractive, had been kind enough to come to welcome her visit. To his relief she grinned and put out her hand. "Evelyn will do Brynne, we'll sort the rest out later."

Thank God for that, thought Brynne, *I love her already.* "If you have no plans of your own at the moment we might go and have some lunch and sort out how I can begin to assist you; in line with my instructions."

The crestfallen pilot stood, like a shag on a rock, until out of politeness, Brynne asked if he would care to join them. They may well have had some other arrangement together but he wanted to quickly establish where he stood with this beautiful woman so that he could move on. He had to let her know that he had been put at her disposal as a resource person, for whatever length of time she had in mind. It couldn't be done in an airstrip lobby.

"Yes. Thanks I will join you for lunch Brynne, I'm Kevin MacDonald, from New Zealand."

They put their bags in the tray and then they squeezed into the seat of the ute. Kevin asked if they could drop off his bag at the TAA aircrew house and then they drove down to the harbour side pub, The Cosmopolitan.

"The counter lunch here is usually quite good" said Brynne as he parked the vehicle in view of the pub garden, which had several thatched sun shelters over tables and chairs inside low hibiscus bush and coloured croton borders. A humid breeze wafted across the blue water, rustling the fronds of the palms and dispersing the pungent sweet scent of pink and white frangipani flowers which grew profusely along the edge of the deep storm water drain around the garden. While Kevin went to the bar for drinks Brynne hastened to make his position clear before he came back.

"Evelyn I don't want to rush in here but I do need to tell you what my duties are toward you. It seems your family is well connected in high places and strings have been jerked to smooth your stay here. I have somehow earned a reputation for being a guide and mentor to visiting scientists and important jokers from the UN. I'm told you are planning to write a thesis for your PHD in anthropolgy.

'Some people think I should take you on an extensive bush patrol and generally show you around so that you can decide how you want to do it. You may have very different views on all this and I will have to adapt to whatever you have in mind; so please don't think I'm in any way trying to direct you. I just have to make sure you get home safe and sound."

Evelyn looked at him with a frown, then she gave a resigned sigh.

"Are you to be my chaperone as well as guide and mentor Mr Lewis?"

Brynne shrugged his shoulders and wished he was somewhere else. "Sorry Evelyn, my qualifications are limited for that role. My mum was here a while ago and I couldn't even chaperone her. Not that I tried. I'm a live and let live sort of bloke."

As the Kiwi pilot plonked down three dewy South Pacific Lager stubbies on the table she smiled and clinked the bottles. "Cheers boys, Rabaul looks like a fun place."

"It is as far as I'm concerned," said Brynne. "Do you mind if I go over to the next table for a sec, I have some business with those fellows who just came down from the bar? Oh by the way Evelyn, have you been taking anti malarial medication? The advice is to start three weeks before you land here."

"No, I don't mind if you visit your friends and yes I am up to date on the medication. Is there anything else I should know Brynne?"

Brynne stood up and replied with a grin, "Good, you're on it. Thanks for the beer Kev, I'll be back shortly."

Strewth! She's hard work, he said to himself. Kevin the Kiwi clearly had designs on Evelyn's virtue and Brynne was glad to get out of his road. He really didn't have any urgent business with his acquaintances, he just wanted to get used to the job of dealing with this confident and assertive woman.

The men under the other 'haus wind' were all small ship captains with whom he had travelled between islands. One wizened and sunburnt fellow had a slobbering boxer dog beside his chair with which he shared his beer. The dog expertly slurped the beer out of a glass without tipping it over and his master drank out of his stubby. Both man and dog were a little groggy but while the dog remained quiet his owner was boasting in a loud, rough voice that he knew "every bloody reef and passage from Honiara to Wewak." The other men teased him about going aground on a New Ireland reef years before and he began to swear at them as they grinned behind their beer.

One of the men, a tall, very black young man threw his arm round Brynne's thick shoulders and glanced across at Evelyn and the earnest Kiwi pilot, who was earbashing her in a quiet voice. She wasn't taking much notice and kept her eyes on Brynne and his friend.

"What's up Taffy? Don't tell me you found yourself a girlfriend mate. She looks alright too. I thought you'd marry a nun."

Henry Sinclair thought himself a bit of a ladies man and he flashed a broad white smile at Evelyn when they made eye contact. Henry boasted that he was an Englishman; because his grandfather had been one. He got his native girlfriend pregnant and the son that was the result was Henry's dad. He was sent to school in England and when he came home he married a coal black woman from the Shortland Islands. Henry turned out as dark as his mum and was sent for a good education in Australia. He became the owner and skipper of a copra boat named *ELIZABETH //* and made a good living. He often had young women tourists as passengers and for many he was a romantic trophy memory to take home.

Brynne chuckled at Henry's interest in Evelyn, he knew all about his exploits.

"Nah, she's an anthropologist Henry. I have to look after her for awhile and make sure she gets home, virgo intacto, without a scratch on her. You remember that Yank I had with me last year collecting sea horses on the reefs. It's that kind of job."

"Wow! You sure get some cruisy jobs Brynne. Where will you take her? I'm going to pick up the Catholic Mission copra on the Duke of Yorks next week if you want to come along."

The men at the table were falling out after too much beer and boasting so Brynne and Henry went back to Evelyn and Kevin. The latter was looking a bit discouraged so Brynne surmised that she had not encouraged his efforts. He introduced Henry to his guests and was surprised at the instant radiance that bloomed from Evelyn, whose eyes were locked on the flirtatious smile on Henry's face.

Just then the grumpy skipper and his dog stumbled away from the laughing mob at the other table and headed for the plank across the storm water drain. It started to bounce and the dog lost its balance and fell on his master's feet and they both pitched into the bottom of the muddy drain. Thunderous laughter burst from everyone, including guys up in the bar. Kevin wasn't in a laughing mood, he just remarked drily,

"So much for the great navigator, his bearings were a bit off there."

This remark sent Evelyn into contortions of laughter and Brynne and Henry were pulled into her orbit for a moment.

Henry ran over to pull the old skipper out of the drain and then he whistled to a taxi driver to take him down to the dock. He gave the driver a couple of notes because he would have to wash the mud out of the cab.

"Take care Nelson" he yelled as the car drove away and then he came back chuckling to the table.

"Poor old feller, the tumble is going to haunt him for awhile. That mob won't let him forget it. Say Brynne, are you playing this Sunday? I might come down and watch. My little brother is having a run for Comworks."

"Yes do come Henry. We play Comworks in the four o clock game. I'll see if I can smash young Simon right in front of the stands."

Henry grinned, "Yeah right, if you can catch him, yuh fat bugger. At school they call Simon 'The Black Flash'. I used to be 'The Flash Black' I still am I guess."

Evelyn was now eager to participate in the conversation.

"I suppose you are talking about a rugby match Brynne. I'd like to come to that. I used to watch my brother and always enjoyed it. I even played on a girl's team myself."

"Certainly Evelyn, but Sunday morning you must come to church with me. I'd love to see your reaction when you hear the children sing at the Vunapope Church.

"They have a beautiful choir."

"Hmm! I'm not at my best on Sunday mornings but if that's your passion I'll come along. How is it that a Welsh chapel lad is into Catholic Church choir? It must be your genetic proclivity for singing,"

"Yes quite right Evelyn. My parents are singers and I'm not too bad myself. The missionaries have done a great job encouraging choral music and the people have embraced it across all denominations. They put their heart and soul in it"

Kevin was becoming bored with them and rose to leave, muttering about what he had to get done in the afternoon. He sat down again when the waiter brought out an excellent lunch of grilled fish and salad. He ate quickly and rose again to leave. "Hang on a bit cuz" said Brynne, "I'll run you back up to your quarters."

Brynne then quickly finished his light lunch. "Excuse me for a moment Evelyn, I'll be back directly."

As he drove out of the parking area Kevin beside him heaved a big sigh.

"Jesus Brynne, that sheila is as cold as a maggot. She doesn't respond in any normal way in conversation. She just looks you in the eye and answers a question with an unrelated one of her own. You won't be into her drawers anytime soon I reckon."

Brynne Lewis grinned at Kevin's discomfort.

"I imagine Evelyn is used to being hit on by blokes like you Kevin. She won't bother me. I'm in the role of loco parentis with her, like the great white hunter on the safari. I just have to help her with her task. She has some high ranking connections, Lords and governors and wankers like that. I don't have any romantic notions."

"What do you mean 'blokes like me?'" growled Kevin, "I just invited her to a dance at the golf club tomorrow night but she didn't even acknowledge the invite."

At the air crew house Lewis pulled into the driveway between high fences and croton bushes and saw an air hostess in a thin house coat hanging her dainties on the Hills hoist. The sun shone through her cool cotton garment, revealing a shapely silhoette.

"Now she is a pretty woman Kev. How is your security in this place? Rabaul can be a dodgy town for a woman."

Brynne waved his hand to the smiling young hostess.

Kevin yanked his six pack of beer out of the ute and stood beside the door.

"We haven't had any bother, except for the odd Peeping Tom in the mango tree.

'Old Pedro the house boy fixed that. He stapled thorny Bougainvillea branches up high where you can't see them from the ground. He didn't catch any of the bastards but he sometimes sees blood below the tree and he yells so triumphantly you'd think he won a lottery. Thanks for the lift Brynne and good luck in the bush. Hope you don't have to carry her ladyship out on your shoulder."

Back at the Cosmo Hotel Evelyn was in animated discussion with Henry Sinclair and Brynne felt like an intruder as he pulled out his chair. The blond head and the black one drew further apart. Evelyn was pink and breathless while Henry had a grin a mile wide and gave Brynne a wink. He stood up and patted her shoulder affectionately, then shook hands with Brynne.

"See you on Sunday Brynne, I'll warn the young feller that you plan to trample him beneath your farmer boots."

Henry walked nimbly across the plank over the storm drain and strolled over to a three ton Bedford truck with a dozen native men in the back. He climbed in the passenger side door and waved to them as it drove away in a cloud of grey dust.

Evelyn and Brynne went out across the bouncy plank and as they drove onto the road she said. "Your friend Henry is a lovely chap Brynne. What a romantic life he has, sailing around on *ELIZABETH //* carrying passengers and copra and doing diving charters for millionaires. It's about as free a life as one can imagine. Have you ever been with him on a trip?"

"Yes I have. Henry always treats me like a millionaire guest. He is the same with everyone, plantation labourers or rich Americans. He makes a little money but really doesn't care as long as he can cover his bills. His father is the one who does well. He runs a barge that can unload directly onto the beach so he gets chartered by all kinds of people."

When they drove up onto the lawn in front of his house Evelyn felt like the Queen stepping off the *BRITTANIA*. Half the village emerged from the bushes, with Albert in the lead followed by Iambata and a crowd of beaming children. Brynne introduced them and then Iambata escorted her along a line of people with whom she had to shake hands. Evelyn kissed the first child and then had no option but to repeat the process for the whole line. There was a tug of war to carry her bag into the house until Albert clapped his hands and told everyone to go home. Iambata stayed as Albert made tea and Brynne explained to Evelyn how the girl could help her during her stay.

Iambata was still excited and she looked charming, with hibiscus flowers in her woolly hair, a smile of perfect white teeth and wearing a snow white Mother Hubbard blouse and green laplap. Evelyn opened up like a flower and gave the girl a sisterly hug and thanked her for her tasteful bouquet.

Then she had a look around the fibro cottage. Brynne and Albert were nervous but encouraged by her nods of approval, even at the primitive bathroom and the copper boiler behind the kitchen for washing clothes. Albert took the tea pot out to the gazebo with its panoramic view of Blanche Bay. She glanced at the tin of Nestle condensed milk and then took pictures of the bay and Iambata by the gazebo. The reception had all turned out much as Brynne had hoped. He realised he was tired from the tension of his unusual assignment but as he sipped the tea and crunched a ginger snap biscuit he relaxed and realised that this had been the easy part. He still had to get her across the Bainings Mountains without putting his foot in it.

"Evelyn, one of the things that bothers me about this job is that I might find myself out in the bush with someone who doesn't really want to be there. It has only happened once but by the time we got back me and Albert were plotting murder. I mention this because you seem a little ambivalent about the trip.

'Do you have any doubts or questions?"

She sipped her tea and looked out at the blue expanse of Blanche Bay and the green volcanic cones on the far side. Then she turned her lovely calm eyes to him. He liked this of her, the way she gave considered responses without blurting out the first thought in her head.

"Brynne, rest assured, I absolutely want to be here. A great deal of planning has gone into this venture. Several people have been involved and you should feel proud that your ability as a mentor and facilitator is highly regarded. I had a meeting with Pim Trautman who you looked after for several months in this district when he was doing a study out of ANU in Canberra. That interview is why I am here.

'I'm sorry if my reticent nature gave you the jitters. We will get along very well.

†I'm quite tough and self reliant and will not challenge your authority or leadership and will heed your advice in all things. I already feel comfortable with you and Albert and Iambata and I'm eager to set off. Does that make you feel better?"

"Yes indeed it does Evelyn. I'm glad Pim spoke well of me. He was a fine chap, good at his work and fun to be with. We shared a passion for port and cigars and fishing on the Bay with his wife and children. I should have paid to do the job with him and felt quite lost when they went home."

"It's a lovely spot here, don't you have a nice girlfriend to keep you company on weekends?"

He could tell she was trying to tease him a little, or was maybe a little apprehensive that such a girlfriend might show up and embarrass him with her presence.

"No, I don't make much of an impression with the ladies I'm afraid. Most of the white women in town are nurses or secretaries. I'm not a party goer so my friends are mostly sports people and male. When I do socialise it's usually at the mixed race clubs or the Kuomintang Club in Chinatown. I'm a legend at the Bossanova and the Twist by the way."

"Oh! Can I come too Brynne? The New Zealander invited me to a dance at the Golf Club but your venues sound much more appealing to me. When I was a teenager my father was posted to Trinidad and Tobago and I had the wildest time of my life there. I had a lovely black boyfriend and I enjoyed more ganga, rum and calypso sex than I thought possible. Father was upset and shipped me off to Cambridge to save my soul. It was a case of 'out of the frying pan into the fire' for the first year. After that I got down to work and found I was a good student. How about tomorrow night? It's a Saturday so there's sure to be something brewing."

Iambata was smiling but had no idea what ganga, rum and calypso sex was. She thought it might be some kind of dance with the black boy friend. She was too shy to ask but it probably was..

Brynne chuckled at her candid nature. "Ok we can do that but I don't want to be up all night drinking rum and coke and dancing my boots off. I have a football game on Sunday to think of and I want to get up early to enjoy the choir at Vunapope.

'If you promise to come home before midnight it's on, at least for me. You might wish to make other arrangements, given your predilection for ganga, rum and sex."

"Thank you Brynne. I promise not to be too much of a handful. I'm more grown up now than when I was seventeen."

"Well that's encouraging. Don't forget where you are Evelyn. Be a bit 'street smart' with your personal safety."

She made no comment on that piece of advice but it had made an impact.

"I'll give you a checklist of things you'll need in the bush; and I stress 'need' as all our equipment and supplies will be carried in steel boxes on a pole between two carriers. There aren't very many able bodied men in some villages so we have to keep our baggage to a minimum. Albert is very good at keeping clothes washed and dried even in the rain and fog of high altitudes. He hangs them by the cook fire, so they quickly smell smoky. You'll get used to that.

'The most important thing to remember is look after your feet and legs. Scratches can quickly become inflamed, especially on new chum legs. Tropical ulcers are a painful danger which can be prevented by disinfecting the tiniest scratch. Tinea between the toes and the crutch and armpits is also lurking for the careless so we take lots of talcum powder, tinea powder and metho to dry the skin. I have a full tropical first aid box as I often have to treat people in the villages. Once we get going we have no outside communication. The only way we can get help is by sending a runner to the nearest mission.

'It's all routine to me now but you can see why I'm a bit nervous about looking after someone else. You look fit and healthy Evelyn so I'm confident you'll come through without any worries. Let's go indoors and you can check my list and we can pick up your kit in town tomorrow morning. I urge you to use cotton drill long pants rather than shorts. Natives are turned on by shapely female thighs, God bless them. And bare legs are also attractive to leaches and thorny lawyer vines. You can charge all this stuff to my account and I'll claim on it after we come back."

He then thanked Iambata for coming to meet Evelyn and promised her he would get her some kit for the trip. She ran off with her little sister, still full of excitement.

After dinner Evelyn sat at the table with a lantern and diligently went through his patrol check list and made a list of her own. She was still at it when he went to bed.

He was pleased to hear her fill the shower bucket and take a cold shower before she too retired. He would have boiled some water if she had asked; he liked her self reliant streak.

Evelyn Pemberton Davies lay naked and barely cool under her green mosquito net, thinking through the events of the day. The genuine warmth of the village and the excited affection of Iambata delighted her. She was less enthused about the pilot's unwelcome, tentative attention. Brynne Lewis was more reserved but she suspected that he too was biding his time before making some clumsy proposition, despite his obvious good advice. She had been getting good advice all her life and realised she had became less tolerant of those who gave it as she grew older. As she pictured the inviting smile of Henry Sinclair she felt a stir of desire, like the first time she met Ambrose in the West Indies. She looked forward to seeing him again on Sunday; already there was an unspoken attraction between them which she had no intention to resist.

Before the sun was up the next morning the road beside the cottage had become busy, with people walking by, loaded with produce, to catch a truck to town from the corner by Navuneram Primary School, about a half mile away. The main road from Toma and the Warengoi Valley swept around the bend there. Drivers stopped to load people and garden produce and by the time they pulled into the Rabaul market they were usually grossly overloaded. Brynne and Evelyn ate a leisurely breakfast in the haus wind and enjoyed the magnificent sunrise to the east as the sun came up behind the unusually clear blue mountains of New Ireland and reflected from the distant coral beaches of the Duke of York islands, a ring of atolls around a central lagoon. Brynne loved those islands and wished he had more reasons to go there than once or twice a year.

"Is that the island that Henry Sinclair is going to on Sunday Brynne. He said he has to pick up the copra from the Catholic Mission plantation on Monday?"

"Yes Evelyn. It's about a two hour trip from Rabaul but he usually takes a day or two, picking up people and the things they bring to town to sell. Last year I spent a month out there with a marine biologist from Honolulu. He had a ten thousand dollar grant to travel every island group in the South Pacific collecting little sea horses so they could be classified. Great job. Too bad you are an anthropologist who wants to traipse through the soggy Bainings Mountains." Brynne gave an exaggerated sigh.

"It's not all beer and skittles in this job."

Evelyn piled another bowl with red pawpaw, banana and passion fruit salad.

"This fruit salad is marvellous Brynne; no wonder you are so beautiful. That's probably why you get all these good jobs."

He grinned at her teasing. "Thanks Evelyn I'll write to my mum and tell her what you said, and I'll add 'and she is an anthropologist too so she knows what she's talking about'. We'll head down to Rabaul shortly so bring some swimming gear and something to wear tonight. I'll show you around and when you get a place in town it will all be familiar"

"What! Are you trying to get rid of me already Brynne?"

"No. Of course not. I was told you plan to spend six months doing research for your PHD. I can't imagine you camping here without power and a hot shower. Also

I'm often away for weeks at a time and this is an isolated spot for a young woman to live alone. Once this expedition is over you can then decide how you will complete your assignment. By the time we get back you will be glad to see the back of me."

"Oh! Ok. I thought you were to be my Man Friday for six months."

Brynne Lewis laughed in genuine amusement. "Are you serious? Even his lordship or whatever your connections are couldn't swing that. I have lots of other jobs to do but you can count on me to assist in any way I can. I'm looking forward to being involved in your research. I had a good time with Pim and I read all his notes and observations and we discussed a great deal of it together."

She looked out at the blue expanse below and waved to some children passing by. Her confidence seemed to have dipped a little. "Yes. I see what you mean."

She stood up and picked up the breakfast tray and as they walked across the lawn she said, "It's just first day jitters Brynne. I can be as wild as a tiger and timid as a fawn. One day I hope to be as steady as a guide dog."

"It will probably be about the time you need one" chuckled Brynne.

They drove down the steep, bamboo covered hill into the sweltering, sulphur tainted air of Rabaul. For a newcomer the smell of the Matupit volcano was a little unnerving. Lewis mentioned that silver spoons were tarnished by the slight amount of gas in the air. As they drove by, the sweet odour from the copra crushing mill overpowered the sulphur and further into town the air was heavy with the fragrance of frangipani blooms, jasmine and camellia. They parked some distance from the 'Bung' or market and walked to it among a crowd of all races. Piles of tropical fruit and vegetables were in line under tin roofed shelters and native women sat and squatted among their produce and basket ware, nursing babies and haggling with buyers. Brynne walked along the rows explaining what everything was to Evelyn and telling her the value of the various items. He didn't buy anything but he kept up to date on produce supply and values through the year, as part of his job. Urban natives with no gardens bought all their food from the market and the Chinese were important customers, white people too. Albert did all the food shopping for Brynne's household, except for the few items he purchased at the Burns Philp and Colyer Watson stores.

Many people stopped to shake hands with Brynne and a group of elderly, partially crippled women struggled to their feet and embraced him as if he were their grandson. Their daughters and grandchildren smiled at him and shook his hand and a few brawny men grabbed him, like football players, shaking his hand and patting him on the back after a game.

Occasionally white people greeted him and he introduced them to Evelyn with a brief, defensive explanation that she was on an assignment, so that they wouldn't speculate on any romantic notion. Some young men who he knew through sport grinned knowingly and made comments like, "Yeah, right Brynne, you play the dark horse and here you show up with a movie star."

Evelyn was delighted with the market atmosphere. Iambata appeared before them, full of smiles and excitement and took her by the hand to meet her former school friends. Brynne stood in the shade chatting to his Papuan pal, Les Gorore who was telling him how he had already fallen off the motorbike but was quickly getting better at it. Les introduced his beautiful sister, who worked as a nurse at the hospital and by the time Evelyn came back Brynne was surrounded by a group of giggling brown girls. She could tell they were speculating wildly about her relationship with Brynne so to add fuel to the fire she put her hand behind his neck and kissed him on the cheek and whispered, "I love the market Brynne, it's so alive and colourful."

The girls applauded with claps and giggles, as they did at romantic movie scenes.

Brynne blushed and was lost for words. As they walked back to the car he smiled ruefully at Evelyn and said, "Jesus Evelyn, you sure know how to wind up the troops. Those girls will be whooping ooh la la every time they see me."

"Good! I love these girls Brynne, they are so open and full of the joy of life. I'm so impressed that everyone likes you. Those poor old ladies who struggled up to give you a cuddle almost made me cry. Why are they so fond of you?"

"I'll explain it all on the way to PilaPila beach. It's up over the hill on the north coast."

As they drove out of town he told her about a dreadful accident that had happened on a Saturday morning a couple of years back. "You saw how steep the hill is coming down to town and the sharp curves as it winds round the cliff. A fully loaded market truck lost control and went over the side and plunged into a bamboo thicket. Several people died and those old ladies were badly injured. The insurance company for the truck owner had no idea how to allocate damages and was fearful some UN human rights lawyer would turn it into a multi million dollar case.

'I was asked to calculate the income they would forgo for the rest of their lives because they were too badly injured to work their market gardens. It took many months of measuring their plots and calculating the yields they could sell and what they needed to feed their families. By the time it went to court I knew exactly how much they could grow and what they could get for it at the 'bung'.

'The amazing thing was that it worked out to around $4000 a year. I had to go through all my calculations in court, under

73

cross examination. The company didn't try to contest the figures once they saw how I had made them. Then the question was how does an illiterate old woman know how to handle fifty thousand dollars of compensation?

'When I suggested an annuity that would pay them a hundred dollars a week for life I ran across the bows of the native affairs people, who felt that the agriculture department was encroaching on their territory. I backed off but the lawyer for the old girls kept an eye on the outcome. Finally they all agreed to bank the money and pay them every week through the rural co-op in the village.

'Now they think it was me that made them rich. That's why they always make a fuss of me. I think they give away most of the money every week but that's their business. They are important people now and everyone treats them with the respect they deserve."

"That's nice Brynne. How many people can do their job and have such a rewarding outcome? I wonder what would have happened to those women if a less thorough person had backed their claim. It seems all the young ones like you too. You had lots of fans when I came back with Iambata."

"Yes, they are nice girls, all Papuans from Daru. One is Les Gorore's sister.

'He's a bit of a star now that he has my old AJS motorbike. I hope he won't take them for a ride on it until he can ride it himself. He already scratched up his knees."

As they reached the crest of the hill Brynne stopped the car on the side of the road and opened his door. "Just hop out a minute Evelyn I want you to see this."

She stood beside him looking back across the town and out to sea. The distant islands around an aqua marine lagoon looked beautiful, and closer, inside the bay, a couple of steep peaks rose from the water.

"Those two little islands are called The Beehives and we are standing on what was once the rim of a huge volcano. That grey mass beneath the three green peaks is Matupit. It's still active and it's where the sulphur gas burps out from time to time. 'The whole thing blew up in 1937 and no doubt it will blow again someday. Whenever I drive over this hill I always have visions of what this huge volcano must have looked like in its prime. I link it to the huge craters one sees in telescopic photos of the moon. We seem so insignificant in the scale of time."

Evelyn took pictures of the scene and one of Brynne in which she posed him pointing toward the sea. She realised he had tried to share his awe of nature and time with her and she felt a bit embarrassed that she wasn't sure how to respond without sounding trite. As they drove on towards the beach she remembered a massive volcano she had seen in Patagonia on a trip to South America.

"If you want to see a living replica of what this area was like Brynne I recommend a trip to Patagonia, or Japan for a look at Mount Fuji."

"I should do something like that Evelyn. Usually on leave I just hang around at home or take in some shows in Sydney. You sure have been around. I hope this trip will be memorable for you."

"It's only just beginning," she said as they arrived at the black sand beach. Families were setting up picnics under shady trees and children were diving off a small pontoon anchored fifty yards from shore. The water was calm, blue and inviting with the humidity and temperature nearing peak values before the wind had begun to stir. She quickly threw off her white wrap around frock and ran down to the water in her pink bikini. It wasn't as tiny as those worn by the exhibitionists on Bondi beach, in fact it was only a few square inches less than a modest two piece, but as her form had the classic proportions of a Greek statue, every eye on the beach, both male and female, focused on her.

She quite took Brynne's breath away. She swam strongly towards the pontoon and was on it skylarking with kids before he even reached the waters edge. He was joined there by the men who had been loafing in the shade, some of whom he knew. After some hurried handshakes and introductions they all swam eagerly toward the pontoon while their wives and girlfriends frowned and fiddled with the picnic tables.

Evelyn winked at Brynne and whispered in his ear, "How popular you are Brynne; you have so many friends."

He grinned at her flirtatious body language and admired her awareness of how powerful she was in her effect on men. He rolled off the pontoon and swam ashore to flirt with the mildly resentful women, while she engaged in playful games with the children. One of the ladies he knew casually began to tease him a little.

"I hope you'll introduce us to your little sister Mr Lewis. Is she here for the school holidays?"

"Not exactly a holiday. She is on a university study assignment for a couple of months. It's to do with the way men interact with women in the sultry heat of the tropics."

Five pairs of eyes locked on to Brynne; if they were mares their ears would have been pricked up and their hind hoof would stamp. Before they could regather their wits to comment, his self control broke and he burst out laughing that they had swallowed his hook. The ladies all relaxed and chuckled at the ease with which he had pulled them in.

"Are you to be her guinea pig then Brynne? She might find you a hard old nut to crack, even in the volcanic heat of Rabaul."

"Well Glenda that would be a nice idea. The truth is she is a graduate student and I have to be her guide and helper sometimes. I don't know why they always pick me for these shitty jobs. Maybe your Tom could help out, he seems to be interested."

Out on the pontoon Evelyn was balancing on Tom's shoulders to do a graceful dive into the water. She swam toward the beach while Tom was delayed, doing the same trick with the children.

"Somehow I have to keep her occupied until this evening. It's going to be a long hot day. I promised to take her to the Kombui Club tonight."

"No worries Brynne," said Glenda. "You can spend a few hours at our place to fill in the day. If Tom gets a concentrated perv for a few hours today it might make for an interesting three minutes tonight."

Glenda's friends were shaking with laughter as Evelyn came up the beach but they wouldn't share the joke. One of them filled a plastic container with water from a drum in the truck and rinsed the salt water from her hair and body. She made a few new friends right there and Brynne thought she would soon find more congenial lodgings.

By Saturday afternoon she had bought all the gear she would need and it was safely locked in a steel box bolted to the tray of his truck. Brynne had purchased a few items for Iambata including a pair of canvas and rubber jungle boots and some army surplus trousers the same as Evelyn's. He knew the girl's feet were accustomed to being bare foot but climbing on muddy tracks and stony creeks was not her usual terrain, nor were the lawyer vines, stinging plants and leaches.

Lewis was trying too hard to entertain Evelyn Pemberton-Davies. He knew it but didn't know how to pull back from the commitment he had made. Fortunately for him a regular troublemaker was creating a scene at the Kombui Club so he drove down to Chinatown and took her for dinner to the ChungChing Restaurant. They again joined several people he knew for dinner and he was able to head home afterwards with a clear conscience. They sat in the gazebo drinking a glass of scotch whisky, enjoying the silence and the silver moon on the bay. This part of the day, just reflecting and arranging his thoughts before bedtime was sometimes his most productive time.

"Thank you for a lovely day Brynne, the market and the beach and all your attractive and interesting acquaintances. There is a unique buzz to Rabaul, I could feel it all day. I'll be awake tonight, absorbing it all and speculating on what is to come. I feel like a child going on holiday and eager to catch my first glimpse of the sea."

"This time next week we'll be high in the mountains, sitting in a thatched hut, digesting a feed of brown rice and corned beef. It may well be raining and you'll be writing up your days observations beside a dull lamp which will attract a buzzing swarm of little bugs. But it too will have its rewards Evelyn and when you come back to Rabaul it will seem like the most luxurious place in the world. One of the good things about my job is that I see the joy of new experiences of my guests. We will have some fun together on this trip. Your positive attitude is encouraging and that is all you need, to get the most out of your time here."

"Well we had some fun today, except for the unfortunate fracas that kept us out of the Kombui Club. I wonder why that chap was so angry. Nobody seemed to take much notice of him. Have you any idea what upset him Brynne?"

"Yes I do. His name is Ben Ah Ping and you noticed he was a brown skinned half caste. He is normally a pleasant fellow but he's bitter about the way he is paid. He is a workmate of my friend Lesley at the public works motor pool. Both are good at their work but somehow the administration has them on different pay scales from expatriates. Les is on native scale, Len in the middle range and white mechanics on top scale. Australians won't come here on local wages so the idea is that as the locals become competent the expatriates will not be offered a new contract at Australian pay levels and a future public service will be affordable.

'The wizard that came up with the plan didn't consider the racial tension he had installed. You saw the young white blokes going in the club but Ben and Les can't go into the New Guinea Club or the Kokopo Club. Even you Evelyn cannot enter the bar of the New Guinea Club. If I were Ben I'd be a bit grumpy too. Some handle it well but for Ben it's a lingering toothache that flares up after a couple of drinks. He doesn't see the big picture, like the wise admin people, only a sense of being undervalued.

'Men like Henry Sinclair aren't affected because they are self employed. The Chinese are the same, they don't work for wages, or if they do only until they can start up on their own. I told Ben to do the same and offered to invest a little to get him going. He doesn't quite have the confidence yet."

Evelyn nodded in understanding. "Wage differentials are a touchy point in every workplace. I see clearly the added dimension of race. Just the fact of being white can make others apprehensive. It's a problem like the weather Brynne, you just have to hope the sun will shine because you can't do anything about it."

"Yes, there is some truth in that. If policy gurus spent a bit more time among the people they administer they might add the right ingredients. One day we will all be kicked out so I hope everyone will be content. All these clans and racial mixes don't realise yet that we are the only neutral force. When we are gone they will have to face up to their own differences. I'm sure they will but they might miss us for a while.

'I'll keep you from your room for a few minutes while I shower and shave for tomorrow. Don't feel obliged to come to church tomorrow. I have some friends among the people in the choir who appreciate my enjoyment of their singing so it's a sort of duty to be there when I can."

"Ok Brynne, I might give it a miss this time and have a lazy Sunday sleep in. Good night."

He left quietly the next morning and drove down through NangaNanga village, slowly so as not to kick up too much dust. By the time he reached the coast road to turn right to Vunapope the back of the ute had several passengers plus two cheeky little boys beside him. He realised he would have to impose some number limits, especially coming home. The local people, especially the young were capable of squeezing a dozen people onto a small utility. It was a catch twenty two situation where you made friends with the riders and enemies of those refused.

The singing was soaring to new heights of perfection since the choir festival and he had to resist the urge to applaud, since he was in church. Afterwards he told his eager passengers, who were already in place by the time he returned to the vehicle, that they would all have to get down as he had business in Kokopo. It took a few minutes before he could leave and complete his business; a game of snooker at the Kokopo Club and breakfast with the manager.

Then he drove down to Takumbar beach and watched the water skiers skimming around on the bay. Most of the people were plantation staff who enjoyed a Sunday barbeque, which often included fish when early morning anglers stopped by to cook their catch. Brynne liked the atmosphere and the people but had no affection for riding the skis. There was sometimes a bit of tension in the air. A few men among the planters felt resentment toward 'admin people'. Australian politicians of the left had angered plantation owners by implying that their days were numbered, like the white farmers of Africa. Brynne Lewis was not a target since he was an agronomist but he was sometimes aware of resentment toward native affairs and other departments who were suspected of supporting the view that planters and business people were in some way colonial oppressors.

When he arrived at home Evelyn was in the gazebo with Iambata, who was giving her a lesson in pidgin English. She rose to leave but he said, "No stay Iambata, I want to see you teaching missus."

He was impressed with the girl's gentle and patient explanations and the care with which she taught the humour and nuances of a quite colourful language. Evelyn was attentive and eager to learn so he left them to it and relaxed on his bed on the veranda. He woke around two o clock to Evelyn calling gently to awaken him.

She had on a light blue wrap around dress with a yellow sash around the waist to keep it all in place. Her floppy white hat and sandals had reappeared and her army rucksack, looking quite full, sat on the table. *A very fetching outfit*, he thought, but he didn't make any gallant comment. He had plenty of time before the game but it wasn't too early to leave. His football gear was all washed, ironed and packed in the kitbag so he threw it in the back of the car. Iambata, urged on by Evelyn, wanted to come to see the football game so he told her to ask Albert for permission. He didn't really want her along, but with Evelyn as well it would be ok. Rabaul was an easy town to start scurrilous rumours.

He parked the ute some distance from the football ground so that the women could see all the various sporting contests going on in Elizabeth Park. Two soccer matches were being vigorously contested by native players, all playing barefoot in front of cheering fans. It was the first season since the game had been banned for a couple of years. A player had suffered a broken leg and huge fights erupted when one team was accused of sorcery in the incident. Many native policemen were posted to prevent a recurrence. Women were playing basketball in a wild, rough and tumble style and athletes were racing on the grass running track. The spectator stands were where Brynne's mother had seen the choirs from all the schools for miles around.

The early game, in the heat of the sun, was being played when they climbed into the shady stand at the football ground. People were hurrying in to get a seat in the shade for the big game and soon they were joined by Henry Sinclair and his young brother Simon. Henry was trying to stir up some rivalry but Simon and Brynne just grinned and ignored him. Brief but heavy scuds of rain passed over the ground and by the time the two players left for the changing room, pools of water had formed in places on the field. Brynne enjoyed cool wet conditions, when opponent's legs became slippery and spectacular slides occurred in high speed tackles. Soon after the starting whistle both teams were well coated with mud and players were fooling around trying to push their opposite number's face in the mud as they got up to play the ball. Brynne tried it with Simon after bringing him down right in front of the stand. Simon was not amused and got up in a rage, throwing wild punches at Brynne. He quickly cooled off when Brynne ran behind the referee for protection and he heard Henry screaming with laughter in the stand. Simon's team emerged victorious by two points so he threw his arm around Brynne in forgiveness as they walked off the field.

The showers were cold but refreshing as they took turns to rinse off most of the dirt and sweat. Usually Brynne went down to the Cosmo beer garden for a few drinks and a post mortem of the game but he wanted to get Iambata home before it was too dark. He would have liked to take Evelyn there to experience the blokey atmosphere of after rugby beer but she had wanted the girl to come with them and he couldn't take a sixteen year old native girl to a beer garden full of bawdy ruffians.

Nearly everyone was gone from the stand except a few wives and girlfriends waiting for men still in the changing room. Iambata sat alone on the bottom row, looking unhappy. She stood up as Brynne approached with his bag of smelly clothes.

She looked embarrassed and shy and his first thought was that someone had made unwelcome advances toward her, as Evelyn was not there. Before he could ask where she was Iambata burst out in pidgin, "Missus go wantaim Henry long ship masta."

It seemed no big deal to Brynne, he thought she had gone down to the dock to have a look at *Elizabeth//* before dark. He told Iambata it was ok, they would drive by the waterfront on the way home and pick her up. He was surprised when Iambata told him the ship had left for the Duke of Yorks and she had been told to tell him Evelyn would be back on Tuesday.

Well how bloody dumb am I? He thought. Briefly he considered going round to Bob Gifford's house to let him know she was no longer in his care. The need to get Iambata home promptly became his priority. Evelyn is free, white and over twenty one, he told himself. Gifford was capable of sending a policeman in a boat to bring her back. That would go down like a lead balloon with a free spirit like Miss Evelyn Pemberton Davies. Besides, she was safe with Henry, except for her virginity, which was apparently long gone anyway.

If she was like other women who went with Henry on his boat, she might be gone for a couple of weeks, like the two German girls he had taken to Kavieng a month or so back. Henry had form with female backpackers. Brynne realised he was disappointed in her. It was uncomfortable to face the reasons why. The last thought he had as Iambata ran off home was that with or without Evelyn he would still take her to the Bainings. The girl was so excited about the trip that he couldn't bear to disappoint her.

Later, as he lay under his mosquito net waiting for the crickets to sing him to sleep he realised that Evelyn had planned this excursion with Henry Sinclair while they were in the beer garden on the day of her arrival. That accounted for her full knapsack and her request to bring Iambata to the game. He pictured her walking toward the terminal shed at the airstrip and remembered her knapsack looked flat and empty. "She is one tricky unit" he said aloud. It wasn't really a breech of trust on her part, but it would have been better if she had been open about it and just said she wanted to go with Henry to the islands. He had more obligation to her than she to him, since she was part of his job. As he drifted off to sleep he hoped that Henry's legendary stamina in the bunk would keep her away until he had left on the scheduled Bainings patrol.

He wondered if she was fair dinkum about her studies or whether she was just a wealthy dilettante with time on her hands.

Evelyn had briefly considered telling of her plans with Henry but in the heat of her desire it was easy to dismiss the notion. She told herself she was not obliged to discuss her personal life with a hairy legged rugby player she barely knew. She was not attracted to people with strong, dimpled chins and burly shoulders. The classic beauty of men like Henry filled her with desire and in such moments she sometimes overlooked things that she would normally consider good manners. She had invited Iambata along solely to ease her defection with him, without considering Brynne's responsibility for the girl.

Chapter Six

"The mill cannot grind
With the water that is past"
Sarah Doudney

Brynne woke at six o clock to the rattle of Albert tipping a kettle full of boiling water into the red shower bucket. Momentarily he had forgotten about Evelyn, until he walked past her suitcase into the bathroom. He enjoyed scrubbing off the remains of yesterday's sport blemishes and shaving neatly before his new mirror. He gave a sigh of frustration, that soon he would be confronted with questions about the missing guest, by every inquisitive child that passed the house. Iambata would have spread the news and it would ricochet throughout the village. It was a beautiful clear morning, with no heat haze over the sea but he had his pot of tea and fruit salad indoors at the dining room table, to avoid the kids who usually stopped for a visit when he had breakfast under the Poinceana tree.

Albert crept around in uncomfortable silence. He had the full story from the girl but was too shy to mention it. Brynne said nothing to ease the tension. Instead he resolved to escape for a couple of days down to his camp in the Warengoi Valley. Part of his job there was to monitor the development of the soldier settler plantations. They were obliged to plant four hundred acres of cocoa trees with the capital that had been lent to them. Most were good men but a couple were drunks and difficult to manage so he sometimes spent a few days at a time with them. They knew they could be evicted if they failed to meet their commitments to the Soldier Settlement Board so Brynne Lewis had some tense moments. He felt in the mood for a bit of confrontation. He took a change of clothes and some food and told Albert he would be back for lunch on Wednesday.

As he drove away he felt quite triumphant, having escaped nosey questions from the villagers and fired up about exerting his authority with a couple of ingrate settlers.

The plan worked well and he was unusually assertive with his resentful clients. They made the usual derogatory comments that they had been fighting the Jap's before he was born and they didn't need advice from a bludging public servant. In a rare loss of control Brynne assured one man that he had checked his service record and found he had been an airfield labourer who had never seen a Japanese soldier in his life. He further told him he was a fraud and more deserving veterans were waiting for a block so had better shape up or he would be out by Christmas.

This outburst was therapeutic and after a couple of congenial visits with better men his good humour returned. He tried to tell himself that he always felt bad when his guests went home, so his sense of failure with Evelyn was irrational. By the time he went home on Wednesday though he had admitted to himself that she had got under his skin and hurt him. The self- evident truth was that he had no right to feel that way and she had not made any attempt to encourage such feelings.

In this rather pathetic and unsettling state he drove up onto the lawn and saw her, behind him and to the left, sitting in the gazebo talking to Albert's wife. It was an awkward moment and all he could do was wave his hand and carry his bag into the house and unpack the few items. Albert came in from the kitchen and said in a flat tone,

"Missus he stap," and pointing his nose toward the gazebo.

"Yes Albert," he said shortly. "Are you ready for tomorrow and Iambata too?"

In his laconic style Albert lifted his nose again to three galvanised patrol boxes on the veranda. Brynne didn't need to ask again if everything was packed. The two of them had been on many bush patrols together. His personal box needed the addition of a couple of good books and some rum and pipe tobacco, his personal vices that he reserved for evenings in camp.

Evelyn came into the house with the unabashed confidence of a teenager, about to tell lies to her father.

"Hallo Brynne. As you see, we are all packed and eager to go. I havn't seen Iambata, today but Albert has packed for her. Where have you been? I thought you had gone off in a huff because I went for a trip with Henry."

Brynne felt himself blushing and at a loss for words. He looked directly into her eyes for a moment to try to take the heat out of his feelings, it didn't work.

"Yes. I was a little peeved that you slunk away like an Arab in the night and left Iambata alone in the grandstand. I was made responsible for your safety Evelyn, it would have been better if you told me what you had arranged at the pub with Henry."

His direct approach confronted her own and brought some colour to her cheeks.

"I'm twenty five years old Brynne Lewis. It's a long time since I had to explain myself to anyone, or ask permission to do anything. I apologise though for my neglect of Iambata. In fact I do see your point; I should have told you what I wanted to do."

"Ok Evelyn. Your response is as honest as one could wish, so we'll move on. Try to be considerate of the duties of others. Four weeks together in the bush requires a bit of patience and tolerance and the ability to soak up discomfort without moaning."

It was clear to her that Brynne was hurt and unhappy. She felt both complimented and concerned. Other men had fallen in love with her, with what she considered very little encouragement on her part. Eventually they had become tiresome. Henry Sinclair was one. He had matched her urgent lust, but when it was satiated he didn't want it to end and asked her to come with him on a long trip to pick up a plantation labour force from Wewak, hundreds of miles to the west.

"Why do you want to wander in the jungle with Brynne, covered in all the mud and leaches and rain when you can come cruising with me, like the Queen in my luxurious royal yacht?"

She had giggled in his embrace and grabbed his crotch, saying huskily, "Are you Henry the Eight then your majesty?"

It wasn't true that Henry had become tiresome; she had enjoyed her time with him in the Duke of York islands. It was as sexy and adventurous as her time in

Trinidad and Tobago when she was a girl. The short break was but a welcome prelude to some serious work and she knew that her academic ambitions were genuine.

Conversation seemed strained so Brynne excused himself to write up his Soldier Settlement Journal. He was utterly candid in his daily journal but more circumspect in his official reports, which required diplomatic language and selected accuracy.

The delicious aroma of roast lamb was wafting from the kitchen stove where Albert was cooking a last fresh meat meal before the weeks of canned beef and spam.

Lewis busied himself at his cramped desk on the verandah and then finished packing his patrol box, which was the only one with a lock on it. They ate a light salad lunch in the gazebo together and gradually the mood returned to normal. Iambata came by with her mother and shared tea with them but she had trouble looking directly at Evelyn and tried to keep her head down. Her mother was bold and direct and told Evelyn that she expected her to take good care of her daughter. She shook hands with Brynne and looked him in the eye, but she made no further comment. They both knew that her daughter was in his care.

Later that evening, after the wonderful roast lamb dinner, they sat outside in silver moonlight, sipping port. Brynne began to relax again, telling her what to expect from tomorrow onwards.

"We will begin our journey tomorrow from the village of Gaulim Evelyn. It's the first of the Baining villages and we can drive to it. From there we will have to walk across the mountains to the north coast. You will see the people get less sophisticated as we move along, to the point where they are almost at pre contact level. You will find them dour, serious people who seem devoid of interest in humour, sex or festivity. Your anthropology antenna will be on high alert as soon as we get there.

'Of course Gaulim is a little different, famous for the elaborate tapa masks they make and the annual fire pit ceremony where people run through a bed of hot coals carrying pythons and carpet snakes. The village grows cocoa and is used to a little cash, the people speak some pidgin, but they don't have much contact with their Tolai neighbours. The headman is a self appointed bully named Tanke. He is a pain in the neck. Albert told me he is also a paedophile who has intercourse with little girls, one in particular. He should be arrested and thrown in jail, but he is also the leading figure in a cargo cult and has an evil influence way down through the South Bainings to

Wide Bay. He has convinced his followers that he has the answer to getting access to cargo, like white men. I was in Wide Bay a few months ago and found he had convinced the people they didn't need to plant their food gardens because soon he would have access to all the goods that are in the stores in Rabaul. When I addressed the village and told them they should care for their food gardens in case Tanke was unsuccessful, the reaction was quite frightening. The facial expressions were savage and deeply suspicious, like the old photos one sees of frightened, first contact people. Sergeant Binus whispered to me to put a sock in it and get out of there as he sensed bad vibes. He pulled back the bolt on his .303 service rifle and pretended he was loading it. Then we left. He is never issued with ammunition for that thing.

'Tanke has been to town and seen people fill up a trolley on account and walk out of the store without handing over any cash. This to him is proof that the whites have a magic secret. He sells cocoa and receives cash but figures it's a con. In the village he has built a store, with shelves and a padlocked door, like a Chinese trade store. He claims that one day he will open the door and voila; it will be full of cargo.

'He tells the people that he has had a dream that a giant python had wrapped itself around the summit of Mount Sinuwit to lure the Americans into revealing the secret of cargo. His proof is that an American Navy helicopter had made gifts to the python totem on the mountain. The Americans had indeed dropped off material there, namely a petrol generator and some drums of fuel and a radio station and transmitter of some kind. He has convinced the people that white men will try to dupe them and has told them they will die mysteriously if they talk to whites. Anyone who dies now is suspected of having been a traitor and of course a few people have indeed passed on.

'So this awful man has erected a shield of ignorance around himself so no one is brave enough to arrest him and provoke an outbreak of lethal violence. The only man currently standing up to him is a black Methodist missionary named Jeremy who denounces him in church and to his face as being an emissary of the devil.

'We may see this bloke tomorrow morning. He has a massive haematoma behind his left ear and people call him 'Man bilong buk' or the man with a lump. The carriers for our gear will be there, from Malasait village, which will be our first stop. It's about a three hour walk. I feel the people we will meet are not impressed by Tanke. In fact not much seems to impress them at all. If you can get the women to talk candidly with you I will be very interested in what they tell you."

"I've heard of cargo cults before, I think from the New Hebrides. That was to do with Americans and their massive access to military supplies. I also saw in the papers that someone offered to buy Vice President Johnson. I'm sure some Republicans were eager to sell too. Thanks for that background Brynne. This trip is all set for some interesting encounters."

The road down to Gaulim badly needed grading. Deep washouts ran across it on slopes and the flat areas were dusty and corrugated, making a bone shaking, neck wrenching ride in an International truck and Land Rover troop carrier. With relief they arrived a little after eight in the morning to be greeted by Jeremy, the Methodist minister. He had built a magnificent native materials church and took his work very seriously, especially as he had a resident Satan in the village. Brynne gave him a parcel of exercise books and a couple of boxes of soft pencils and thanked him for taking care of the field workers who stayed in the village teaching the people how to look after their cocoa trees. The men were brought back to the extension centre for weekends and in fact were quite self sufficient. Even so, Jeremy was kind and supportive toward them.

A group of squat, tough looking men, wearing a piece of dirty cloth around their waists began to shove thick bamboo poles through the hoop handles on the boxes and lashing them with strips of vine. Sergeant Binus, the big black policeman inspected their work and shook hands with a couple of them. He wore his black, wool serge police tunic, trimmed around the edges and the V neck with red and his sergeant's stripes. On his head was a police beret and in his hand he carried a .303 Lee Enfield service rifle. The rifle was a prop to emphasize his authority. A wide, polished leather belt with a shiny brass buckle encircled his waist and had several mysterious pouches on it. His powerful frame and assertive manner worked and he was treated with respect. Later on he would wear khaki shorts but once in a village he would again don his full uniform until the next move.

At a signal from his hand the men, as one, picked up their load and filed out of the village, watched by dirty, pot- bellied children, even more pot- bellied mothers and a pack of skinny, scrofulous dogs. The sergeant fell in behind them followed by Albert, Iambata and Evelyn with Brynne Lewis in the rear. Everyone carried a machete, shiny with use, except the policeman and Evelyn.

Soon they emerged from the rows of cocoa trees and walked through patches of tall forest, interspersed with open food gardens containing banana groves, mounds of sweet potato and taro with huge leaves resembling elephant ears. Conical towers of sticks, like great wigwams were covered in yam vines. In the open places in full sunlight, bushes and vines grew profusely over the track. Everyone slashed them off with their sharp bush knives in a rhythmic motion, like a horse swishing its tail against flies. Under the high forest canopy there was no ground cover and the path became soft and muddy as they plodded on in single file. When the track sloped upwards feet began to lose traction and cut the path up quickly so that Evelyn was soon breathing hard as her boots and trouser bottoms became wet and muddy.

Brynne was bringing up the rear and watching Evelyn's shapely bum straining along bravely. Just when she thought she would have to take a break they crested a ridge and began the descent down an even steeper incline of mud and twisted tree roots. Brynne lopped off a couple of strong sticks to assist the descent, as Albert and Binus had already done. She grinned at Brynne as he gave her the stick but said nothing for fear she would show how breathless she was. Her shirt was black with sweat, which also dripped off her nose and darkened her fair hair.

At the bottom of the hill a broad, clear green river swept around a bend over a bank of gravel and then disappeared into deeper, and even greener water, reflecting the overhanging forest. The carriers walked straight into the water and waded across up to their waist and without hesitation climbed quickly up the steep bank and on into the forest. Iambata stooped and swept water up over her head and cupped her hands to drink. Her beaming smile was back. She was relishing the adventure. Soaked with mud and sweat, Evelyn sank thankfully into the cool water and smiled up at Brynne.

"Just when I thought I had hit the wall we come to this delicious river. Now I feel

I could walk forever Brynne."

"It's not that far, we are nearly halfway. You've done well Evelyn. It actually gets a little easier soon," he lied. "Push up now, we don't want to be left too far behind."

She looked up and realised that everyone had gone, even Iambata, so she plunged across the river and strode manfully on, encouraged by Brynne's praise and determined to do well. It was as exciting as the Outward Bound course she had done as a schoolgirl in the Scottish Highlands. Blasé at the time, she now realised how valuable that experience had been to the confidence she needed now. She was unaware that Brynne was keeping the worst till last and had not picked up the unease in his voice when he urged her to keep up with the carriers.

The narrow track had dissolved into mud where it passed through low areas. This had slowed down the carriers and soon she could hear them not far ahead as the ground rose steeply in a cathedral of mighty trees, where high overhead stars of light penetrated the thick canopy and vines hung down as if waiting for some hero of the film world to swing by. Underfoot, surface roots were hidden in a thick mulch of rotting leaves which made very arduous climbing. The men were streaming with sweat and holding grimly onto the slippery bamboo poles on their shoulders, which were trying to slide back down hill. The maximum load per box was only eighty pounds but she looked with pity at their struggles and felt sorry for the man on the bottom on the steep slopes. As the going got harder the men started a low chant of deep grunts that seemed to unify them, although it was not like an army marching song or a heave ho chant to co-ordinate effort on a winch or set of oars.

The prodigious effort for twenty minutes brought them to the crest of a steep ridge where they put down their loads and stood beside them with their chests heaving. Evelyn noticed the physique of the men for the first time. As they sat on the boxes or scraped sweat and mud away with their bush knives their powerful shoulders revealed how they could cope with the work. On each mans shoulders a thick pad of skin, as tough as on their feet had formed from using carrying poles since they were boys. Their thighs were powerful and their chests deep, from living in country where the terrain was either up or down. They were not beautiful in the classic sense as their thick eye brow ridges, broad noses and jaws and thick necks gave them a brutish aspect. What was beautiful about them was their power and endurance and their mutual pride in their ability, like a gang of Welsh miners coming off shift with a song of pride in comradeship and shared hardship.

Sergeant Binus moved around among the men, not saying much but sometimes shaking a hand of the leaders and checking the bindings on the poles to make sure one of the boxes would not slide back on a slope and injure the bottom man. Evelyn saw him speak to a boy who was rubbing his knee and looking a little anxious. Binus gave the boy his rifle and when the march resumed he took his place on the front of his pole to take the strain on the downhill side. His mighty body made the other men look small. Although he came from the Sepik district he had none of the tattoos or split earlobes and pierced nasal septum common there. On his right shoulder blade began a band of cicatrice scars that curved upward and then descended down the right side of his spine. His mother had protested about that blemish but was overruled by the elders who insisted he pay proper respect to the mighty crocodile of their environment. His successful career as a policeman was a source of pride and vindication to his mother, who had absorbed some education as the servant of a priest in a Catholic Mission. Had she been a white woman she may well have been described as 'liberated' because of her disregard of custom and bold advocacy of modern ideas.

Brynne checked briefly that Albert and his niece were travelling well and then fell in behind the group. Everyone had cut a stout stave to help their descent and now the discomfort was felt mainly by the men on the front of the pole. Evelyn watched the struggle before her with some trepidation. She had planned a six month study and would have to spend a lot of time in the field between sojourns in Rabaul writing up her findings. She began to wonder if she really wanted to do this study. Eventually the slope grew less severe and after crossing numerous small creeks they came to a larger stream with a fallen tree across it. To her surprise the leading team with Binus at the front, stepped onto the log and marched resolutely across the swaying trunk. The other teams followed without hesitation until the boy carrying the rifle limped across. Albert and Iambata followed with only a slight degree of hesitation and looked back anxiously to see how Evelyn would cope.

Her heart sank as she approached the trembling log. The sides of it were covered in slimy moss and lichens, but the top surface had been rubbed fairly clean by the traffic of bare feet. In spite of her courage and resolve to step straight onto the log and walk across, her heart was pounding, her mouth was dry and her anus felt an uncomfortable tremor of fear. Brynne spoke quietly, just in time to overcome her hesitation.

"The water here is quite deep below Evelyn, at least enough to break your fall. If you take a bath I'll be with you in a second."

His calm presence was enough and she stepped up onto the tree and marched across as though it were a zebra crossing. As she stepped onto terra firma she turned to Brynne with a triumphant smile as he walked across, with the benefit of experience. She was about to make a smart arse quip but desisted when she could tell from his expression he was pleased with her. He made no attempt to praise or flatter, other than to pat her shoulder.

"That was an easy and safe one. We will cross several more with long drops and rocks below. I have a rope and a couple of riggers belts for anyone who wants to use them. The carriers ignore them but Albert and Binus are not so foolhardy."

She nodded but kept her mouth shut to maintain her brave aura and walked for another hour with renewed confidence and sense of accomplishment. Then they emerged from the forest onto a cleared plateau on a ridge and were walking along a path through a young coffee plantation. The rows between the coffee and shade trees were trimmed and neat and merged into gardens of sweet potato vines and banana groves until they came to an open compound with a thatched, bamboo guest hut on head high posts. Nearby was a thatched hut on the ground and a wall less shelter with a rock fireplace in the centre. The sweating carriers were squatting around as Binus and Albert arranged the galvanised steel boxes under the house. A hundred yards further and a little lower down the slope the village of Malasait clustered in two rows on each side of a swept, bare red earth area, like a wide village street.

Iambata was leaning on her stave looking out across the high, forested mountains toward the halo of cloud around Mount Sinuwit. Although she was in awe of the mountains she had a worried expression as she limped across to Albert and sat down on a box under the house. Blood oozed out of her right foot where a sharp, broken stick had cut her instep. He immediately applied a dab to the wound with some cotton wool wound around a stick, which he dipped in a large beer bottle of iodine.

The girl winced at the sting but made no complaint and Albert moved around checking everyone for small nicks and scratches; his first duty at the end of a walk.

Brynne stood with Evelyn looking out across the mountains and pointing out to her the direction their journey would follow. She was aware of the smell of his sweaty shirt as he raised his arm to point and she smiled inwardly that she was probably a little aromatic herself. Below them, from a small wooded ravine with a spring in it came a line of women and girls carrying pails of water on their heads. They were naked except for a small tuft of grass in front and a bunch of leafy twigs behind. They had no ornaments or shells, only a little woven bracelet around the left arm. Some were mature women with wide spaced and somewhat pendulous breasts and a couple were young with half formed buds on their chest. All had protuberant bellies but were otherwise slim, dirty and fit looking. Their feet seemed large and flat and they walked with a pigeon toed, swinging gait. None of them had spilled any water on the climb up the ravine and they lifted down their pails and tipped them into a large Shell oil drum in the cook house. Then, without expression or acknowledgement of the presence of anyone, they made their way back to the village.

"Those are some of the ladies you will be talking to Evelyn. They just delivered cooking water, which they do every time a patrol arrives. Its part of the head man's duty to ensure supply of water and firewood to the government rest house. I don't envy your task. The only thing they seem to understand in these hills is work. You don't even see children playing, other than mimicking the work of their parents."

"Yes, I've noticed how quiet the people are. Even now when their work is done the men seem indifferent and joyless. I don't see any of them smoking and only one chewing betel nut, thank God. There Brynne, see how impatient I am, one of them is shaking hands with Sergeant Binus, I wonder what prompted that?"

"He is the leading man in this group of carriers and Binus is about to pay them. I always stay in the background at this time to allow him to represent the authority of the government. See how he is miraculously back in full uniform with his belt, beret and rifle. I'm just a 'Didiman' concerned with food and crops but Sergeant Binus represents the majesty of government. He does it bloody well too."

Evelyn stood back with her camera watching the process of pitching camp and taking a photograph now and then. The policeman sat on a canvas director's chair behind a small fold out table, handing out shilling coins and writing the names of the men in his book. Behind him Albert was unloading some of the boxes and helping Iambata to carry things up the stick ladder into the house. He directed a couple of men who carried some boxes upstairs and others to the cook shelter. A group of women brought baskets of sweet potato and green vegetables, including snake beans nearly a yard long.

It seemed odd that they made no acknowledgement of anyone, just put down their baskets and walked away. She saw three women approaching along the path through the coffee seedlings. All were naked except for the leaves fore and aft on a string that hung over their protruding buttocks and under their belly. They had woven bark straps around their forehead to support the weight of baskets of food and piles of firewood that lay across their lower back. Little girls, completely naked but with child size loads on their backs and head straps like their mother's brought up the rear.

They evinced no interest at all in the visitors. They couldn't lift their head because of the weight on their forehead but Evelyn was surprised to see that they didn't even lift their eyes or show any sign of curiosity. None looked at her as they passed close by. She felt discouraged that she didn't even get to smile at anyone. They all seemed utterly indifferent. She remembered reading Captain Cook's logbook and his observation that the Australian Aboriginals showed no interest at all in the items he usually gave as gifts to new contacts. They simply walked away from them, even steel knives and axes.

The contrast between the happy, vivacious and businesslike women she had met at the Rabaul market and those in front of her seemed like a thousand year gulf. She was still glowing with a sense of accomplishment from the way she had coped with the trail, even though it was in good conditions with no rain or major obstacles. The thought of crossing that log bridge in the rain made her shudder. Brynne came and stood beside her again as the carriers moved off to the village and Binus carried the folding table and chair up into the house. Albert had set up the primus stove on a bamboo bench in the cook house and was busy with Iambata preparing lunch.

"Well Evelyn you are now a veteran. The rest of the trip will be much like today, maybe wetter, steeper and a bit like the movie Lost World. The people get more unsophisticated in some ways but there is a chance there has been a change since the last time I was through here.

'Some of the carriers we will have later have just completed two years in jail for mass murder. Sergeant Binus was up here for their arrest and had a lot to do with them during their sentence. He's a smart cove and he took the opportunity to learn their language, and the prisoners, all twelve of them, learned pidgin. They trust him and he is held in high regard. From now on when you want to interview people you would have better results if you form a team with Iambata and Binus.

'By the way, when you address Iambata you don't have to say the whole name, as in 'Yambata'. She will be more comfortable if you just sound the m as in 'mmm', so it comes out as mbata."

"Well thanks Brynne. I love the way you trickle out information that we will be using mass murderers and Binus has no bullets for his gun. After a week in her company you tell me how to address Iambata. Do you have any more juicy details I should know?"

He grinned at her as Albert called them to lunch. In the hut he had set up the small folding table with two canvas chairs and he brought up an aluminium plate piled with cold lamb sandwiches and a large pot of tea and some enamel mugs and condensed milk. "Enjoy the bread and cold lamb because we'll be on bush tucker by Sunday. These big tomatoes are delicious Evelyn, this seems to be the best place to get them."

She felt awfully smelly and sweaty but enjoyed the lunch and tea especially as she saw their three companions eating the same in the cook house below.

"Tell me about the mass murderers Brynne. Are they as awful as one imagines?"

A little catch in her voice belied the apparent calmness of her demeanour. Brynne felt a moment of shame; he hadn't meant to frighten her and paused to pour out the tea and dribble some sweetened Nestles tinned milk into his mug, in a vain attempt to pretend he hadn't picked up her concern. He chose his words even more carefully.

"The crime was as awful as you can imagine but the motive was understandable and that's why they only spent two years in jail. In fact they weren't even in jail much of the time. They were out on a work party round Rabaul collecting sanitary cans and putting in clean ones. Sergeant Binus spent a lot of time supervising them and did such a good job that he got promoted.

'Briefly the background to the story is that a group of plantation labourers absconded from a plantation on the north coast and set out on foot for Rabaul to complain to the government about ill treatment by their employer. Their leader had seen a patrol officer come through the plantation to be picked up from the beach so he knew there was a track across the mountains to Rabaul.

'Halfway across, they came to a village, which we will visit shortly. The people gave them food and a hut to sleep in. While they slept the village men discussed the suspicious strangers, who had no white man with them. The people at the time had barely been in contact with the administration. They didn't know that New Britain is an island and they had a folk lore of terrifying stories of people who burst out of the forest and massacred people. Not long ago there was such a tribe here called the Makolkols, who are said to have used axes with a seven foot handles. They disappeared around 1937, but the men didn't know that.

'They concluded that although the labourers were unarmed they were probably an advance party of spies, sent to gauge the strength of the village so that they could return in overwhelming force and wipe out the people. In the morning they gave the visitors food for the journey and let them leave the village. As the track descended into a hollow the ambush fell upon them and clubbed them to death. Only one man escaped and made it out of the mountains to report the crime. Binus was one of the policemen sent out to arrest the murderers.

'The judge in the case realised that it was a tragic misunderstanding and urged that the men be exposed to civilization for two years. Twelve innocent men died in that incident and another twelve or more guilty ones were brought into the 20th century by an enforced exposure to civilization. All those men speak pidgin now and know about the outside world. Binus speaks their language from daily contact with them and he understands their culture. The men are deeply ashamed of their crime and the ignorance that prompted it.

'So there's nothing to fear from them and that's why the gun Binus carries has no bullets. But I have thirty rounds in my patrol box. Not for protection from people but to shoot any water buffalo we come across. Before the war a planter on the south coast brought in working cattle from Indonesia. They were released into the bush when the Jap's arrived and are now a wild herd. Problem is they carry bovine TB so we have to make an effort to destroy them. I got three a few months ago near Wide Bay. I doubt we'll see any up here."

Evelyn sipped her tea, thinking about other instances she had encountered in her reading where suspicion, treachery and fear had hatched dreadful tragedies. The death of Captain Cook came to mind as well as numerous missionaries, traders and whalers. The incident Brynne had related carried all the ingredients of a typical South Pacific crime. The agricultural department depot at Taliligap was a classic example from the past. There on the site a chief named Talili had organised the massacre of some Fijian missionaries who had been trained in New Zealand to bring the gospel to cannibals. The spot went down in infamy as Talili's war, or crime; Taliligap.

The story had been related by Iambata to Evelyn in the hushed tones of shame.

"Thank you Brynne for that account. One feels encouraged at how far we have come. Not long ago a punitive expedition would have been launched, like in the days of gunboat diplomacy when the navy would blow a village of grass huts to pieces.

'I suppose there has to be a fear factor in the early stages of civilization to allow the penetration of trade and missionary zeal. When I was thinking about this project I read a lot about the early contacts with isolated people. I recall especially the observations of Rev' Charles Fox of the Anglican Mission in the Solomon Islands. He had some marvellous early photographs of people in the very first stages of contact with missionaries. Everything in their expression showed fear, curiosity, cunning and treachery. They reminded me of caged silver foxes I had seen on a fur farm in Sweden, one cringed at the wildness in their eyes.

'There was none of the 'noble savage' about them, as fantasized by the charlatan Rousseau, after he heard about the Tahitians. Fox also showed a contrasting picture of the happy, open faces of people who had imbibed the Christian message and had the burden of fear and sorcery lifted from them. I'm sure it went down well among the gentle souls among whom he sought donations to help civilise the heathen."

Lewis looked at her with renewed interest and liked her thoughtful approach.

"Yes. The 'noble savage' idea was always a bit of a stretch. But there are philosophical questions in this kind of work. Was it God, or just contact with western ideas? I link it to some of the thoughts of Tolstoy when he discussed the education of the peasants in 'Anna Karenina'. Many Russians with so called progressive ideas felt they should educate the peasant children. Levin, a big land owner disagreed. He felt that if you educate a man and leave him as a peasant, you have neither an educated man, nor a contented peasant.

'My job is to introduce cash crops to these people so that they can earn some cash to spend to improve their life. I'm doing it but somehow I don't feel any sense of achievement. It's an uncomfortable frame of mind. The United Nations mandate is to develop an economy and make a modern nation. When you see how self sufficient and content people like these are you get the uncomfortable feeling that you might be unwittingly destroying something of value. Change has always been difficult.

'Do you agonise over philosophical questions in your anthropology observations Evelyn or do you just observe and record what's in front of you?"

"You know Brynne, I'm beginning to wish I hadn't met you. You are like a hair in my soup. The Hippocratic oath declares that the number one rule for a physician is, 'First, do no harm'. In our case it might be 'Do no intentional harm'. I guess I will have to strive to objectively study what is in front of me, as you suggest."

"Bravo Evelyn! On the first day out you have discovered that I am a pain in the arse. I have a nit picking habit of asking myself 'what if?' I'll try to avoid disturbing the peace I promise you. Now I must go and have a wash before I disturb your nostrils. Down over the hill there is a little stream with a split bamboo aqueduct rigged up to drop water onto a rock. It's a perfect shower with no labour involved. When I get back you can take mBata with you. You will see she can have a great wash without taking her clothes off. You may not be so bashful but you'll figure it out. When you get back bring her up here, I want to have a look at her foot injury, we can't have her limping along for another month. Later on Albert will rig up a canvas shower bucket with hot water but he'll need a bit more time to make a privacy screen for you and mBata. I'll be back shortly."

As he strode off down the ravine in dry leather boots and a towel over his shoulder Evelyn noticed that below her, under the cooking shelter Albert had placed a clothes iron over the kerosene stove and had taken some green drill shorts and a shirt out of a patrol box. Before Brynne came back he had ironed the clothes on a towel over the top of the box and they were neatly folded on the box for his return. No instructions had been given and clearly the simple task was a well oiled routine, hardly different from the system at home. MBata had taken the canvas bed tubes and placed them across a hibiscus bush in the sun and Binus had placed his spare uniform beside Albert so he could iron it while his tool was hot.

She felt a warm admiration for the way they all worked together so smoothly. When Brynne came back she took the girl with her to wash off the mud and sweat of the journey and instantly joined her in soaping the soiled clothes and pounding them on the rock before rinsing and ringing them out under the falling water. At first they giggled and were a little bashful with each other but the camaraderie was established by the time they came back up the hill, changed into clean dry clothes. Brynne called mBata up to the hut to check her cut foot and Evelyn watched him with interest.

The cut was quite deep on the softer skin of her instep. He flushed it with a syringe of hydrogen peroxide and dried it gently with some kapok. Then he opened the cut and puffed some sulphanilimide wound powder into it before making three sutures in it from a pack with sterile needle and black silk thread. Mbata made no sign of pain as the curved needle pushed through and the knots were drawn together.

Brynne then applied a dressing soaked in yellow acriflavine and bandaged the foot neatly. He still wasn't done and found a small vial of anti tetanus vaccine which he scored with a nail file and snapped off before injecting a tiny dose under the skin of her arm.

"Just sit quietly for a while Bata. I want to see if you react to the shoot, before I give you the full dose. In this box I have some socks and jungle boots for you to wear until your foot is healed. We have to take care because we have a long way to go."

Behind them Albert and Binus were tying the carrying poles to form a row of crosses and then they pushed poles through the canvas tubes and stretched them over the crosses and tied them off. Within a few minutes three beds were ready for the night and mosquito nets rigged above them. After Brynne completed the anti tetanus shot Bata tried on her new green canvas and rubber boots. "Him nau, one pela soldier he stap" teased Binus.

At this point Brynne wandered off in his neatly pressed clothes to meet the headman and have a look around the gardens the village had established with the seeds from his last visit. He was gone until almost sunset during which time he explained to the chief the work the Missus wanted to do.

"This pela missus him he like kisim savvy long all fashion blong yupela man/meri long this pela hap. Him he like toktok plenty long ol meri wantaim namba one polis man to turn him tok."

His explanation was that Evelyn, with the assistance of Binus would like to have plenty of conversation with the village to find out all their customs and habits.

The chief was ok with that and wanted to know what the little woman, Bata, was to do. Brynne explained that she would help the missus so that the women were not afraid of her and Binus. The only reason that Brynne could give him as to why missus wanted to know all about bush kanakas was that it was an unfortunate habit of white women that they wanted to know everyone else's business.

The chief nodded sagely and Brynne almost burst into laughter at his instinctive understanding of the nature of women. Then he got down to business and asked the chief if he had any broody hens sitting on eggs. The chief said he would find out and Brynne told him he had some eggs from number one chickens. He then pulled out from his pack a picture of a magnificent Rhode Island Red rooster and told the chief that the eggs he had were laid by the rooster's wife. The chief was very animated and keen to go find a broody hen. Village chickens were often scrawny, bantam types, very hardy and self sufficient. He went with Brynne to the visitor's house where he was introduced to Evelyn and Bata. He was polite but eager to get the magic eggs.

Binus warned him, in his own language, against eating the eggs and said he wanted to see the super rooster on his next visit. The chief held his hand and laid his forehead on Binus's broad chest in solemn assurance that the eggs would be hatched.

Evelyn took a picture of the chief holding the egg carton and the picture of the rooster which Brynne had given him. Because it was dusk with an orange sun sinking quickly behind the black mountains she used the flash on the camera. The poor old man was so startled he almost dropped his eggs. He stumbled away with his head down at the awesome responsibility he had been given and fearful that another flash of lightning might greet him if the eggs failed to hatch.

"You scared the shit out him with that flash Evelyn. If those eggs fail to hatch he will dread meeting me next time I come by."

Bata was giggling and bending over as if she was trying to hold in an urge to pee. Binus looked at her sternly for laughing at the chief's fear of the camera flash. She felt a little ashamed and said apologetically. "The bush kanakas don't go to school yet, that is why they are funny."

Evelyn watched this little scene with silent interest and then took a few more pictures of them as Albert and Bata began to prepare supper. The girl was to sleep in the middle bed but she would eat in the cookhouse with Albert and the policeman. The meal was quite a pleasant assortment of sweet potatos, green beans and a dark spinach called aibika with a tinned corned beef and tomato hash with a liberal splash of hot chilli. In the cookhouse the trio also had a pile of brown rice.

Brynne and Evelyn ate without much conversation until she observed.

"Did you ever notice what beautiful hands Bata has Brynne? They are such a nice colour and texture, despite all the garden work she does."

He was surprised by her question. "No I can't say I have noticed, but now that you mention it I agree. She does have expressive and pretty hands. She is young though so I expect many kids are just as beautiful. Thinking about it I recall her mother has slim hands and nice features. Bata is as fortunate as you Evelyn, inheriting some fine genes."

"Why thank you Brynne. I wish I could say the same about you, even though you do have a lovely dimple in your chin."

Brynne chuckled but made no further comment. He opened his box and drew out a can of instant coffee, a bottle of dark rum and his pipe and tobacco. Albert had placed a steel thermos of hot water on the table. He poured a mug of coffee and splashed in a good tot of rum and grunted to Evelyn, "Help yourself."

When the pipe was going he opened the box again and drew out a thick book before adjusting the lamp behind him and putting his feet up on the box. The only thing he didn't do was erect a "Do not disturb" sign, but she got the message and adjusted her own lamp in order to make up her diary. Around eight o clock heavy rain began to fall and at nine Brynne folded his book and put his rum and pipe and book back in the box. Then he brushed his teeth and went outside for a pee before going to bed.

The two women were fast asleep by the time he crept under his mosquito net and he quickly went under himself, to the music of the rain.

Chapter Seven

Some men live to eat, I eat to live.

Socrates

The patrol remained several days at Malasait. Evelyn worked hard all day with Bata and Sergeant Binus talking to any villagers that were approachable and watching how they went about their daily lives. Most of the information came from Binus who was more confident and articulate than the women. He tried hard to give Evelyn the background to the shy and unco-operative villagers, concentrating on his English.

"These people are indifferent to new outside influences," he said. "Long before the white man came here they had been eaten and enslaved by the powerful Tolai people. They also had enemies within these mountains so their numbers remained small and restricted to their home area. Even now they often live in family size groups around their gardens. The government wants them to have proper villages so they do what they are told, but at the same time they do what they want to do.

'The thing they care about is food. They don't buy rice and tinned meat like other people and don't care about those things. Their main topic and culture is about their gardens so if you want them to talk to you it is important to start off by talking about food gardens.

110

'They had a hard time under the Japanese and had to flee deep into the forest to grow their food and escape from Japanese work and punishment. Since the war the missionaries and the government have been telling them what to do. They don't rebel but they go their own way and try to be invisible. Mr Brynne understands them and he doesn't talk play with them. He just looks at their food crops and gives them some seeds to try. He shows them how to grow their coffee gardens but he doesn't push them or talk about rules or what the government wants.

'The thing they love about Mr Brynne is that he takes pictures of them and when he comes back next time he does a slide show so they can see themselves. That's when you see them smile and laugh."

Binus had pretty good English but when he got into difficulty Bata was able to confer with him in Pidgin and then explain in English.

Evelyn remained patient in her approach and paid very close attention to her two helpers, developing a deep respect for their intelligence, tact and sensitivity. They walked for miles in the forest, visiting small garden clearings and the scattered families working them. Binus always yodelled and made a noise as they approached the gardens so that people were ready for their appearance. As they rested by a small waterfall she asked him if he was following a Baining custom by his yodelling calls.

Binus and Bata were embarrassed by the question. The girl giggled behind her hand and if Binus had been white he would have been blushing. He got up and moved away down the creek with a brief signal to Bata to explain. Evelyn knew she had put her foot in it but had no idea why.

"Missus, Binus is shamed by your question. In our culture men and women play with each other in the garden. We don't have bedrooms like white people so a garden is the private place for the man and his wife; like in the bible. In Australia it would be rude to walk into a bedroom without knocking on the door. When Binus sings out he is knocking on the door."

Evelyn was by no means a bashful person, in fact she could be downright bawdy in her private moments. She felt her colour rising with embarrassment that she had not been perceptive enough to realise what Binus was doing. He was so respectful of her dignity as a missus. Looking at his broad, muscular and scarified back she realised that he was more a gentleman than any toff she had met in England.

"Bata, please go and tell Binus I am sorry for his shame. It is my shame for asking him a silly question. He is our father in this forest."

The two came back, holding hands with Bata pretending to pull an embarrassed policeman and Evelyn stepped forward and shook his hand. The situation was resolved with mutual affection all round and a sense of family grew stronger as the trip went on.

Brynne Lewis kept his distance from Evelyn's activities, knowing she was safe with her two companions. He accepted the fact that he was very attracted to her but he drew no comfort from that acceptance. It was uncharted territory for him to be dealing with the pangs of love for someone for whom he was no more than a necessary part of the equipment. He smiled grimly to himself that he was the pathetic lover in a country song, like Hank Williams 'Cheatin Heart.' The last time he had felt similar feelings was years ago at university. At least that affair had blossomed briefly until his lover became impatient with his lack of ambition. She wanted an ambitious, successful man, eager to become wealthy. He wasn't and had to admit it, to their mutual disappointment.

The only resolution to his dilemma was to complete the next three weeks and get away from her presence without making a fool of himself. When they were together in the evenings he made a conscious effort to be affable and polite, even doing more than necessary to avoid the guilty thought that he might be perceived as sulking. He carried it off quite well until he could bury his nose in his book and then she intuitively withdrew into her own sphere or went out to the fireside to chat with Albert and Binus.

On their last night in Malasait he invited his companions to come down to the village for his slide show, using a small battery powered projector. They hung a white sheet on a tree with a stick top and bottom and set up the projector on the folding table. The people loved the brief show. He had slides of roosters and pink pigs and men receiving money for bags of coffee which they then spent in a store. He knew it was propaganda for the government agenda but it was just a curtain raiser before he showed them pictures of themselves from his last trip. This is what they loved and everyone became animated and merry, exclaiming at their own image and copping the remarks of their neighbours on how they looked. When he walked around with his camera round his neck they were as vain as a movie star before the paparazzi to have their picture taken; they knew he would show them on his next trip.

White people rarely ventured into the mountains more than once or twice but Brynne had become a regular visitor and his slide shows were eagerly awaited. His effectiveness as an agricultural extension worker was dramatically enhanced by his low key approach and his camera. As he flicked through his small box of slides he said to Evelyn, "Do you see the secret to good public relations here? If you plan an extended study of these people Evelyn this is what they see as fun. It's only a small thing but for such a dour, hard working mob as this it's a chance to make them smile."

She put her warm hand on his arm, sending shivers down his spine.

"Yes Brynne you have tickled their fancy. I can't remember who made the observation that 'The proper study of mankind is man' but your 'stone age' instincts are spot on tonight."

He couldn't figure out whether or not he had been complimented, but he wished she had left her hand on his arm a little longer. Later, relaxing before the long walk facing them the next day they sat at the folding table listening to the rain dripping from the thatch. She shared rum and black coffee and tried a puff on his pipe. Brynne promptly opened his box of medical supplies and drew out a small corn cob pipe from a bag of them he kept as presents for people who had been extra helpful.

"Here aunty, try your own pipe, the meris will admire you for it."

Evelyn loaded the pipe and puffed away nonchalantly with a grin on her face at his astonishment. She didn't mention her experience as a marijuana smoker but he guessed accurately where her smoking background had occurred, probably as a student or with her pals in the West Indies..

"What have you been up to while I've been wandering around with Sergeant Binus? You seem to keep your distance from us Brynne."

"Not at all Evelyn! I have just followed my normal routine. These people are totally dependent on their food gardens so I like to keep up with the health of their crops. A few years ago one of their favourite varieties of taro was afflicted with a leaf disease and they have had to adapt to other staples. In some parts of the country a leaf mosaic has reduced the yields of sweet potato and corn crops have been damaged by a disease called blister smut. It's quite a demanding task to visit most of their gardens on the lookout for pests and diseases that might make them dependant on government handouts, like rice and canned food. If that should ever happen its mighty hard to get them back to being self sufficient.

'That is probably the most important part of my job. I do introduce new crops like beets and carrots but one has to be careful with plant introductions; one mistake can be disastrous. As we go higher, above two thousand feet the options get narrower for traditional crops. Even when new crops are successful the people are reluctant to eat them. There is no haute cuisine around here. They can eat the same thing everyday for years and the only requirement is quantity."

"Yes I understand that point. On my father's estate there is a long term crop rotation that's been in place since ancient times to keep on top of weeds and pests. I suppose the local habit of moving to new ground after every crop performs a similar role. With Bata and Binus I have walked up hill and down dale visiting people in their gardens.

'I say Brynne, did you know that people conduct their sex life in their gardens?

'Bata explained it to me when I was silly enough to ask Binus why he yodels when he approaches a garden. The poor fellow was embarrassed and had to walk away while Bata explained." Evelyn giggled as she recalled the conversation.

"She said the people were like Adam and Eve in the garden of Eden; unlike white folks who have privacy in their bedroom."

"Bless her for that Evelyn, how tastefully done. I always thought there was something extraordinary about that girl. She should go to high school, she has a natural grace and wisdom beyond her years."

Chapter Eight

The houses, built with axe and knife,
were neat and trim
And the smell inside, of old fires, not in the
least unpleasant.

Caroline Mytinger

The packing up for the next stage was finished before the sun had
risen above the white fog that lay across the mountains. Lewis
urged Evelyn to eat another bowl of oatmeal porridge, drenched
in sweetened condensed milk.

"Today we may well take eight or nine hours to reach Yalom
and hard going, harder still if we have rain. We change carriers
halfway and may well be walking in the dark if anything goes
wrong. Put this army poncho in your pack Evelyn. It won't keep
you dry but it will keep you from cold rain on your shirt. Take
care of Bata, she's not used to a long slog like this, although she's
young and fit.

'We have some dangerous bridges to cross but Albert has our
rope and slings lashed on top of a box. They may not stop you
falling but you'll be safe if you do."

Evelyn was becoming used to Brynne's laconic manner but
she gulped nervously at the ordeal she faced. How cunning he

was to make her responsible for Bata, to mask her own fear. She grinned sheepishly and punched him lightly in the belly.

"Don't try your bloody psychology with me Mr Lewis. You know I'm scared to death about walking across these log bridges, so is Bata. We are in your hands so be careful yourself. If you go down we'll all be in the hands of Sergeant Binus."

He grinned and pulled her into a cuddle under his left arm.

"I'm not trying to make you nervous Evelyn. I've done this trip several times and I know you are more than up to it. My warning is only to give you time to prepare yourself for a challenge. Albert would have told Bata and has probably asked her to take care of missus. Tonight, when you're by a warm fire and drinking a mug of hot Oxo and rum you'll feel on top of the world."

As the patrol filed out of the village in the sunshine the people stood on each side of the path watching them go. Evelyn was pleased to see some of the women were smiling at her and reached out to touch her arm as she passed by. Naked children ran along beside them and a few skinny dogs wagged their tails, as if catching the congenial mood. Soon they were alone, walking in the used air behind the carrying line, which left a scent of sweat and native tobacco in its wake. Conditions were perfect in the descent down the side of a broad valley. The path was wide with no vegetation to interfere with progress. The only negative aspect was the knowledge that the further down they went the further up they would soon have to climb. The air was cool and the sunshine had yet to turn to cloying humidity.

After an hour the long descent met with a river where the ford was chest deep on the far bank. Brynne watched anxiously from a little downstream, ready to plunge to the assistance of anyone who lost their footing. The water was cold and the current strong but the expedition climbed the bank unscathed, although cold and shivering. With a couple of whoops the men marched into the uphill stage on the other side and within ten minutes the cool dip was forgotten as sweat began to trickle down backs and chests heaved with the strain. Now they were beneath the thick, dark canopy of the forest again and sounds seemed to echo as if in a cave. Higher and higher they climbed until on reaching a narrow plateau Sergeant Binus called a halt to rest and drink from a stream falling down over rocks in a red clay bank. The march continued in a steady rhythm with a break every hour, where men changed positions on the pole.

They crossed numerous log bridges without mishap and walked along the narrow crests of ridges where breaks in the forest revealed spectacular views across the mountains. To Evelyn and Bata it seemed they were walking across the top of the world and they frequently smiled at each other with each new scene.

Just before noon, clouds could be seen forming in the distance and the air began to become oppressive. At a steep and plunging waterfall they met the carriers from the next village. This dour, muscled and unsmiling group lined up to embrace Sergeant Binus with a few grunts of greeting and then they picked up all but one of the boxes and left, with an energetic spring in their step, to mount the log bridge and disappear into the forest. From the last box Binus retrieved the pay for the tired carriers who also embraced him and left to return home. Brynne stood beside the trail and thanked them for their work but they barely acknowledged him, other than to slap his outstretched hand. The last box was then hoisted onto the brawny shoulders of the two remaining carriers from the new line and they too crossed the bridge and disappeared.

At this point heavy rain began to pour down. Binus took one end of the nylon climbing rope and walked across the bridge, above white water roaring over black rocks. On the other side he took two turns around a tree and two half hitches and waited while Brynne took a turn around a tree and pulled the rope tightrope taut by passing the fall through two wagoners hitch loops.

"Who's first?" he grinned to Albert, Bata and Evelyn. He knew Evelyn would step forward first. She did, but she was swallowing nervously while trying to appear calm. He snapped the brass clip over the rope and let her fasten the safety belt round her waist. She glanced into his eyes but he offered no encouragement nor did he betray any sympathy for her obvious fear. Without a backward glance she stepped up onto the log and walked across, trailing the retrieval string behind her. Binus smiled and shook her hand and Brynne pulled the belt back across. Albert and Bata followed with the same procedure. Then Brynne undid the rope and tied it to the belt around his waist and walked across while Albert and Binus hauled in the slack. Without any further ado Brynne coiled the rope and slung it over his shoulder and they all set off in the deluge in pursuit of the cargo line. Despite the exhausting conditions and the cold rain Evelyn and Bata glowed with pride in their new confidence. They knew now that they could do anything Brynne asked of them. Several hours later they staggered into the village, where the tired carriers were standing under the rest house shivering, waiting for Sergeant Binus to pay them off. Someone had built a blazing fire on a rock fire platform filled with clay in the middle of the house. The two women couldn't resist the allure of the fire and soon they were standing in a cloud of steam as the heat began to dry their clothes. Brynne whispered to Binus to pay the men extra for their hard work in the rain and then he set to work helping Albert set up the camp for another week.

While the women stripped off their wet clothing and dried themselves behind a hanging blanket Brynne surprised them by tossing a couple of army sweaters with leather elbow and shoulder pads over the blanket. Before he had a chance to get into dry trousers himself they emerged and giggled at the sight of his hairy white bum. He too put on a sweater and they sat on bamboo benches around the fire, like relaxing soldiers. The rain had eased off a little but the air was cold and raw and the fire heat most welcome.

A large billy can over the fire began to simmer so Brynne dropped a few Oxo cubes into it and stirred it with a stick until they dissolved. Then he poured in half a mug of rum and called Albert and Binus to come up for a hot drink. Both men were still shivering and became much more cheerful by the heat of the fire, with an enamel mug of hot drink in their hand.

It had been dark for two hours before Albert managed to bring up a pot of boiled sweet potato, fried spam and tinned baked beans. Soon after dinner everyone except Brynne went to bed and he was able to relax with his book and pipe and rum laced coffee. This simple routine at the end of a hard day was the bliss of the pioneer, soon to be ruined by massive taxation on spirits and tobacco and the rage of wowsers.

Just before he decided to turn in himself Albert crept up the ladder and whispered that Binus was sick.

"Sikin blong im he hot masta. Him guria guria."

Brynne had noticed that Binus looked unwell but he was so used to his robust vigour it didn't register. He dug out his medical case and a flashlight and followed Albert down to the cook's hut. Binus lay on a sleeping mat on a bamboo bed, shivering violently under two blankets. He had a temperature of 103deg.

They raised him up and gave him four chloroquine phosphate tablets and three aspirins. Brynne listened to his chest with a stethoscope and was relieved to hear it was clear.

"You had better come upstairs Binus, it's too cold and damp down here. You too Albert, come and sleep by the fire."

He helped Binus up the stick ladder while Albert gathered up their bedding and arranged it around the fireplace. When the men were settled he left a lamp burning low and went to bed himself, planning to check on the sick man through the night.

The exertions of the day overtook him, until he woke with a start at two a.m with Bata shaking his arm.

"Binus has big kus Mr Brynne and his sikin is hat."

She had woken to hear Binus coughing in shallow and painful gasps. This time the stethoscope revealed bubbling and crackling congestion in his lungs and Brynne recognised a rapid onset of pneumonia. Binus was taking shallow breaths and trying to avoid the pain of coughing. Brynne selected from his medical kit a vial of crystalline penicillin and another of sterile water in which to dissolve it. This he injected into the left buttock and then gave him four cc s of procaine penicillin in the other buttock. Later that night he also gave Binus four M and B sulpha drug tablets.

Despite all this he couldn't sleep with a seriously ill man in his care so he stoked up the fire and went back to reading his book, 'Quiet Flows The Don' by Mikhail
Sholokov.

He stayed in his chair, reading until dawn and was relieved to find his patient recovering. His chest sounded better and his breathing more comfortable but he was far from well. He gave him more tablets and a cup of sweet black tea from the billy can stewing gently by the fire and then crept wearily into bed. Bata was up and sitting with Binus so he told her to wake him if there was any change in the patient. Evelyn had woken from time to time and watched the proceedings but her legs were burning from the long walk and she had nothing to offer except kind words for Binus. She knew that Bata was a far superior nurse.

In the misty damp of dawn Albert arranged a banana leaf screen across a corner of the house and behind this he hung the steaming canvas shower bucket from a beam. Evelyn had lived in some luxurious homes over the years but the memory of the hot shower that morning, followed by warm damper, tinned butter and strawberry jam for breakfast would stay with her forever. The hot water and Sunlight soap suds ran over her and down through the limbom palm floor and her hot green towel, smoky from drying beside the fire, seemed the height of luxury. By the time Brynne woke up Binus was gone and he ran out anxiously looking for him. He found him sitting in the sun on the east side of the cookhouse, drinking a mug of tea. His temperature had eased and he breathed more comfortably so Brynne gave him another round of anti malarial tablets and aspirins. An hour or so later he also gave him more sulpha drugs and told him to stay in bed by the fire for another day or two.

Nobody was in the mood to do any work but Brynne walked up to the village with Bata to talk to the headman about someone to help Evelyn, while Sergeant Binus was laid up. The men in the village were fluent in pidgin after their two year spell in jail and two of them were willing to talk to the missus. Bata explained to them what they were doing and they responded with an uncomprehending nod. They looked at each other but could not think of a question. With that more or less settled Brynne went down to the creek with his soap and towel and enjoyed an icy cold bath while Bata sat on the bank laughing at his gasps and chattering teeth.

Evelyn could now proceed with her study with the help of the locals and Bata while he looked forward to a lazy week. The village had been indifferent to his efforts to interest them in coffee, or food crops they considered exotic. They weren't even interested in his pictures, so he lost interest in them in return. He had a whole week to compile a report on the state of their health and food resources and he had several books he was eager to read while he nursed Binus back to full health.

To his surprise a woman appeared below the house carrying a couple of baskets, piled on her head. Her unencumbered man stood beside her as Brynne walked down the dog proof stick ladder. The gift was a basket of red potatoes and another with foot long carrots and a large cabbage, grown from seed he had handed out on a previous trip. Delighted, he examined the blemish free potatoes and congratulated the couple.

Just when I was about to give up on this mob, he thought, feeling ashamed of his impatience. He gave them some packets of seed and asked to be shown their garden the next day. They refused his offer to pay for the vegetables.

In the evening as they ate a western dinner of vegetables, corn cobs and cold corn beef and mustard he felt a certain glow that at last he had made an impression. His boyish pride in the gift was noted by Evelyn. She had begun to be a little irritated by his easy competence and command of every situation, without considering that she was, so to speak, on his turf. It was this mood that led her into a minor confrontation later that evening.

With Binus and Bata beside her near the fire she was planning and making notes of the questions they would begin with the next day when they were introduced to the people willing to talk to them. Brynne, reading some distance away with a dim lantern hanging over his shoulder, could hear the conversation. He stopped his concentration on the book and thought about how she was going about her study.

An hour later, when Bata had gone to bed and Binus was snoring beside the fire, she came over to sit across the folding table from Brynne. He poured hot water from his flask and made her a half mug of black coffee and poured in a splash of black,

Buka Meri rum. She took a pinch of his tobacco for her little corn cob pipe and as she struck a Greenlite match was pleased to see he had not picked up his book again.

"It's good to see Binus getting well again. Is there anything you can't do Brynne Lewis?" She didn't realise it but she was looking for a squabble and sounded a little arch. He watched her, without immediate reply. When she was about to add something he grinned and said,

"Nothing comes to mind at the moment Evelyn; I'm sure you can think of something for me."

It was annoying that he had so easily gauged her mood. She blundered on, without realising she wanted him to be defensive. She wasn't used to men who did not defer to her rather commanding presence.

"You seem so content roaming about the bush, influencing simple people. But for a young virile man you seem to live like a celibate monk, as the years pass you by.

'Do you ever reflect on the future, or even the present?"

Brynne was momentarily taken aback at this line of personal enquiry and made a flippant response to give himself time to think.

"Yes. I do reflect and become a little ashamed of myself. For years I've had fantasies of a beautiful blonde with a curvy bum blundering into my life and just when all my dreams come true, she pisses off with my best mate. Like an erotic nightmare that doesn't quite come off. You can imagine the blow to my self esteem. I'm getting over it though and I will have to recalibrate my imaginative fantasies, taking into account my obvious defects, like my dimply chin and hairy arse.

'Your advice would be much appreciated."

Evelyn was almost pitched into a defensive position herself and felt even more annoyed that he should refer directly to her fling with Henry Sinclair, which was none of his damn business. She ignored his reply and responded to his request for advice.

"My advice, as you well know, is unnecessary. You live surrounded; well, not surrounded, but exposed to numerous beautiful women. All your friends at the beach and the market and those we met at the restaurant in Chinatown. I'm sure there are many others; and yet you live in splendid isolation in one of the most scenic and romantic spots in the South Pacific. I would be astonished if you should admit you are queer, so that's what intrigues me."

"Bloody hell Evelyn! How can you be so personal? How would you feel if I asked you how many times you bonked Henry on your first night on his boat?"

He was about to blurt out more protest but Evelyn, interrupting, said candidly

"Seven. Please continue."

Astonished, he suddenly burst into laughter, waking up both Binus and Bata and probably Albert too, down in the cooks hut.

"Jesus! That is priceless. Seven, *please continue*. Poor Henry!"

It took him several minutes to regain his composure, by which time Evelyn had lost her desire to provoke him and was grinning at his reaction to her characteristically open nature. Eventually he was able to give her a measured response.

"The fact is Evelyn I'm not in the position to act the libertine. I deal with a wide section of the community and I can't have them wondering whether I am more sincere about my interest in their women than in my business with them. That goes for everyone. It doesn't preclude me from the odd affair but I have to consider my position against the potential for raising hackles among the people who trust me."

"Well Brynne, you disappoint me. One is reminded of Don Jose in Carmen; torn between his ardour for Carmen and his

Pavlovian response to the regimental bugle blowing reveille. Women adore a passionate man."

"You've got me Evelyn. Alas. I lack passion and ambition and the desire to be desirable. That's how I lost the girl I loved at university. She wanted a man who was going places and I just didn't fit the bill. She got so pissed off that she married a urologist for God's sake and now she lives in a leafy suburb in Brisbane and socialises with medical people who work themselves to death while their wives make futile attempts to 'do something with their lives'. Imagine the dinner table conversation when the urologist comes home.

'Darling today I saw the most distended bladder on record. It took a catheter an hour to drain it'.

'It's not all bad, being a little boring, but of course, one does miss out on sex compared with more vivacious and stylish people."

"Brynne, havn't you noticed that everyone has primal needs? Even the most primitive, it's an important part of the way society is constituted. Courtship, marriage and sexual attitudes are a big part of my anthropological studies."

Thank God we've turned the corner thought Brynne, I'm off the hook now.

"Yes I heard you discussing possible lines of enquiry with Bata. I hope you aren't practising on me. My experience has been that when I ask a series of questions

'I find they answer with what they think I want to hear. It is a very natural thing to try to be agreeable in this way. It's an unreliable research technique for someone like you.

'I suggest lots of empirical observation and widely spaced questions to different individuals so you don't indicate a direction you may be heading before you realise it yourself. Sometimes unconsciously pre conceived notions can do that to you. Any detective knows this is so, I'm sure you have come across it before. You could start off with the topic of adoption. These people swap kids all the time, I have no idea why"

"Heavens above! Now you are telling me how to conduct my research. I have a lot to do in a short space of time. How can I do it without talking to people?"

Brynne could see she was feeling the pressure of thinking he was judging her in some way. It would only get worse unless she felt more relaxed with his leadership.

"Well, as I said, possibly you could limit your questions to each individual so that they don't pick up a trend. I've made my point out of the goodness of my heart my dear.

'Would you care for another spot of rum Evelyn? It will help you sleep; without nightmares about my sex life."

She pushed her mug forward and clumsily lit her pipe for the umpteenth time. Her irritation with his smug self containment had eased but she was still upset and angry that she didn't know why.

"I'm not your bloody dear, don't patronise me."

They sat in uncomfortable silence for a few minutes. Brynne could feel her sense of frustration about something; he could go neither forward nor back so he waited patiently for her to break the impasse. He had been in this situation before when in remote areas with people who became discontented. There were still nearly three weeks to go before she could be relieved of his presence. He resolved to be very careful and avoid any hint of friction with her, if possible.

"Why are you so enamoured of these gloomy Russians you read so avidly. Sholokov, Tolstoy, Gorky. Are they an indication of your intrinsic nature or a passing phase?"

"You may be right Evelyn. I do love the Russians but it's not a topic I have ever discussed with anyone. They are beautiful writers. I don't find them 'gloomy' at all. I'm not just reading; I'm in the book. Here, for example, on this page, is a picture of the brave Cossack, Gregor Melekhov, sitting in the long grass on the bank of the Don with his lover, Aksinia Astakov. As she laments the brutality of her cruel husband Stepan, who knows of the affair, he watches the warm steppe breeze move the soft, fair curls at the nape of her neck. He knows a day of reckoning awaits him and Stepan.

'Sholokov was said to be a fellow traveller because the Reds allowed his books to be published. That he told the truth seems clear to me and I love him."

Evelyn was silent as she imagined the scene he had just described. She knew about the fearless intoxication of love and momentarily she too was in the book, wishing she could support the recklessly brave Aksinia. She looked into Brynne's eyes and saw a different man from the hairy legged sportsman image she had tagged him with. He was moved by that scene in the grass by the Don. She remembered his love of choral music and the happy children who treated his home like a playground. Her inexplicable anger toward him softened and almost prompted a meek apology.

"Are you on that page at the moment Brynne?"

"Yes. Here, read it yourself. You will be captivated by Aksinia. Russian heroines are always brave and passionate."

As he made that observation he knew in his heart that he was looking at a woman with just those qualities, with an added dash of recklessness. He remained silent on the topic, fearful he would blunder into some provocative indiscretion. As he watched her reading he could tell that the magic of Sholokov had caught her in his web. Would she be drawn to the characters in a different way from his own? Would she see in Aksinia aspects of herself, as he did with Gregor?

He waited patiently while she read and turned the pages, making no attempt to hand back the book. Before he ran out of patience he grinned and hid behind his enamel mug to suppress his chuckle, as the words 'please continue' crossed his mind.

That joke was over. It would be indecent to mention it again. Instead he took his feet off the patrol box and searched inside for his toothbrush and medical case so he could do a final check on Binus and then go to bed.

"If you want to read that book Evelyn just go back to the beginning and get the whole story. I've read it before so I won't miss it."

Another spark of irritation flashed in her, that he should tell her how to read a book. She looked up at him and tried to hide her mood, saying. "Are you in the habit of reading books over again then?"

He hadn't noticed her slightly sarcastic tone. "Why yes I am. On the first reading I am curious about the characters and the plot, but on second reading I know how they feel and can picture their environment better, so I find it a richer experience. Like a second marriage I suppose, one is able to explore the meaning between the lines. It seems silly but it works for me. I've been doing it since I was a boy."

Evelyn nodded slightly. "I know what you mean, but it seems a bit odd. Most people are so busy that they rarely read a book at all let alone savouring it for a second or even third time. Do any of your friends do it Brynne? Maybe it's a habit of men who spend a lot of time alone that makes them identify with characters in a book."

He couldn't think of a sensible response. Her cool blue eyes unnerved him so he murmured, "No, I don't know how other people read. It's just a habit I developed after I read 'Treasure Island' again when I was a ten."

Down in the cookhouse he dipped out a mug of water to brush his teeth and thought about her comments. He had the uncomfortable thought that he might be a little 'odd', as she had suggested. It soon occurred to him that his main concern was not that he was odd, but that Evelyn might think him so. He grinned as he thought she might be a little 'odd' herself, but he certainly would not be impertinent enough to say so.

He had a chat with Albert and Binus by the cookhouse fire. The policeman was feeling much better and would be fine by the time the march resumed in a few days. The weather had turned and they could look forward to a few rain free days and clear cool nights. Albert enjoyed walking through the food gardens with Brynne admiring the skill of the people and the crops he couldn't grow down at sea level. The villagers were used to him as well so he usually came back to camp with a variety of gifts.

The cold nights by the fire were a rare pleasure and Bata relished the sensation of watching the vapour from her breath as she pretended to smoke a small stick, giggling as Brynne smiled at her antics. The days were warm and sunny after the thick fog burned off and she enjoyed walking out with Evelyn and sometimes with Brynne to distant food gardens and camps or helping Albert wash clothes on a rock in a stream. She was a close observer of every move of the two white people and had not missed the eager reading of Sholokov by Evelyn as soon as she had completed her records in the evenings. Bata felt a little irritated that Evelyn had taken the book when she knew he was less than halfway through it. Brynne came to the village when she was eleven years old and she had grown up watching him reading and listening to the radio and playing records. When he ran in the evenings he always had a troop of tireless kids with him and when he sat under the poinceana tree they would watch his beer glass and poise themselves to race to the fridge for another can at the slightest of signals.

They all knew it was a game, which he enjoyed as much as the children. Bata didn't realise she had a sense of ownership over him, which she shared with Albert. It made them a little resentful of Evelyn.

One morning, when Evelyn was out at the toilet hut Bata asked him bluntly,

"Why has Evelyn taken your book?"

He was surprised at the question, unaware that she and her uncle observed every interaction between him and Evelyn. He thought about the question before making a reply, wondering what prompted it and what sort of answer was expected. He knew Bata was far more intelligent than the giggling teenager she appeared to be. She had told his mother, Gwen, that she had read the bible from beginning to end. He never mentioned the fact that he knew this but his regard for the girl was now tinged with respect. That bible was probably the only book she had. He was sure there were even missionaries who had not shown her perseverance.

"Evelyn didn't 'take' the book, I gave it to her to read because she asked me a question about it. She liked the answer I gave her, that's why she reads it at every spare moment."

"What is in the book?"

Brynne had not missed the slightly aggrieved tone of the original question and was a little puzzled by it. In his reply he made a conscious effort to avoid any hint of being patronising, unaware that Evelyn's critical comments about him were bearing fruit.

"Well Bata, it is a big book so there is a lot in it. Mostly it is the story of a family whose lives are shattered by the war between Russia and Germany from 1914. As you know the Germans were here in this country and your grandparents would remember them. I have heard old people refer to the German time as 'Good time blong before'. You may have heard that too.

'In the family, whose name was Melekhov, there is a father, a mother and two sons and a daughter about your age. One of the sons is a handsome man named Gregor and he loves a married woman named Aksinia Astakov. Gregor's father Prokofei is furious at his son for bringing scandal to the family name. Aksinia's husband Stepan is jealous and cruel and he wants to kill Gregor. When all this happens the men have to take their horses and go with the army to fight, leaving the village with only old men and boys to do all the work.

'So the whole book has these people weaved into it but it is really the tragic story of the civil war between Russian people who liked the old ways and the communists who wanted to live without the king and all his people ruling their lives."

"Would I be able to read the book like Evelyn?" Bata asked nervously.

Brynne knew that his response would be taken personally so he had no hesitation in answering immediately in the affirmative.

"Yes of course you could. Although the scene is in a distant country with a cold snowy winter, the people in many ways are very similar to New Guineans. If you keep in mind the similarities you would soon be thinking like a Russian villager as the story proceeds. Gregor's hiding in the bush with Aksinia would be just as much a scandal as in your home village. You know the saying that in a village there are two kinds of trouble: trouble blong pig and trouble blong meri. Stealing women and animals is a crime in any village.

'Also many young people want white people to leave and local people to run the government, just like the Russians who wanted the Czar and all his people to go and local people run the government and share all the rich people's wealth. Here they want to take the plantations and that kind of thing.

'So the answer to your question Bata is yes, you could read that book and make the connections between your people and the Russians. If you want to read it I will be glad to lend it to you and answer any questions you ask me. Right at the beginning of the story Gregor's grandfather comes home from a war with Turkey and he brings a woman he has stolen. The villagers are afraid of her. She can't speak their language and they think she is a witch. When some animals die they think she has made magic on them and they kill her. The furious grandfather kills people with his sword and has to spend some time in prison. So Gregor's family history is different from other villagers, just as yours would be if your grandfather had married a woman from China or Australia.

'That sort of crime happens here sometimes and you hear about it on the radio. As soon as Evelyn is finished with that book you can have it. I'm sure you will love the people in that book as I do."

Bata was like any young girl or boy eagerly listening to a story. Already she was hooked by Brynne's brief introduction of the characters in 'Quiet Flows the Don'. For the rest of their time in the bush she watched as Evelyn turned the pages and had pangs of fear that she would not finish by the time they got home and would take the book with her.

Brynne had become aware how curious she was about his relationship with Evelyn. He noticed how she often watched Evelyn reading, with her hands fidgeting in eagerness to hold the book. This will make a great letter to mum, he thought, knowing how fond she had become of Bata on her visit. He understood that the child like joy of hearing a story had grown into the intellectual curiosity of a young woman.

In the days that followed he too watched Evelyn's progress through the book with as much interest as the girl. He soon realised why Evelyn was a scholar, by the speed of her reading. She wasn't just skimming the book but reading it at about double his own reading speed. If their routine stayed normal Bata would have that book in her hands within a week.

Chapter Nine

It is not good that man should be alone.

Old Testament

"Tomorrow we head for Raunsepna. It's even higher than where we are now so let's hope for good weather. There is a German priest who is good company but you may find him as mad as a hatter Evelyn. He is a kind and generous host but we have to humour his eccentric ways."

"I'm glad to hear that Brynne. In what way do you consider him eccentric? You're not exactly run of the mill yourself you know."

"Yes. I lost some sleep when you hinted that I might be a bit odd; but I'm ok with it now. Father Michael is from an industrial part of Germany and he is very zealous in his work. Apparently it's a German trait. He is convinced that the people are malnourished and that it affects their brain development. He is also concerned about sin, especially as it relates to sex. You may have noticed by now that sex for these people is not a preoccupation like it is in our society. It's just part of life in the natural order of things.

'Also he has decided they need milk in their diet. He tries to crack down on polygamy and is almost obsessive about it, even though it's not a significant problem.

'I expect by now he has his cows so it will be interesting to see how the people react.

'You may be tempted to laugh at this bloke Evelyn. Zealots can be dangerously amusing."

She almost resented his warning but he had put it very well so she just nodded and went back to reading her book. Brynne lit his pipe and watched her beautiful profile. He was again impressed by the speed with which she turned the pages and the amount she had read of quite a thick book. He thought it may be an acquired skill which he should attempt. Early the next morning he did a check on the condition of Binus and Bata's cut foot. Both were much improved and capable of the long walk.

Again they were lucky to have sunny weather but from daylight to nine a.m they walked in white, damp mist. By ten the sun was hot and they sweated along in thick humidity until a heavy deluge of rain in the early afternoon caught them just before they reached their destination. On the last stretch they walked along a grassy meadow with a rocky stream running through it. Mist was gathering around the tops of surrounding hills and Evelyn was again reminded of the Scottish highlands she enjoyed as a girl on an Outward Bound course. She could see far up the valley the grey, corrugated iron buildings of the mission and the almost black, thatched huts around it with smoke seeping through the thatch.

Brynne pointed out to her a small hut high up on the side of a steep green hill. It too had smoke seeping out through the thatched roof.

"That little house is where menstruating women go until the condition passes. I'm sure you will want to find out why. I have never been indelicate enough to ask the question; but I'm not an anthropologist."

As they came to the impressive government rest house, made of native materials, a small group of people began to appear. Some approached Sergeant Binus and held his hand for a few paces and then greeted Albert and Brynne. Twenty yards from the house an elderly man sat beside the stream, with six women of various ages gathered around him and a couple of small, naked children. While Binus set up his table to pay the carriers and Albert and Bata started carrying boxes up the stairs Brynne walked over to the old man and shook his hand and then the hands of the women and had a brief conversation with them. Evelyn walked around taking pictures of everything and everyone.

She was impressed by the size of the house, the thickness of the thatch and the huge central fireplace that sat on a great box of earth made of interlocking logs. There was even a rough chimney hole in the peak of the roof, made from a piece of folded roofing iron with a hat on it. When she took pictures of the group Brynne was talking to he introduced her to them. She was the first white woman they had ever seen. The old man seemed unimpressed but his women rose and touched her hands and arms, sniffed her and looked closely at her face. They didn't smile or exclaim but curiosity and wonder were expressed in their actions and comments to each other.

"These ladies are the sinful women that are eating the soul of the priest. He wants this man to put them aside and choose one wife and sin no more. But he refuses and despises the priest. Some are widows or abandoned wives and they cling to this kind old man. They live and work happily together and often have children with them for weeks at a time. Next time I come by there may be no children or several different ones. The priest seems to imagine the old bloke spends all his time copulating furiously with his harem. That, Evelyn, is why I think he's a fool. I hope he has become a bit less dogmatic since I was here last."

Evelyn looked at the small, contented group and suppressed a smile at Brynne's allusion to the old man copulating furiously.

"Someone should suggest to Father Mike that there's not much else to do up here on a cold night" she said mischievously, trying to goad Brynne into a grin. She was unsuccessful until they went up into the house.

"You nearly got me there Evelyn. I hate to laugh in front of these people for fear they will think I'm laughing at them. They're not a jolly and humorous bunch like Bata's people."

Bata looked up with a grin and said in pidgin "Olosem wonem?" which means what's up and is literally 'All the same what name.'

Brynne was free to laugh now so he said, "Evelyn thinks the lapun plays with his women at night to keep warm."

Bata slapped her thighs with a squeal of laughter and again replied in pidgin, as she usually did when making a joke.

"Nogat ia, ol lapun sleep tasol."

Albert grinned, as did Binus who said "Shame on you blong talk play." He really didn't like to laugh at the expense of the mountain people so there was a little bite in his remark. Albert and Binus began sorting the baggage. To get out of their way Brynne and Evelyn left to visit the priest. "You come too Bata. Father Mike has a couple of your wantoks looking after him, young nuns from the mission in Kokopo. I'm sure they will enjoy talking to you after months up here in the mountains."

They had to wait while she had a wash in the cold stream and changed into clean dry clothes. She wished she had a present for them and when she told Evelyn why she was searching through her box in vain she was delighted when Evelyn gave her a bottle of shampoo and a bar of orange Lifebuoy soap. She didn't know the nuns, but knew she would be welcome with the small gift. While Bata was combing out her big hair in front of a small mirror, with a bamboo comb Evelyn remarked quietly to Brynne; "Do you realise that you have a tendency to treat Bata the way an older brother treats a little sister?"

He thought for a long pause and as the girl came down the house steps he smiled at Evelyn and agreed with her observation. "I suppose you're right. I hadn't noticed it but I don't have a sister and if I did have I can't think of a better model."

None of the group was aware that they were observing and thinking about each other every day. They were thrown into close relationships by the circumstances of the journey, in much the same way as anyone in a normal workplace. As they walked off Albert grinned and cautioned Bata in a joking way to beware of falling under the influence of a priest and his nuns. "Ting ting gut long giamon lotu" he said.

His village followed the Anglican Church and like the other Protestant groups they were taught to regard the Catholics as a false church or 'giamon lotu'. The Catholics of course made the same observation about their Protestant neighbours. But they all got along with each other and competed joyfully in the annual choir festivals.

As they approached the mission buildings they could see some activity at a set of bamboo stock yards. Tan and white cows and calves were in the enclosure and boys were hopping around making a noise. The little priest was in among them. He scaled the fence nimbly and approached with his hand held out in welcome to Brynne.

"You are chust the man I vant to see Mr Lewis. The cows are very angry and the people are afraid of dem."

He greeted the women with vigorous handshakes and Brynne explained that Bata would like to visit his nuns, who were her wantoks from Vunapope.

"Yes yes yes Bata. They will be very happy to see you. Just go to the big building over there and sing out for Sister Miriam and tell her ve vill haf guests for dinner."

The eager speed of the girl to visit the nuns made Evelyn smile as watched her go and then she turned her attention to the cows. There were four in the yard with four calves skipping around them while naked men and boys sat on top of the fence, like spectators at a rodeo. One cow was imprisoned in a narrow chute and a hesitant boy was reaching through the bars trying to milk it into a jam tin. The animal's horns were tied with rope and all four legs were tied to the rails but still it kicked and struggled furiously.

"The cows are angry and ve haf much fear and get little milk. When ve do the cow kicks the tin to the ground no matter how tight ve tie her legs."

Brynne walked over to the animal in the crush and motioned the boy to get back out of the way. Then he undid the mass of knots in the leg ropes until the cow could stand freely and he loosened the head rope. He started to stroke the cow and talk softly to her as she flinched from his touch.

"Father Mike this cow is afraid of all of you. She will not let you milk her until you are her friend. See how already she doesn't mind my hand on her back. Now I will stroke toward her head until she calms down."

He beckoned the boy who had been attempting to milk the cow and addressed him in pidgin, hoping he would understand. The boy could see that the cow was much less aggressive and he too started to stroke her back and gradually along her neck.

"I suggest you leave the cows in the pen and separate the calves so that they cannot suckle the cows. Ask your people to cut grass for them and bring water and tomorrow morning we will try to milk them without scaring them to death."

The priest could see that his own fear and that of the people had communicated itself to the animals and with his hand on Brynne's shoulder he gave the instructions as Brynne told the people to be as friendly with the cows as they were with their dogs. He stepped back and stood beside Evelyn as the priest and his flock tentatively stroked the cow in the chute.

In a quiet aside to Evelyn he said. "This bloody idiot has the idea that the people are malnourished and in need of fresh milk, like he was after the war. I have my doubts that they will even be able to digest it, even if he can milk the damn things."

"Yes it is a crazy arrangement. I've never seen a friendly old Guernsey cow make such a fuss. Do you think you will be able to milk those cows tomorrow Brynne? You could be in for a few bruises."

"Well we'll see. Tomorrow they will have an udder full of milk and they'll be bellowing for the calves. These cows came from a plantation down on the coast. I've seen them handled properly down there. I did TB tests on them last year and I know they are just ordinary docile cows who have been frightened out of their wits."

It was mid afternoon when they walked up to the corrugated iron house of Father Mike. It looked a substantial and permanent building of two storeys with big verandahs, water tanks and a rough but massive stone chimney from the ground floor fireplace. There were no windows, just hinged shutters held open by stout wooden props, exactly like those in Brynne's fibro cottage. At the back of the main room a big kitchen with a wood burning range and a couple of kerosene powered fridges filled the back

141

wall, then a timber work bench and toward the centre a massive wooden dining table. It looked like a lonely spot for one man to eat.

There could be heard some movement and laughter from above and soon, down a broad stairway Bata descended with a couple of jolly young nuns in blue habits. The priest introduced his helpers and shook hands with Bata before the three young women went to the kitchen area together and began preparing his evening meal. He motioned to Evelyn and Brynne to sit in cane chairs on the west side of a broad, stone floored patio with a view across the mountains. To their delight he quickly returned with some frosty beer Steins and a tray with cold cans of VB beer.

Brynne expected nothing less having been a guest there before. The red sun, sinking quickly beyond the distant dark hills made a rewarding backdrop as they clinked their pots. Then Father Mike produced some fat Dutch cigars and began to exhort them with his grandiose plans for the mission. Evelyn listened to his passionate enthusiasm and thought to herself; this fellow is here for the long haul.

From the kitchen Brynne caught snatches of the giggles and gossip and grinned as he heard one of the young nuns ask Bata whether both she and the white woman were the 'friend' or lover of the didiman. She asked the candid question in Kuanua, Bata's native language, unaware that he was fluent in that tongue. He could imagine how embarrassed Bata was by the question; she knew he would have heard it. After that the conversation in the kitchen took on a more subdued level as she warned the Tolai nuns that he would hear and understand them.

The priest was so glad to have receptive ears that he took full advantage of them to expound on all his problems, from recalcitrant cows, polygamous elders and lukewarm responses to the message of the bible. It was a revelation to Evelyn and she hung on every word and made penetrating observations and personal enquiries about his background and motivation. He told stories of being a child in the ruins of Essen, on the verge of starvation and in fear of everyone, from his equally desperate neighbours to the occupation forces. It was a plausible explanation for his chosen path, the peaceful life of a priest, well supplied with the minor luxuries of life. Many others for the past thousand years had chosen the monastery for no doubt similar reasons, and not all lived a chaste and celibate life.

His nuns produced a fine dinner of baked pork chops, spinach and Spetzler noodles, made with potatoes and flour, along with a couple of glasses of wine and brandy and coffee. One of them gave Bata a lantern when it came time to find their way back down to the rest house in the cool and misty air. The fire in the house was a pleasant greeting as they joined Albert and Binus beside it and answered all their questions. When they went off to bed Brynne lit his pipe, expecting Evelyn to also comment on their pleasant evening. She remained silent, looking into the fire and not picking up her book.

"I find men like Father Mike a bit of a puzzle" said Brynne. "And I've met a few. It seems against nature for a man to isolate himself from his own people and live a celibate life in a remote outpost in order to spread the gospel. One hears of the occasional hermit whose only desire is isolation. It must be some form of mental problem. I suspect some may be latent homosexuals with feelings of guilt or confusion. I'm sure that has been a motivator for hundreds of years."

He was being deliberately provocative. Evelyn had shown some empathy for Father Mike. She glanced at him with a hint of a sneer in her smile before she said,

"His life is not markedly different from yours. At least he has a couple of nubile young nuns to keep him company: a good

143

old Catholic tradition according to Chaucer and countless other commentators.

'When you look at his background it's a pretty attractive career path to live in a place like this, where he is at the top of the food chain and has no pressure from his own kind or fear of being sacked. I found him a charming host in fact."

"I agree Evelyn, I didn't mean my comment to be critical of Mike; I'm not an ingrate. I do find these men a conundrum though. It's hard to grasp the way a person's brain can become so fixated on a faith or belief to the exclusion of so much other experience in life. Often it's as if experience of life drives them back into their acquired mind set, like a rescued horse galloping back into the burning stable."

"Brynne. You could drive yourself crazy thinking about the foibles of human nature. Some people are drawn to the eternal question of why we are here; millions in fact. The best we can hope for is that they won't hurt each other, itself a forlorn hope. I too think we are at the beginning of a post religion age, after thousands of years of religious mumbo jumbo and superstition when there was nothing else to fill the empty brain cells. It will take a long time to mature into universal humanism, not in our lifetime anyway.

'If I were you I would just help Mike to milk his cows tomorrow without thinking about his motivation. At least he isn't doing any harm."

He was glad he had provoked her into revealing a little of her personal philosophy. She was in tune with the times in her, 'live and let live' nature. He chose to remain silent on his personal observation that most of the people in the world seemed driven by either the most ancient or the most fashionable fads circulating among their peers.

"Later on I'll ask Bata if she was attracted by the life of the young nuns she met today. We may be as surprised by her observations, as I often am on many topics.

'By the way, she is eager to read Sholokov's book. She asked me why you were so engrossed in it so I gave her an outline of the story."

Evelyn looked up in surprise. "Really Brynne. Could she read such a book and understand it with only a primary school education?"

He grinned as he stood up to go outside. "Well she's read the bible; why not? How many people do you know who have read the New Testament from cover to cover? I think she'll find "Quiet Flows the Don" a much more ripping yarn."

When he came back in she was still gazing into the fire. Bata was snoring gently, like the purring of a cat, under her blankets and Albert and Binus were sitting out by the cookhouse fire drinking tea.

"Brynne in some ways you resemble Father Mike. You seem dedicated to work and averse to women. I'm trying to picture you in ten years time. Will you still be here, in this country, with a coloured or exotic wife and children climbing on your lap, or will you maintain your social isolation in your little rented cottage with the best view in the world?"

Here we go, thought Brynne. She's getting personal and trying to shunt me into a defensive position.

"I think none of the above Evelyn. Rumour has it that my position as a permanent public service officer may soon be terminated to make way for a suitably trained local person. There are a number of young men in Australian universities who may well make me redundant. I know some police officers who have received a generous compensation package to quit and go south. One can't make any long term plan nowadays.

145

'As regards a choice of a wife I havn't given it much thought but I don't think I'd marry outside my own people. Plenty do. It seems all the go to marry Chinese these days. Ten years ago it was unheard of. Lots of my friends have brown wives and girlfriends. Things are changing faster than me I guess."

"Are you prejudiced against local girls then? You seem to have such an easy rapport with everyone. Why would you not consider a non European as a wife?"

"I didn't say I had anything against the local beauties. I guess I'm just too lazy to adapt to another culture on a personal level. Marriage is a pretty personal arrangement; in case you hadn't noticed."

"Yes I had noticed. It's probably why I'm still single myself. I'm sorry Brynne, I should be more considerate and less personal in my conversation. Is there any rum left in that bottle?"

Brynne grinned and looked into her beautiful blue eyes. "Now that, Evelyn, is what I call a personal question, especially as this is the last bottle."

With that he tipped the last shot of rum into her coffee mug and they clinked cups and said "Salud."

The patrol was drawing toward the last few days, supplies were low and a boat was scheduled to pick them up from the beach on the next Monday. Although she had enjoyed the experience she was having private second thoughts about an extended study of the Bainings for her Phd. It was beginning to look like a bit too much dedication for a few extra letters on her curriculum vitae. Already she was thinking about how she could slip away when they got back to Rabaul, without having to explain herself to Brynne. This made her angry with herself for feeling she was obliged to explain anything to anyone. She went to bed without giving any hint of her mental turmoil.

She awoke at dawn to the sound of moisture dripping from the thatched roof and the rather strangled, pathetic efforts of the native roosters up at the village and the cries of hungry calves. Thick white fog billowed around outside, soaking everything with dew; the air was chilly and damp. Brynne and Bata stood by the newly rekindled fire drinking mugs of tea and enjoying the warmth on their legs. Then he left and Bata sat down beside the fire. Cosy and warm under her blankets Evelyn turned over in her stiff canvas bed and went back to sleep.

At the stockyard, Father Mike, in a thick sweater, waited eagerly for Brynne to attempt to milk his recalcitrant cows. He tied only the near side leg back a little to expose the udder and asked them to release her calf. He wanted the cow to let down her milk but an outburst of anger from the cow made it obvious it was not her calf. The animal was wrestled back into the calf pen and when the right calf came out and started to nurse, the cow settled down. Now Brynne got down on the stool and elbowed the calf aside and began milking the small teats, slippery from the saliva of the eager calf which butted and slobbered against his broad back. He milked fast with little interference from the cow. He drew about a gallon of milk from her before he stood up and let the calf milk her out.

The priest was delighted with the amount of milk he had drawn from one cow. By the time the other three cows were milked he needed more bucket to hold all the milk. It was rewarding for Brynne to see how happy Father Mike was. His project was now a success that answered all his dreams and he begged Brynne to stay one more day to teach him how to do it. Then he invited him to breakfast. The whole village had assembled to see this marvellous event but Mike would not give anyone a taste of the milk until he had put it through all his new filters and cooled it in his bank of refrigerators. He had read books on this for months and everything about milk became a ritual of almost religious significance.

They stayed two more days in the village and when they left to walk down to the coast everyone wanted to carry something. Evelyn and Bata had missed the whole performance in the stockyard and were surprised at the air of celebration that accompanied them on the long downhill walk.

Brynne had urged Father Mike to castrate the two bull calves; which he was reluctant to do. He then explained that Channel Island breed bulls can become dangerous and if one of the people was hurt the project would be untenable. He then showed the people how to throw the calves and he castrated them so fast the priest could barely follow his movements.

"There Mike, next time I come by we can have roast beef for dinner."

He hoped there would be a next time. The way things were unfolding he could be out of a job and back in Australia before he was scheduled to visit the area again.

Chapter Ten

Everything that exists in time,
Runs out of time
Someday.

Bruce Coburn song

The heat and humidity of the coast hit them like a wall as they descended the last couple of miles down the mountains and walked through the tall coconut palms of the coastal plantations. Copra cutting labourers and men slashing grass between the palms called out and waved to them as they passed by down to the beach. The resident plantation manager was not renowned for his good nature or generosity so Brynne skirted by the main establishment and headed straight for the beach, where he was relieved to see the government workboat anchored just offshore, with the laundry of the crew fluttering gaily in the breeze from a rope above the cabin.

By the time they had paid off the carriers most of the party had been picked up in the tender and they were soon heading east into a gentle swell, back to Rabaul. He was in his usual euphoric mood at the conclusion of a successful patrol and looking forward to cold beer at the RSL Club and sleeping in his own bed again. He smiled at the analogy of the man who felt so good, when he quit bashing his own head with a hammer. That's how it felt heading for luxury after mild privation.

Bata had found a shady spot and was about to become engrossed in the first pages of the book Evelyn had finished the night before. Albert and Binus had their fingers hopefully on the taut trolling lines, baited with the stringy white roots of arum lilies to look like a swimming squid and Brynne was hearing all the latest news from Rabaul from the pointy headed Arawe skipper. He was one of the last babies to have had his skull bound to make it come to a point. It wasn't grossly deformed but he favoured a haircut that exaggerated the cone shape of his head, which is easy to do with the tight curls of Melanesian hair. Brynne had enjoyed many journeys with Isidore, who had a fund of ancient stories to tell and was a fine seaman. He told of a rowdy strike by the town police force the previous day. The policemen were angry at the constant delays in being issued with the promised new uniform.

Brynne looked back at Sergeant Binus in his black, wool serge tunic with red stripes and piping. He closed his eyes to imagine him in a smart blue shirt with shoulder boards, darker blue shorts and beret and polished boots and knee socks. Binus might take a little while to get used to it.

Evelyn stood beside Brynne, easily following the conversation in pidgin and admiring the tattoos and facial markings of Isidore. She clung gently to Brynnes arm, to steady herself to the lift and surge of the swell. It was as physically close as they had been in the month or so she had known him and Brynne mused at how nice it would be if the weather blew up a little. It reminded him of the time he had taken a girl for a ride on the back of a motorbike when he was sixteen and how she clung to him as he made exaggerated sweeps around curves in the road. He grinned as he recalled wishing he had a bigger fuel tank so he could ride forever in such blissful circumstances.

He coaxed Evelyn over to where Bata had started to read and interrupted her.

"Bata we wanted to ask you if you were impressed by the nuns up at Father Mike's mission. Would you like to be one yourself?"

She giggled at the question. "No, it's not something blong me but they like it. They say that Mike is doing God's work and by caring for him they too are doing God's work. But I don't believe it."

"What don't you believe Bata?" asked Evelyn, genuinely interested in her reply.

"I don't believe in God or his work. It's all ting ting something. I believe Jesus was a good man and his father was a carpenter, that's all, not God in the sky."

"Well Bata I'm surprised to hear that. What do you think about the missions and the church and everthing?" Brynne was surprised at how the conversation was going.

Bata looked at him with no hint of a grin or shyness and said. "Altogether something is good, the church, the missionaries, the schools the hymns and ologeta something, except God in sky. That is ting ting blong me."

Her tone indicated she didn't want to discuss it further. Brynne gently stroked her pile of soft hair and smiled down at her. "Thank you for your honesty Bata" he said.

By the time they rounded volcano point where the Mother and Twin Daughters rose in perfect, forest covered peaks, the sea had become as flat as a mill pond and

Evelyn had made her way out to the bow, where she stood in the pulpit like a classic ship's figurehead, with her fair hair fluttering in the breeze of the vessels motion.

The familiar sulphur smell of the Matupit volcano on the starboard side turned all heads toward the brooding and menacing grey slopes, still bare of vegetation since the nineteen thirty seven eruption. Across the harbour the long ridge of Vulcan was as green as the rest of the hills around Rabaul. Whenever Brynne returned to the town he was always amazed at the verdant and heavily populated Matupit Island. Only a few feet above sea level and not far from an active volcano he found it hard to understand the daring indifference of the islanders to potential catastrophe. There was a causeway to the mainland but even so, the situation gave ominous meaning to the biblical phrase 'the quick and the dead'.

As they tied up to the government wharf he said to Evelyn. "I'm going up to the office to get the ute, do you want to come and have a cuppa with Bob Gifford, I'm sure he'll be glad to claim a few brownie points if he can report that you had a successful patrol."

"Ok. I'd like to thank him for placing me in the care of the great white hunter

Brynne Lewis: for a whole month. You took good care of me Brynne and I do appreciate your generous and kind understanding. I can be difficult I know, so seriously I do thank you for a wonderful trip."

He gave her a hug without further comment and told the others he would be back with the ute shortly. Then he shook hands with Isidore and his crew boy before walking up town to the office. There Bob Gifford was in conversation with a smart and athletic looking young man who was quite obviously a Tolai from the local area. Bob sprang out of his chair and his guest rose politely as he was introduced.

"Penias this is Brynne Lewis and Miss Evelyn P Davies. They have just returned from a month in the North Bainings and

I'm glad to see they are none the worse for wear. Penias has just graduated in agricultural science from Sydney University and may soon emulate your trip for the department. How was it Evelyn? Did you find a suitable area for further study?"

"Yes indeed Bob. I have reams of notes and observations to organise as well as a brain bursting with new experiences which will take a lot of quiet reflection to sort out. It was a wonderful month and Brynne lived up to his reputation in every way."

Gifford looked at Brynne Lewis with a lascivious lift in his eyebrow. He had never heard Brynne referred to as a romantic Lothario but somehow her look and the way she had phrased her response led him to imagine all kinds of erotic possibilities. This was not lost on Evelyn and was the exact response she had been seeking. Brynne looked a bit embarrassed until he noticed her wicked grin and then he knew she was playing with Bob Gifford. This relaxed him again and he had a brief conversation with the new man while Evelyn had a more serious conversation with Gifford.

As he walked out to the parking lot with his car keys he had the uneasy feeling he had just met his replacement. While he was arranging transport for his people and equipment his mind was preoccupied with the possible end to the life he had enjoyed for the past six years. Suddenly the thought of saying goodbye to Albert and Bata and the village he had grown into overwhelmed him with melancholy. First he dropped off Sergeant Binus at his quarters and gave him a hug and a handshake in their usual routine. He also stopped at the police station to tell the officer in charge that Binus should go for a medical check up after his illness in the bush. The officer was a new bloke and he asked if Binus had done his duty. With his thoughts already in turmoil about his own imagined situation Lewis was surprised and then offended by the question.

"Of course he did his bloody duty. Binus is a magnificent fellow and has a powerful influence in the Bainings. I suggest you check his record mate, you won't find a better man in the entire police force."

He regretted the outburst immediately and then changed his mind again. Sometimes new police officers from Australia were less than respectful of native police. He hoped the sergeant stripes would give Binus the stature he deserved with the new man.

The joy of coming home had gone. He had no desire for a visit to the RSL or a meal at the ChungChing. His mood was subdued. Evelyn thought he was sulking about something. He couldn't hide his feelings but he didn't explain, it would make him look pathetic. He paid Albert and Bata at the house and indicated with a glance that now was the time for Evelyn to do the same. Albert was told to go home for a week off while the two women hugged each other in genuine affection. Bata had big tears rolling down her smooth brown cheeks, as if they were parting forever. New Guineans are always emotional when parting from friends and relatives and she could not imagine they would meet again.

After they had left for the village he trimmed the wicks on the refrigerators and topped up the kerosene tanks before relighting them. There was still a half bottle of scotch in the kitchen cupboard but it would take awhile before they had some ice.

"Evelyn come, look at this. We've been away for five weeks and the house has been open and unlocked all that time and still there's half a bottle of scotch in the cupboard. This has to be one of the most civilised villages in the world."

There was a bit of a catch in his voice as he said it. She noticed but didn't understand why until later in the evening when they were sitting in the gazebo in the moonlight, where he could not keep quiet about his foreboding for the future. She listened attentively and was moved by his obvious love for the village and the people in it. When he was finished and feeling embarrassed that he had spilled his innermost feelings she paused momentarily and then said. "That's life Brynne. I'm sure your apprehension is well founded but usually in life people move on and later wonder why they were so upset. What do you have in mind, or is it too early to consider your next stage?"

"You're right Evelyn. I am momentarily rather glum. Not at the likely end of my job but at the thought of saying goodbye to people who have treated me with love and affection. New Guineans are used to parting from expatriate friends who 'go pinis' as they say. It resembles 'die pinis' for someone unconscious or 'die pinis ologeta' for someone who is actually dead. I have the Welsh propensity to display emotion in moments of stress so I'm afraid I'll lose it in front of the whole village. It's like feeling you are deserting them and don't love them as much as they love you.

'Maybe if I can stretch out the departure over a few months it will all be ok. I have to train Penias for his role and that will mean a lot of travel around my beat to introduce him to the people he will be working with.

'The good news is that as I'm on a permanent appointment I may get a golden handshake to bugger off. I know a couple of coppers who have gone south with two years salary. I won't hold my breath but I'm sure Bob will sort something out if I do a good job with young Penias."

Evelyn felt for him but couldn't think of anything more to say. If he wasn't so hairy and brawny, she smiled to herself, a bit of sympathy sex might be in order. She was feeling quite the opposite emotions from Brynne and looking forward to getting back to her flat in Canberra. She didn't mention it though.

He left her the next morning to arrange all her papers and belongings and drove down to town to front Gifford and clarify his position. He felt better after a comfortable night at home and was ready to deal with his new situation. His boss wasn't expecting him back in town and was piling up old patrol reports and surveys on a desk next to Rosemarie the typist, where Penias was flicking through them while trying to suppress a yawn. Brynne got straight down to business and ushered Bob Gifford outside and suggested they have a private chat in a shady spot at the New Britain Sailing Club. Gifford was hesitant but he knew Brynne Lewis could be very direct when he needed to be so he decided to get his unpleasant duty over with so they could both move on.

"Bob you know why we are here so don't fuck around, I need a time frame."

"The 'winds of change' have reached us Brynne. As you know you were one of the last expatriates hired on a permanent basis. Everyone since you are on two year contracts. My instructions are to offer you a golden handshake if you plan to go south at the end of the year. If you want to stay on the Director has indicated that from next year you will be on a temporary contract basis.

'He wants me to emphasize this is in no way a reflection on your exemplary service to the Department. We are all under great pressure to localise the public service before the country is granted independence sometime in the next few years.

'People like Penias Tavui are graduating in increasing numbers and we have to get them up to speed in all government services as fast as possible.

'The boy looks like a pretty slack unit to me to tell you the truth. I'm sure other heads of department are in the same boat. Time marches on mate and soon this country will have to sink or swim without us. If you go for the exit I can assure you of a decent compensation package to get you started in a new career. All we want is that you take Penias under your wing for a few months before you go so that the work you have done has some continuity.

'I'm sorry Brynne. No one likes change when they love the present. I'm sure I won't be far behind you. Penias may be humped into my job in a year or two. No doubt the last whitey to leave will have to turn out the lights but I'm sure sooner or later the locals will figure out how to switch them on again."

So there it was. He was glad Bob had been so direct. He caught the eye of a waiter and ordered a couple of cans of VB. "Its early Bob but let's drink to the end of an era."

That was easy thought Bob with some relief. Somehow he knew it would be this way with Brynne Lewis, no whining or bitterness, just mature acceptance.

"So how was it out there in the mountains Brynne? Did you get an aristocratic bonk in the bushes? That girl had a saucy look about her when I asked about her trip."

"That's the way she is Bob. Just when you think you might be in with a chance she makes a dope out of you. But she was a fun person, very bright and agreeable; I'll miss her for sure."

He didn't mention her brief elopement with Henry Sinclair. Gifford was a bit of a stuffed shirt on that sort of thing. She hadn't expressed any urge to hunt down Henry again since they got back but he expected she might be feeling a bit restless.

"It would be good if you could take her off my hands Bob. I've done everything you asked but I've been with her for five bloody weeks. I can't even fart in my own house anymore mate. I want my freedom back. All your kids are down south at school and Joanna is with them for a few weeks. You might be just the colonial gentleman Evelyn has been craving all this time."

Gifford's office wallah complexion reddened as erotic possibilities flooded his rather innocent mind. He felt uneasy at his guilty thoughts; before he agreed. Brynne grinned mischievously at the effect of his saucy suggestion. He hoped Bob would not take him seriously.

"Ok Brynne it's a deal. I take Miss Davies off your hands and you take Penias Tavui back up to your place and start breaking him in."

"No fuckin way sport, I rent my house for me. You can billet Tavui somewhere else. I'm sick of company and yearn for peace and solitude. I'll bring Evelyn down tomorrow and then I'm taking a week off to relax and write up my report."

He stood up and shook hands with Bob. "Its premature I know Bob but I have enjoyed working with you these past few years. I want you to know that."

Bob put his hand on Brynnes shoulder as they walked back to the office.

"What do you think you'll do Brynne? Have you ever thought about life down south?"

"Yes I have sometimes given it some thought. I got an honours degree so I hope it might be enough to get me into veterinary college. I want a 'hands on' job rather than selling chemicals for Shell or pissing off farmers with unsolicited advice in a government job. Something will turn up before my golden handshake money runs out, I hope."

"Sounds good Brynne, you can't keep a good man down. Bring that goddess down tomorrow and I'll see you in a week or two."

As Brynne got into the ute Penias rushed up to the car and blurted out.

"Mr Brynne, as you will be writing reports this week I would like to use the government vehicle to explore my area of responsibility. The typist said you usually take a few days on your reports."

Brynne Lewis could hardly believe what he had heard. It took the department six years to issue me with a vehicle, he thought, and this prick wants it on his first day on the job. He switched off the engine and tried to think of something to say. Tavui looked expectantly down at him. Then he started the engine, looked him in the eye and said forcefully "Fuck off."

All's well that ends well, he thought and then laughed at the crazy turn of events until he was at the end of Malaguna Avenue.

Back up at the house Evelyn was sitting at the table, surrounded by little baskets of eggs, tomatoes, passion fruit and snake beans. There was more stuff in the kitchen and children were playing under the trees. She was looking around trying to make sense of it all.

"Don't you love the chaos Evelyn? Lets have a party and get good and pissed tonight. I have plenty of wine and port, there's whisky and ice and tomorrow you're leaving to stay at Giff's house. A farewell party you might say."

"What! Are you kicking me out already? What have I done?"

"It's not what you have done Evelyn. It's what I've done. I did everything Bob asked me to do with you for five or six weeks; now I want my life back. I like being a solitary rogue male in my own space, without wearing a cloak of good manners and observing delicate habits like deodorant and underwear. The slob in me is yearning to break free."

She threw her head back and laughed till tears fell.

"This I must see, the maggot emerging from the egg. Can't I stay until you are fully formed and chewing up the lace curtains and pissing on the lawn?"

"Of course you can. Before I take you to town tomorrow I'll have plenty of time to emerge into my full blown horror, especially if we behave like licentious sailors newly ashore tonight."

"Shiver me timbers Brynne. Will I be a sailor or a whore on the shore?"

"Fuck! I never thought of that, I should've stopped at the bank on the way home. I guess you'll have to be a shipmate arter arll."

She knew there was no harm in Brynne so she pushed the nonsense further.

"And just one thing before we start our carouse Brynne, are we the poncy Royal Navy or a bunch of sturdy pirates? Mateyness is a broad church, matey."

Brynne grinned, he had had enough fooling around. "I'll make omelette and salad and I bought back a chocolate cake for your farewell party. It should make a lovely chunterous mixture for after the party."

It was a grand party. They danced to his Frank Sinatra records until the batteries on the turntable died. They ate biscuits and cake and cheese and drank wine till three in the morning out in the gazebo, where Evelyn lost it all over the side before she went to bed. All around, curious eyes watched their carouse, including Bata, too shy to approach.

In spite of all the booze they consumed neither revealed their innermost thoughts or mentioned their future plans or other personal details or observations about each other. It was like a Christmas office party where no one goes too far.

They slept late and finally left for town in the early afternoon. They said little on the way down Burma Road but as they passed by the copra mill Brynne looked across at her and felt a pang of sorrow they hadn't become closer and that she was now out of his life. He recognised that he loved her but it was as futile as Don Quixote's love for Dulcinea.

"If you need clarification on anything as you go through your records just post them up and I'll try to help out. I'll be around for a few months yet."

She was glad he spoke up. She had some regrets of her own after a month and a half of mostly harmonious friendship. "Thanks Brynne. I'm sure that will happen. It's hard to imagine returning for further study in those mountains without being with you and Bata."

She put her small, tanned hand on his arm until they arrived at the office. Then their parting was a brief hug and a kiss and he was gone, after a brief conversation with Bob Gifford.

Still feeling the affect of the booze up the night before, he went straight home to the serenity of an empty house. He loafed around reading and smoking and began preparing an advisory manual of procedures for Penias Tavui. It was a list of villages with names of elders and leading growers with some cautionary notes to be wary of certain individuals who might try to take advantage of a new man. He found it boring and spent more time drafting letters for his future plans.

On Saturday morning Bata and her mother stopped by on the way to the market.

She also returned the book and was eager to talk about it. "I'd love to hear your impressions Bata. I'm so glad you read it so fast. Let's do it tomorrow, you can skip going to church and we'll sit in the haus wind with tea and sweet biscuits."

Then he loaded their produce into the ute and drove them down to the main road to wait for the market truck, explaining on the way that Evelyn was staying in town and may show up at the market to look for Bata. At that time he had given little thought to the girl having read a Nobel Prize winning novel.

But the next day as she explained her emotions about the tumultuous scenes and predicaments of the characters, the great love and cruelty woven through the story and how she identified with Aksinia and Gregor, it became obvious she was a person of discerning intellect. There was no sign of the giggling adolescent. Her eyes filled with tears at times but also hardened with anger as her recollections continued.

Brynne hardly said a word until the evening and it was time for her to go home.

Then he said, to her astonishment. "Bata, would you like to go to school in Australia?"

He hastened to explain before she could continue. "I have never met anyone who could analyse a story in such detail and with such feeling. I hardly know anyone who could read that book, let alone the Bible. You are a special person Bata, you can't be wasted growing sweet potatoes in a village."

She couldn't understand how impressed he was that she had merely read a book.

"How could I do that? I finished grade six three years ago. The mission only sends the clever students from high school to Australia?"

"Talk to your mother Bata and I will call Gwen tomorrow. She was the one who said you should go to school in Australia because she could see you are a smart girl. Gwen loves you and she will take care of you. She is unhappy that she never had a daughter, only me and Jeremy. Your parents like Gwen and they know you would be safe. I think you could be a fine student. My mother is a teacher too so you will soon catch up with Australian girls."

"Will Australian girls like me?" said Bata timidly.

"Did Evelyn like you? Did Gwen like you? Did Mrs Gifford like you? Of course they will like you Bata, you smile once and everyone loves you. Off you go home now. By next weekend we'll have it all worked out."

They worked it out. As doors closed softly behind them they nudged the slightly open doors in front of them and had no need to look back. The anthropologist soon forgot about her romantic voyage on *ELIZABETH 11* but she lingered in the memory of the busy vet, Brynne Lewis, cropping up at the most unexpected times, while he performed his grimy duties as a partner in a large animal practise in the Kangaroo Valley of New South Wales.

He followed closely the career of Iambata who had not only graduated from university but was a valuable employee in the office of a senior minister in the government of an independent Papua New Guinea. She made regular visits to his mother Gwen, whenever she had business in Australia.

Time marches on; none of them gave much thought to the rather mundane trek across the Baining mountains or the influence it had on their future. Ten years had passed since they parted, on the day Brynne came home late in the afternoon after a hard job replacing a prolapsed uterus in a valuable, high yielding dairy cow. The animal would have to be sent to the slaughterhouse after her lactation. The farmer was sad to lose her and despite his experience as a busy vet Brynne felt a bit down as he drove along the driveway of his small farm. He saw two vehicles in front of his brick bungalow, a most unusual thing this late in the day.

The red Ford belonged to his housekeeper, Annie Burton but he didn't recognise the blue Holden. His dog ran out to greet him as he stepped out of the Toyota ute and close behind Annie emerged with Bata beside her. She had kindly stayed with Bata since noon to keep her company until he came home. Now she briskly hugged the brown woman and hurried off home to care for her own family.

Brynne was astonished to see the calm, poised woman before him. Tall and slim she was, and fashionably dressed, but the smile of welcome was the same as when she was a girl in a white Mother Hubbard blouse and green laplap. His Welsh genes brought his emotions to the surface and as he raised his arms to embrace her, tears were streaming down his face and he was too choked to say anything as her soft woolly hair caressed his cheek and absorbed his tears. Her arms squeezed him close and they stood embraced as Annie tooted goodbye and waved, with a smile on her face.

When they separated he was surprised to see her brown cheeks as wet as his own stubbly face. "Oh Bata, I never dreamed we would meet again. All the time you were with mum I was at school in New Zealand and then working in Canada. I heard all about you though; how lovely that you came to see me."

"I came to see you because I always loved you Mr Brynne. I'm supposed to be at a conference in Sydney, but I skipped. I'm all grown up now Brynne, you can hug me again if you like."

The next hug lasted longer until she leaned back and put her beautiful hands on each side of his face and kissed him passionately full on the lips and stayed there in pulse racing bliss. By the time they went indoors Brynne's head was spinning, his desire was pounding against his remembrance of her as a child and as he overcame that he became aware of his smelly overalls and was able to gasp. "Forgive me Bata, I smell like a cow barn."

He stripped away his overalls and had a shower and then they sat together on the sofa watching the fireplace, like old times in the mountains. After much reminiscing Bata looked him in the eye, with her small shapely hand in his and said, "Brynne, do you remember when you told me I would be wasted spending my life growing sweet potatoes in a village?"

"Yes I do. We were in the house wind talking about a book. I was right; you would have been wasted, given the success you have enjoyed. Mum said you have been to New York and Geneva and often to Sydney and you're still young with more to come."

"Well Brynne does it surprise you that when I go home I spend my time in the garden, weeding sweet potatoes or pounding my clothes on a rock at the spring and when I go back to work in Port Moresby I always feel homesick."

Her eyes were sad as she explained the loneliness of success and he squeezed her hand and kissed her again. "No. It doesn't surprise me. The late president of Egypt, Anwar Sadat was like you. He liked to go back to his village, put on a caftan and ride around on a donkey visiting his childhood friends. Intelligent people are underwhelmed by grandeur Bata. I love that you value the beauty of your roots."

"And I missed you most of all Brynne, I loved you since I was ten."

Her head fell on his shoulder and the warmth of her face seeped through his shirt, dispelling the social isolation he had felt for years, despite his numerous friends. His world seemed complete. Images of little brown children climbing on his lap were interwoven with the warmth and joy of her presence

She stayed for a week until his parents and brother Jeremy drove down from the Hunter Valley to give their blessing. Every night they lay together talking long into the night. Bata told him she had met Evelyn Pemberton Davies in Geneva at a United Nations function and it was Evelyn who urged her to seek him out and visit him and convey her kind regards. It was Evelyn who had assured Bata that he loved her but didn't know it. Brynne imagined her making that observation, but made no comment.

Evelyn had seen something in him that he didn't know was there.

Chapter Eleven

LOVE AND PERSEVERANCE

The old lady's arthritic hands lay curled and yellow in the lap of her faded red apron. Wrinkled, with swollen joints and brown sun spots though they were, they still resembled the clawed feet of a sick hen. She tried to work a little at her leather trade but what strength she had left was neutered by the pain in her joints. She watched closely as her fifteen year old grand daughter, Lillian, toiled with a draw knife in shaping a saddle tree, clamped to a stand in front of her stool.

Around the girl's bare feet, red chips and shavings indicated how much wood she had removed since the morning, from the aromatic cypress pine block she had started with. Now she was being as careful as a sculptor as she hollowed out the centre, which would clear the withers of the horse when it was fitted. Her grandfather came across from his smithy and leaned on the veranda post beside her while he stuffed his black pipe with even blacker tobacco. His banana thick fingers were about the same dark shade at the end of the day.

"I spose I better get busy and make some straps for that thing," he said.

"Yes poppy, it will soon be ready. I'll do a little smoothing with the hoof rasp before I check how well it fits on Triumphant."

"Well I hope young Josh will find himself a better bag of bones than old Tri" laughed Tom Brace. "But I spose he'll do for a model."

Lillian concentrated on her work. She didn't mind a little teasing from her grandparents. They loved Josh as much as she did, even though he was a Catholic from up at Springers Crossing, half a mile away. His folks didn't like the idea of him marrying an Anglican. At least his father didn't and had vowed not to attend his son's wedding.

Nobody cared about him.

Joshua's brothers and his mother loved her so she felt good about her future.

Josh had just turned nineteen and they planned to marry the day after his twenty first birthday. It seemed like an eternity to wait but there was a lot to do.

The sun was sinking in a red ball behind the black hills and the air was cooling quickly. Soon there wouldn't be enough light to work on the saddle. Other duties crowded in on her so she put down her rasp and stood up to shake the chips and sawdust from her apron. Then she briskly swept the floor with a reed broom and gathered up the material and placed it in a wooden bucket, feeling good that it would be easy for lighting the stove tomorrow morning.

Lily didn't like the long skirts of her gran. She was fed up with washing the dirt out of the hem, so she cut her work skirts off just below the knee. Some thought she was a blowsy tart because her bare brown legs reminded them that her grandmother had been a convict; a thieving fourteen year old prostitute sentenced to seven years in Australia. That was a lifetime ago but still some liked to mutter about the stain on the Brace family name.

They muttered very discretely, in case Tom Brace should hear gossip about what they had said. He used to be respected for his great strength but for most of his life he was such a skilled and clever man that everyone sooner or later needed to do business with him. He was very protective of his wife and on a couple of occasions he had refused to do any work for people whose spiteful remarks had been brought to his attention. He obstinately refused to forgive them, forever, including their descendants; so his sentiments were widely respected.

He was an immigrant blacksmith on the convict ship which brought Emma Gould to Sydney all those years ago. They had never been parted since. Everything that was good in Tom and Emma Brace had blossomed into the perfection of their granddaughter Lillian. They were not a prolific family and they had concentrated their love on their son as they did now with Lillian. There was a void in the family since Lillian's father had gone to sea, several years earlier, in utter despair at the death of his young wife.

He could not bear to live in the surroundings in which they shared so much happiness. In recent years he had been working for an American whaling company and from time to time they received letters from his home port of New Bedford so they were able to send back news from home. In her last letter to him Lily begged him to be home for her wedding to Josh, planned for May 1880. She ached for his reply ever since she wrote that letter.

Lily kissed her grandmother and thanked her for her help and then she rushed away to continue with her work. She put more wood in the black iron stove and lifted the lid on a big pot to poke the corned silverside simmering away there. Then she scraped some potatoes and carrots with a piece of perforated tin, adding them to the pot on the stove with an onion in a cloth, which sat in a tray under the lid. Then she topped up the water in

168

the gutters of the meat safe on the veranda. She took a long drink from the canvas water bag hanging beside it and then skipped around to the laundry. The water in the rum barrel there was comfortably hot but before bathing she had one more job to do. She ran outside and whistled for her dog. It knew exactly what to do and sped off to run the sheep and cattle down to the dam for their evening drink. Lily just had to open the gate. That was the last of her evening chores, grandfather would bale up the calves. Then she ran into the laundry for the most pleasant job of the day.

Here she stripped off her dirty wool skirt and flannel blouse and lifted the lid on the waist high rum barrel and felt the water again. Sometimes it was too hot to bathe and had to be mixed with some cold water in a bucket. There was another barrel of the same capacity in the room above the kitchen. Everyday she topped up the bottom barrel and pumped it upstairs at dawn. Then she adjusted a spigot so that it trickled down via a steel box in the stove into the bottom barrel. That hand pumping was a job she hated but they were the only family for miles around with hot water in the bathroom.

She poured hot water over her head and body with a copper bowl and then soaped herself with an olive slab of home made soap. It was a joy to rinse with plenty of hot water and feel clean and fresh again after a long tiring day. There was lots of water left for her grandparents but they were not so fastidious in their habits and usually had an all over wash on Friday nights. She put on a white cotton shirt and pulled a blue wool dress of regulation ankle length over the top before brushing her fair hair and braiding it into a thick plait, held by a silver clasp. She wiped the steam from the mirror and admired herself with a smile. She wished Josh was coming home tonight.

She heard her gran exclaim and went out to find out why she was cursing. Down the road, a hundred yards away, a sulky with one horse approached and she grinned at her grandmother's irritation. It was the Anglican minister doing his rounds and looking for a free dinner and a bed for the night. Lily hadn't noticed but her grandparents were well aware, that this formerly rare visitor had changed his routine since Lily had rounded out into an attractive young woman. They watched the prurient interest of the young Englishman and although they did not feel at all complimented by his visits, the bush tradition obliged them to be hospitable.

They refused to engage with him on religious topics or allow him to display his vaunted education and superior conversation.

Reverend Hubert Chapman regarded them as poor but hard working yokels, although he was sometimes amazed when Tom Brace displayed his knowledge of British history with a casual reference. Chapman was on the lookout for a well to do heiress of the district squatter class but he couldn't resist the allure of Lillian Brace, poor as she was. He sometimes casually mentioned his duty to visit the poor, when trying to impress some person in authority and he cited the example of lodging at the Brace household, as though it was a cross to bear.

Tom Brace was a long way from poor but he was not ostentatious in his habits or lifestyle. He was content with the comfort he had been able to create, with the family he had and the friends who valued him. The gold and money he kept under a floor slab in the smithy only made an appearance when he needed to make a major purchase, and that purchase, usually of iron, coal, timber or livestock, replenished the steel box soon after it was spent.

Tom carried a discrete aversion toward ministers and those in authority. From his rustic youth in England he had seen the exploitation of rural labourers by the gentry and landowners and their collusion with the indifferent clergy; eager to ingratiate themselves with the rich and powerful

He named his son William Wakly to honour the name of the great Doctor Wakly who lobbied the British Government successfully for a pardon for the Tolpuddle martyrs, whose only crime was a desperate attempt to form a union to oppose rampant wage cutting.

Although Emma Brace too was suspicious of priests and squatters she could be a gracious hostess. While Lily prepared the simple evening meal Emma carried a tray out to the western veranda with tea and oatmeal biscuits and Lily brought a small enamel can of milk from the meat safe, in case the minister liked milk in his tea. Also a saucer with fresh butter for the biscuits. Reverend Chapman didn't realise how honoured he was. Usually the biscuits only appeared during the morning, when they took a break from their work.

Tom Brace was eager to pump the young minister for news of the wider world and asked him questions about Premier Henry Parkes and the political squabbles between the states. Most of the travellers who stopped for a rest at the Brace forge knew nothing but their own cares. Chapman wasn't much different. He knew nothing about the disastrous diseases in the wheat crop or the German colonisation of New Guinea. He didn't even carry much local gossip so they soon lost interest in him. He told Lily it would be nice to see her at divine service and asked if she had been christened.

The answer disappointed him.

At the dinner table he said grace and complimented Lily on the plain fare and the fresh, warm damper. He sensed a cool lack of candour and made no further foray into religious or personal matters. After dinner she showed him the bathroom and the hot water tub with pride and warned him against rinsing his stockings in the hot water barrel.

"If you needs to wash something sir, please dip out the clean water and wash it in the bucket," she said. Other visitors had been ignorant enough to wash their laundry in the barrel, which enraged her as she had to empty it and refill with fresh water.

"I say Lillian, would you mind washing my shirt. I can pick it up on my way back in a couple of days?" His confidence sagged at her uncompromising answer.

Lily looked at him with affront. "Yes I would bloody mind washing your shirt. Wash it yourself, I'm no skivvy for travellers."

She walked angrily away but went out and put his horse in a stall and fed it.

"Next thing he'll want is to have his bloody horse brushed" she muttered under her breath. She did water it though and vigorously rubbed it down around the collar and back with a handful of straw after sponging off the sweat. To Lily it was just natural concern for the comfort of the animal, without thinking it a favour to the priest.

The next morning at dawn she lit the stove and was out letting the sheep and cattle down to the dam for their morning drink while the minister shared tea with her grandmother on the veranda. She took her time, watching the stock until they had all had a drink. By then her grandfather was done with the milking and her dog, Trim, drove them back to the paddock and she shut the gate till evening. She didn't like the animals to hang around the dam, poaching the banks and fouling the water. In fact they had a rail fence at the edge to stop them wading in. Sometimes water from the dam was needed up at the house during dry times.

"Thank you for looking after my mare Lillian," said Chapman, "I forgot about her until bed time and by then you had kindly fed her and put her inside."

He was unnerved by her bare brown legs and feet and her long flowing hair and he drove away quite breathless with admiration, too shy to look back again. She smiled and waved to him, hoping he had enjoyed washing his own shirt, the cheeky bugger.

Her morning chores were to empty the ash box on the stove into a steel bucket for making the next batch of soap. Then strain the milk her grandfather brought in. She took the whey from yesterday's milk and mixed in some oat husks and crushed barley for the pigs, which were already squealing when they saw her go into the dairy. Then she had the tiresome job of hand pumping the water upstairs, which always made her arms ache. By the time Tom Brace had filled the kitchen wood box she was helping Emma to make breakfast. They always lingered over breakfast; one of the luxuries of being self employed. It was as if the long separation of night had to be overcome.

Then she went back to her work on the saddle for Josh. Emma sat across from her and watched the love and care she put into her work. The old lady still had the keen eyesight and hearing of a younger woman but her fingers were swollen and painful for gripping work with hand tools. She could drive a horse hoe and dip clothes out of the copper laundry boiler so she still made a good contribution to their life, even pumping the bellows in the forge from time to time.

"When does Josh expect to catch this horse he's been talking about? As far as I know he hasn't laid a hand on it yet?"

"You know Josh nanna. When he says he's going to do something he does it. He told me he has his eye on a chestnut brumby stallion that runs in the ranges behind the camp. He has seen it along the horse yard when the work mares are on heat and he plans to catch it in the yard he is building alongside. He leaves oats in a trough and the stallion has started to take the bait at night. Anytime now he expects to slam the gate and catch him. Then the fun will start. I hope he'll be careful.

'The boss out there is a hard man named Bruce Thornton. He's always warning

Josh to not waste his work time catching brumbies. That cove wants to be careful himself. The Pringle boys stick together so if he gets too tough on Josh he'll have three angry men to deal with. It's hard enough work already without having a boss like that. I don't know how Josh can spend all week on an axe and buck saw, building railway crossings and bridges and then ride that bloody bike fifty miles home on Friday night."

Emma smiled at her grand daughter's loyalty to Josh. She knew that he was never far from her thoughts. She found it strange that they had been inseparable since they were infants, more like brother and sister, always racing the half mile up and down the road to find each other.

"Well apart from dealing with a brumby stallion I hope he can be sure the squatter out there won't claim him. Sure he has no brand but those bastards will try any trick if Josh catches a decent horse. They hunted Ned Kelly for picking up stray stock and turned him into an outlaw. There's a bit more justice nowadays but lots of people havn't changed."

"Nanna did you know that Josh gave a shearer fifty pounds for that bike so he could come home every second week instead of once a month on the dray with his brothers. I hope he catches him soon. It will be more natural to him riding a strong horse than pedalling that contraption, quite apart from flat tyres and broken chains. Old Thornton doesn't like him to miss Saturday work either but Josh told him to get another man if he wants to, but he won't work a Saturday. He should come home and learn the blacksmith trade from Poppy, but he's saving up his money."

"Well Joshua needs to be a little careful there Lily. Things are getting tough and there's more men looking for work. You've seen them coming through here lately with empty bellies and nothing in their pockets. Maybe there'll be another gold rush somewhere soon and every fool and his dog will head that way.

'The Pringle boys are getting fed up with railway building as they have to work farther away from home. By the time the line gets to Bathurst they will likely run out of work anyway.

'Looks to me that you're nearly done there so hop down the paddock and see how it fits on Tri, then we'll go dig some potaters while Tom fits the straps and stirrup hooks. We'll have the leather on that thing finished before Josh has his horse caught and broke."

Their one hundred and fifty acres had some areas of fine red soil which grew excellent crops of turnips, pumpkins and potatoes. A neighbouring wool grower gave them all the sheep manure under his shearing shed in exchange for some of their crop and the odd job in the smithy. They had to hire men to haul it but the land stayed in good shape with the help of a bean crop, and some barley and oats between potatoes.

Sometimes a few acres of white turnips fed their own sheep and cattle so the little farm was more than enough to feed them and left some produce for sale.

Independence had always been the goal of Tom Brace. His skill as a workman and careful saving gave him the freedom he yearned for at an early age. When young and angry he had been inspired by a seditious copy of Thomas Jefferson's famous speech but the slavery issue revolted him. When he emigrated to Australia he had hopes it would be like America, without the slavery.

Once he had his own bark hut and food security he became self employed and called no man his master, other than his

175

benefactor, Selwyn Lloyd. Several wealthy men had attempted to browbeat him over their unpaid bills but he never made a fuss. He just refused to work for them until the bill for the last job had been paid. A skilled rural blacksmith had little competition because such men were in high demand in the cities and towns, where wages were higher than squatters wanted to pay after enjoying years of convict labour. Not many took him for an educated man, but he could read and write and had a sound understanding of arithmetic and geometry. He never came back from business in Sydney without useful books relating to technical trades. Not to better himself, as he was a contented man; but he was interested in every new idea.

Tom Brace admired Josh Pringle and his brothers. They showed similar qualities. They worked as hard as anyone could wish and demanded good pay. At a time when seven shillings a day was regarded as good pay they wouldn't work for less than twelve, but they provided their own quality horse teams and tools and much of their own rations. Bruce Thornton tried to keep pressure on them but he knew he couldn't find a more productive crew. The Pringles employed a Chinese cook to look after them in the bush. No one could pronounce his name but as he was always singing at his work and had a hoppy leg from an old knee injury they called him Hop Sing. It sounded a bit Chinese and he was happy with it, even regarded it as a term of endearment, which it probably was. He didn't get much wages but like most of his race he had a sharp eye for business so he made money by his obliging and industrious nature. All the jobs he did outside his remit of cooking and laundry for the three Pringles earned him extra money. He never refused a job for people who were honest in paying him and he made more in a day than most in the camp realised.

He had the business man's knack of buying and selling at a profit and he knew what to buy. The Pringles were glad to see him prosper with his initiative and everyone knew they would stand by him in an argument.

At the end of each month when they took a two horse dray home for the weekend, to bring back supplies and a fresh team, Hop Sing came with them. He left orders and money for goods he wanted to buy with Tom Brace and Tom sent them back with the weekly mail service. He also stored Hop Sing's money with his own in the secret spot under the forge. They didn't have much to say to each other but there was trust between them; not many knew where Tom kept his money.

Chapter Twelve

Long before Rebecca Brace, Lillian's mother, fell ill, the family had achieved a degree of comfort and security that would have been the envy of many, had they been aware of the true situation. The ironwork business was busy everyday, not just shoeing and farrier work but also tool and implement making. A very profitable line was the making and fitting of bullock shoes for the teams employed hauling out great wagon loads of wool and timber across the stony ranges. Tom had built a cradle for the job, in which a bullock could be lifted by a winch with wide straps under its belly so the feet could be secured for shoeing. With the advance of railway lines the shoeing of oxen faded but he sold more horse shoes and farm tools as more settlers arrived. The small home farm was productive, worked by Rebecca and her mother in law it produced more than they could consume. They adored each other.

Rebecca had arrived as an emigrant from an Irish orphanage; her passage paid for by the government to try to improve the gender balance in the colony. After a few years of employment in the home of a local squatter she asked his permission to marry William Brace. Many men were interested in her but the shy, reserved and sober William was the one she wanted. Her employer confirmed he was the best man around. She didn't have much competition for William and she planned her campaign by becoming the friend of Emma Brace. Industrious and energetic in her habits she soon became a treasured member of the Brace family, especially after Lillian was born. The child was a mirror of her mother, sturdy and strong with the same fair hair and blue green eyes. The Brace family felt they had been blessed by fate.

Soon after Lily turned eight years of age Rebecca became ill. In two months she fell away to a shadow and died, without a priest or a doctor in attendance. People in the district swore it was a cancer, as she had never coughed or had a fever, nor were any others in the house affected. The only symptom was her inability to eat or drink. Everything she took in came straight back up. No medicine could be given, only hot compresses, which had little affect on her painful abdomen.

The old people had lived through cruel times and seen much suffering, but Will had no such experience outside his happy home. The loss knocked him down so hard he couldn't even bear to look at the child he loved.

They buried Rebecca in a plot way below the dam. Tom carved a headstone and built a wrought iron railing to go around it. He bathed that stone in his tears as he carved it, not only from his own grief but because he tried to carry some of that felt by the others.

There was no Protestant priest around at that time but the Catholic priest who visited the Pringles came by to conduct a funeral service; as much for the shattered Pringle family as for the Brace's. The day after, Will said goodbye to his parents and daughter. He said he had to go away to grieve but he would come back when he had recovered. Emma and Tom feared he would be found hanging from a tree. They exchanged glances before Tom said, "I'll walk along with thee a little Will."

Three miles from home he hugged his son, his face contorted with emotion.

"For God's sake Will, whatever you do, don't break the heart of your mother and child. Everyday that passes will be easier to bear and one day you will come home again. Don't forget us son, you have lost a wife; we have lost Rebecca and our son"

The parting words from his father saved Will's life. Many a time he recalled that parting, sometimes in association with passages from the bible. Though not a religious family his father had insisted he read a page of the bible every night to keep him literate. He remembered 'though I walk through the valley of the shadow of death I will fear no evil' and 'Blessed are they that mourn'. He drew comfort from his bible in dark times.

At that time the railway had reached Lithgow from Sydney and from there he went to the docks with a notion to go to sea and escape everything with which he was familiar, from the scent of gumtrees to the sound of horse hooves and the rumble of wagon wheels. The very first vessel he saw was the American whaler, *Swallow*, unloading barrels of whale oil to be shipped home or sold by an agent on behalf of the owners, Swift & Perry.

The mate liked the look of him straight away, tall and lean, with big strong hands and neatly dressed and shod. He didn't have the look of a tavern bum, in spite of his hang dog expression. When Will put out his hand and said he was looking for a sea going job it was clear he had no experience at all.

"What's your trade then buddy? You don't look like a sailorman."

"I'm a smith Captain, I can do anything with iron."

The American sailor grinned at his promotion to Captain but he was not a man to make fun of a greenhorn. The *Swallow* was likely to be a few men down. The crew wouldn't get the bulk of their money earned from whale oil until they paid off in New Bedford but there were always a few malcontents, impatient to try the next big thing. Australia was coming up with new gold strikes every once in awhile and the lure of a quick fortune overrode the certainty of a good pay day in the distant future. Most of the crew were sober Quakers, like the Captain, but there were Basques and Portugese and a couple of dark boys from Boston who could go off the rails in a port like Sydney.

"Come aboard then smithy and we'll have a visit with Captain Ellis. What's your name pilgrim? I'm the mate Jack Forbusch."

"William Brace sir," said Will, again putting out his hand. The mate was not in the habit of shaking hands with crew. He was more likely to knock a man down with his fist than use it to shake the hand of seaman. He looked up at the tall, raw boned man before him and figured it unlikely he would be troublesome. He knew the courage of a man at sea cannot be gauged from his appearance. He ignored the hand shake without explanation and led Will aft to the Captain's cabin where he tapped respectfully on the door. A short, bearded man opened the door and looked the new man up and down without comment. There was another man in his cabin, standing by the chart table.

"Mr Forbusch I have just arranged to haul out and check our copper. We must be prepared to move to the dry dock on tomorrow's tide. If we can get the job done in time we can likely get back in the water before the change. It sounds as if the holds are empty, is that so?"

"Yes sir it is. We start stowing supplies shortly unless you want to wait until the bottom is checked. This here man, William Brace, wants a berth Cap'n. He's never set foot on a ship but claims to be a journeyman smith. We haven't had such a man seek a berth on the *Swallow* before."

The Captain looked suspiciously at Will Brace. He didn't look like an outlaw trying to skoot the country. A man with no experience could be a nuisance but he dealt with them all the time and it was likely he would lose some crew in Sydney.

Other ships were alongside, trying to recruit replacement crew but his men were aware they had a good pay day assured at home and most had families there. The cooper was unreliable and another man was recovering from a broken shoulder.

He looked up at Will and asked a loaded question.

"Not enough work for a smith around here in Sydney Mister? Or do you just want to go somewheres else?"

Will could tell this was a no nonsense man with whom he should be completely honest. Captain Ellis manner was more direct than his father's.

"There's lots of work, both here and at home, but I do want to go away for a spell. I'm an honest man Captain."

Ellis could sense a troubled man, but he sounded genuine.

"Can you do a cooper's job if we need you to Brace? There is work for a smith aboard but you'll have to turn your hand to any work. Like the rest, like all of us."

"Yes sir, I can do any job with tools. The sailor work I will have to learn."

"He sounds alright Mr Forbusch, show him a berth and put him to work."

With that he turned his back and closed the cabin door. William Brace had begun his seagoing career. He stayed with Captain Ellis for two whaling voyages covering the next five years, the last one venturing far into the north pacific in pursuit of sperm whales that were getting scarce, with a lot of ocean between catches.

They lost Forbusch and two other men in the freezing waters off Alaska when they were fast to a whale that smashed their boat and in rough weather. They recovered the bodies within the hour but they had drowned despite the brave efforts of the frozen boats crew to hold onto them. They lost the whale as well.

The disaster was too much for the indefatigable Captain Ellis and he quit the voyage and headed for Cape Horn. They kept a lookout for whales and in fact caught a huge whale off the coast of Peru that produced two hundred and forty barrels of oil.

The gods smiled on them as they rounded Cape Horn in nothing more than a strong breeze and continued to run easterly for several days before heading north north west on the homeward run. Will Brace knew, days before they reached New Bedford, that he was done with the sea. The loss of Forbusch, who had become a close friend, brought back the suffering from the loss of Rebecca. His bereavement turned into self loathing for deserting his child and parents for so long. He resolved to go home.

Ashore again he took his pay and was advised to seek lodging in town, in fact he was driven in a gig by his employer's black servant, to the boarding house run by the widow of a former employee of Swift and Perry. The owners sold the *Swallow* and became heavily involved in the manufacture and installation of steam engines. They were eager to retain the skills of William Brace and he momentarily forgot his desire to return home as he became engrossed in the magic of the steam age; matching the enthusiasm of his employer. So eager were they to retain him that he was offered a share in the company for every share he could purchase from his accumulated savings.

Will knew that if he accepted the offer he would never go home. By this time he had become very fond of his landlady, Miriam Coffin and her daughter and the little mulatto orphan girl who lived with them. In the evenings, after supper, usually of herring or codfish, they would sit by the kitchen stove and he would tell them stories of Australia. They didn't want to hear about whales and storms and cannibal islands. The children liked to hear about koala bears and wallabies and magpies that chase children in nesting season. He didn't mention snakes.

One evening, in the longer days of spring, they had supper in the garden, away from the heat of the kitchen and he told them sadly, that he planned to go home before the end of summer. The three had become so used to him that at first they were speechless. Then Jessie, the little brown girl looked up at him with her great dark eyes and said simply and in her usual direct way. "What about us Will?"

The pain of the question brought back the words of his father on the day they parted, "don't break the heart of your mother and child."

The other child, Anna Coffin, twisted the knife. "Yes Will, you can't leave us after all this time. What will we do without a father? I'll be the only girl around to lose two fathers, a grandfather and an uncle in five years."

She ran into the house in tears and Jessie followed her in similar distress. Miriam heaved a great shuddering sigh of resignation and put her hand on his great hard fist on the table. It was as if she had expected this moment and was prepared for it, as she had been unprepared for the other losses in her life. Will felt a great lump in his throat as the full impact of leaving them rose up in a flood of emotion. He looked directly into Miriam's eyes and said quietly, "Will you come with me Mrs Coffin?"

Miriam and her girls were unaware that Will Brace had become the centre of their lives over the several months he had been in the house. Other boarders were usually men between ships but Will was employed ashore and his quiet, kindly nature had filled the gulf left by the loss of so many men in the family. He still behaved like a courteous lodger and had made no attempt to be over familiar. Even now with his dramatic proposal she was still Mrs Coffin.

"Yes Mr Brace, I will come with you; with all my heart, to the end of the earth."

They rose from the garden bench and stood together in the gathering dusk, among the heavy scent of roses and the cry of a whippoorwill and the distant sobs of the girls.

They kissed in a warm and suddenly sensuous embrace and right there they were no longer Mr Brace and Mrs Coffin. That night after a long discussion, interrupted by the delirious hugs and kisses of the girls, Will wrote a letter home.

William W Brace
C/O Swift & Perry
Wharf 2 Dock 15
New Bedford
Massachussetts
U.S.A
29th May 1878

Dear Father and Mother and Lillian.

Your letter of last year turned up here a few days ago and I hope this one gets back to you faster than yours got to me. I know how anxious you are for me to come home and I plan to do it real soon. I have been at sea for a long time on two round the world whaling trips under Captain Ellis on the Swallow. We did well to and took over 400 whales so we all made some money.

I have been doing all the iron work but helping with the cutting out when all the men are busy working night and day.

The owners have sold the Swallow and I now work on shore in an engineering shop. Everyone is crazy about steam engines now and whales are getting harder to find so its good to have another job. I am going to marry a widow who came originally from a place called Cape Sable Island up in Canada. Her name is Miriam Coffin and she is thirty five years old. Before, her name was Miriam Doane. Mrs Coffin wants to come to Australia and get as far from the sea as she can. She lost her husband and brother and father to the sea. She says she never again wants to hear a seagull or a wave on the shore.

Soon I'm going with her to her home country and there will be married in the Baptist Church. Then we will take ship to England and find a passage to Australia from Liverpool. I cant tell you when we will be home but I can tell you I will never go away again. It took me three years to accept that Rebecca was gone but Im good now and will soon have a new wife and daughters.

You will all love Miriam the minute you meet her and her daughter Anna who will be thirteen tomorrow. They also have a little brown girl named Jessie whose father was a ship mate of Miriam's late husband. You will have three grandaughters in your old age and a lovely mother and sisters for Lily. I saved up my money all this time and Miriam will sell her property before we leave so we will have enough about us to live in the old way.

I have missed you all every day since I left and coming home will be like the minister says, I will be born again. I will likely be home soon after you get this letter so don't write back to my address above.

Your Loving son and father, William.

Nobody was surprised at the brief letter from William W Brace. He was not a loquacious man. It arrived in the mail four months after it was sent. The waves of joy it generated seemed to be intensified by its long mysterious journey. The whole family knew that the writer could soon be with them. The mail contractor was often surprised to see Lily sitting on Triumphant's back by the mailbox as he urged his team over the hill. He knew why she was there and often felt apologetic that he had no news to bring. He remembered Will Brace and was almost as eager to see him again as the sad eyed girl on the old horse.

She and her grandmother had long finished the saddle for Josh Pringle and he was making good use of it since he caught and branded his stallion. Josh could have bought a saddle for about what he received from the sale of his bike, but like everyone else he was careful with his money and he recognised the love that had gone into making it. Emma Brace had been making and mending horse collars and harness for fifty years so the saddle was well within her capability. He didn't use the new saddle until his horse was broken and quiet, for fear it would fall and break the wooden tree and ruin all the work that had gone into it.

Joshua had grown up with horses but they were not his first skill. The stallion was about three years old and in his prime so it took a lot to calm his wild ways. First he kept him penned in the yards in solitary confinement and on very light rations and water to weaken him a little. Then he asked Hop Sing to visit him a couple of times a day to give him a drink and a little feed until he would come up to the timber rails as he approached. Gradually Hop Sing won the confidence of the horse and he would take Josh to the yard when they got back to the camp after dark and show him the progress he had made. Over a patient couple of months they wore down the stallion's fiery nature and coaxed him into a crush to fit a head stall on him. Soon after, he could be brushed and petted and got used to having a saddle placed on his back and a girth lightly under his chest. When he could be led around Josh decided to take him home to Tom Brace to learn how to be shod and broken to saddle. They led him home behind the dray on their monthly trip home and he was as docile as a work horse. The horse breaker for a neighbouring squatter was a renowned expert at castrating and training brumbies and Josh left him in his hands until he was ready for work. He had to pay the breaker a month of his wages but it was money well spent.

By the time Will Brace came home with his new wife Josh had been riding his horse home every second Friday night for several weeks. In fact he even got a little sleep on these journeys after Spooky got used to the route. The horse was named for the white blaze on his face which made him visible at night. On full feed again he was sleek and beautiful and it was Lily's joy to wash him down and dry him while Josh was fed and petted by her grandmother. He was such a fixture at the Brace household that his mother was often there, just to be with her youngest son. They had all been friends and neighbours for so long that they were comfortable together in either home. The news that William Brace was on his way home was soon common knowledge in the district but the fact that he was bringing home a new wife and children was not divulged, even to Joshua Pringle. Tom and Emma thought it best to keep that information confidential and they had no fear that Lillian would leak it. She was a mature and sensible girl and had no female friends to share secrets with.

Numerous people stopped by the forge to express their joy for the family. Among them was the district squatter, Selwyn Lloyd. He had taken up a vast stretch of land many years earlier and had become wealthy from wool. Everyone in the district loved him for his wisdom and kindness and referred to him as Lord Selwyn.

He was in danger of giving squatters a good name.

He was the employer who had recommended Will Brace to Rebecca. He was also the man who sold Tom Brace his one hundred and fifty acres of land and settled several independent farmers and graziers on land he sold to them at one pound an acre.

Lloyd had no desire to be the master of hordes of labourers, as his family had been in the West Country of England. He needed people but preferred to have self sufficient smallholders who could be called upon when his few full time staff needed help. Tom Brace had been an asset to the district from the start and Lloyd had asked him to select a piece of land to settle on in order to keep him from going back to the city for high wages. It was a fortuitous clash of interests as Brace desired independence above all things. He chose a piece of land with a valley draining down to a creek and a ridge of rough shale country with abundant timber and poor grazing. Along the valley floor there was deep red soil to grow food crops and an excellent site for a dam. Over the past thirty years Tom had excavated a high dam wall, blasted out a small quarry in the shale ridge and developed his red soil into a productive farm. In addition he built a thriving blacksmith and iron working business which enabled him to bring in raw iron, cement, leather and timber from Sydney as back loads on the drays heading out to bring home the wool. Both Selwyn and Tom had grown old together in a symbiotic relationship which had at first seemed unlikely, given their contrasting political backgrounds.

As Selwyn Lloyd walked his latest thoroughbred at a brisk pace toward the Brace home he felt again the satisfaction of having coaxed them into his orbit.

The long, white washed house of shale stone reminded him of the slate houses in Cardiganshire villages. The blue grey slate roof had its connection in that ancient country, having been brought to Australia as ships ballast and hauled out in crates on bullock wagons at huge expense. Ten years of savings from the forge had gone into that house. Built by stone masons brought down from Sydney to erect it and line the circular, underground water tank. It collected the rain water Lily pumped up so laboriously, with a home made pump that Tom designed in his workshop.

"Here comes his Lordship" said Emma as she watched the rider and his three greyhounds approaching. Selwyn was in no hurry as he knew they would be hurrying to make tea and possibly some of the oatmeal and molasses biscuits he had been enjoying for years. Lillian sprang to attention and dropped the stick she had been using to dunk clothes in the copper boiler. She grabbed her dog, which was rarely far from her side and locked him in the laundry. She didn't trust Lloyd's greyhounds, which were adept at killing foxes and dingoes. She moved the black kettle over to the hot part of the stove and put some biscuits on a tray and into the oven, they were a bit easier on the teeth when warm. Then she ran outside to greet the visitor.

"Ahoy there Lily" he shouted as he dismounted. "I've come to hear all the good news my dear."

Lily loved Selwyn and with complete confidence she hugged him and reached up to kiss his smoothly shaven brown cheek. "Yes sir yes, father is coming home. Pray God the ocean is kind to him." Her emotion was clear in the full bright eyes and Selwyn wished he had a daughter who would rejoice at him coming home. Habitually she took the reins of his horse and petted the greyhounds and left him to her grandmother while she put the animals in the stable, taking care to keep her bare toes clear of the iron shod hooves as she loosened the saddle girth.

She skipped up the veranda steps to ring the cow bell to summon grandfather from the forge, but she waited, to avoid interrupting Emma's excited explanation of the news of William Brace's return. Emma sometimes snorted derisively at the mention of squatters, but she loved Selwyn Lloyd and held his hand in her gnarled fingers. Her emotional state was plain to see. He caressed her grey hair, moved by the love and relief in her voice.

"Well that is marvellous news Mrs Brace. I venture to say I am as delighted as you are that Will is coming home. And you Lily, your father coming home at last, his heart healed from the loss of your beautiful mother. Thank God he survived his adventures. When do you expect to see him on your veranda?"

"Soon sir" cried Lily as she jingled the bell. "The sooner the better, I shall hug him till he's blue in the face."

Then she went to make tea while her grandmother took Will's letter from the drawer and carefully unfolded it for Selwyn to read. He laughed out loud and said,

"This is Will Brace to the liver, not one wasted word. Oh my lord, what wonderful news that he has a new wife and daughters. What a mighty family you will have Mrs Brace."

He gave her another hug and clearly needed one himself, he was so happy. Tom came up the stairs and shook his hand. "Ye must keep mum about Will's new wife Selwyn, we havn't mentioned it to anyone else as yet. We don't want people to be gossiping before they meet the woman. She has a brown girl she took in so you can imagine the links some people will make. Will is no fool and if he says this is a good woman you can bet your shirt she will be."

"My word! That is the truth Tom. I shall be as silent as a wombat but it will be hard to keep my mouth shut. If I tell my wife, the news will be in Sydney by suppertime. We must have a celebration when Will is home, everyone will want to shake his hand and hear his voice. Maybe we could have a dance in the woolshed with fiddlers and a big dinner, like the last night of shearing."

"Well that might be something," said Tom, "Will never was a man to make a fuss, especially about himself, but it would be a fine welcome for his family. What do you think Lily? Should we have a big shindig for your father?"

Tom smiled on his grandaughter, he knew she wasn't fooled by his pretending to be hesitant about a 'big shindig'.

"It's a lovely idea Mr Lloyd, I wish it was tomorrow. Can we plan it for seven days after they are home, that way my sisters will be able to help with the preparations, and my new mother too, and ..," here she began to cry and all the pent up misery of losing her father for so long flooded out as she fell on her grandfather's chest as his thick, black, hand fell gently on her back.

Her young emotion connected with the old people, somehow they understood the relief, that all those years of fear he would not return was bursting forth from Lily.

Emma had watched her sadness every time Joshua went back to work in the bush and she realised why she was so attached to the lad. He was the one to whom she turned when she lost both her mother and father in such a short space of time. It was Josh who healed her grief as much as the love of her grandparents.

Selwyn Lloyd watched the cathartic emotion of Lily with a warm regard for her in his heart. Other thoughts crowded in as the words of Will's letter barged in.

"Everyone is crazy about steam" he had said and it was clear he had worked in engineering shops in that line. Lloyd had long been concerned that the district would be without a blacksmith if Tom retired and his son didn't come home. Most countrymen could shoe a horse but there was much more to the trade. He couldn't keep down his fears and ventured a comment.

"Do you think Will can settle down at home after all this time Tom? He has seen many things and is no doubt highly skilled. They are crying out for good men everywhere. The call of the big smoke might be too much for him."

Tom smiled and kissed the top of Lily's fair head.

"He'll stay home Selwyn. He has as much time for the city and high wages as I do. We can do better on our own, with our own home and tucker than all those men in town, surrounded by rum and swindlers. Will can use his new skills right here. I'm so busy I have to twist my own arm to take Sunday off."

Lord Selwyn felt better as he left. Tom Brace knew his son better than he did. He felt a little ashamed as he rode away that his first concern was his own interests rather than the happiness of the blacksmith. The feeling soon dissipated, they were all interconnected in so many ways.

As Emma watched him ride away at an easy canter she slapped her hand into her apron and said, "Darn! I meant to ask him about old Steve Lockyer. He hasn't been around for a month and he's been coming here every couple of weeks for thirty years.

'Lily when you go down to meet the mail man put Sixpence in the trap and trot over to see Steve and tell him your father is comin home."

"I'll go now Nanna and I can catch Fungus Firner on the way back." The mail contractor sported a great fuzzy black beard, nobody remembered what his real Christian name was; maybe he couldn't remember himself.

Lily let her dog out of the laundry and sent him up the night paddock to run the horses in to the yard. They were used to the whirling blue dog coming to get them and the reward of a handful of oats and chaff in the yard, so they cantered down the hill and were in the yard watching her before she had rinsed the clothes from the copper.

She walked over to the yard with a halter and a taste of oats in a wooden bucket to feed the squabbling trio, before putting the halter on Sixpence, her grey pony. She tied him outside the yard and finished her laundry chores before backing the pony into the shafts of the trap and hitching up the harness. Trim sprang into the trap and she went indoors to put on a decent skirt and her soft boots and hat.

Emma admired the smooth efficiency with which Lily ran through her chores and she filled a water bag for the girl to carry on the trap, it was a hot day. Soon Lily was enjoying a breeze on her face as the pony trotted along at a brisk pace toward the mailbox a mile away. Steve Lockyer's place was about three miles from the road on a barely visible track. He too had bought land from Selwyn Lloyd when he was young and valued as a horse breaker and champion at all the rustic trades He was old now and kept sheep and a few cattle which he trained as draft bullocks. Lily was fond of Steve for his kind and gentle nature; a lonely old man who had never married or even employed anyone.

His station was called 'Springbrook' precisely because there was a spring at the base of an escarpment which had never been known to dry out, although it became a mere trickle in dry years. Below it was a billabong full of waterlilies and further down were other smaller pools. It was an ancient abode of aboriginal people long before the white man's germs and greedy land grabbers drove them out of the district. A few had returned since Steve Lockyer bought the land from Selwyn Lloyd and there was a semi permanent camp among the great blue gums which came right down to the water. Steve had fenced off the main lagoon to keep cattle away from the banks but he never interfered with the natives. He knew they were driven away from waterholes in other areas, suspected of killing livestock and he felt sorry for them, being homeless in their tribal country. People said he would be speared to death one day but he had lived side by side with them for thirty odd years without harm. Watching them from his veranda in the evenings had banished his loneliness. He never went out of his way to be friendly or give them presents like tea or tobacco and they had learned not to ask.

When age slowed him down a couple of the men casually began to help him train bullocks to the yoke or shear his few sheep and for this he would share meat when he killed a beast and salted it down. These men had grown to maturity in his vicinity and watched the way he did his work. Over the years Selwyn Lloyd had observed the development of this relationship and although he never raised the subject with Steve, he had modified his own attitude to the blacks, who occasionally drifted back into his own vast domain.

Lily Brace trotted along the dirt track toward Springbrook, as she had done many times before. Her thoughts were far away in the endless blue sky, thinking about her new mother and sisters. The pony slowed to a walk descending to the dry bed of a creek and then threw herself into the collar, trotting up the other side onto the broad flats of tall grass on the last mile before the Springbrook homestead. Trim growled beside her as he saw an aboriginal couple approaching, carrying a small child. Lily recognised a girl about her own age and the young man, both of whom she had played with in the water when she was a child. Her mother used to urge her to play naked with the black children in the billabong and she remembered the delight she showed at the freedom and joy of the native children, compared with her own impoverished and severe childhood in an Irish orphanage. When Rebecca recalled the damp, sour smell of the shabby clothes she grew up in, she felt a surge of admiration for the naked blacks, playing in the warm sunshine.

To Lily it seemed so long ago; her father standing nervously on the bank, unable to swim and depending on the native children to keep her safe.

"Steve him big feller sick, close up die" cried the girl before the pony had come to a stop. Lily shook the reins and shouted urgently "Hup Sixpence." She broke into a canter leaving a small plume of dust behind the trap.

Lily had rarely heard of anyone dying, especially in her own tiny circle. The thought of losing a lovely little man like Steve Lockyer filled her with horror and only prudence prevented her from urging the pony to even greater speed. Well before she came alongside the veranda of the aged, grey, timber slab shack she could see the old man lying beside his cow hide chair. Racing up the steps in one bound her first thought was that he had been speared as he was drenched in congealing black blood down his chest and through his white beard. Flies were crawling over his face and eyes and into his mouth and nostrils. When she lifted his head gently onto her knees he opened his eyes and groaned her name. Now she could see the blood had come from a massive nose bleed and fresh blood was still oozing out.

Relieved he was still alive she pulled him up against the wall and took down his waterbag from a nail on a post and began to wash his face and clean his beard. He came to and eagerly swallowed some water but he didn't try to speak. His face was twisted in a sort of grimace he was unable to change. She went for her own waterbag as more blacks appeared with frightened concern on their faces, but with some relief that it was Lily. They helped her clean him up and carry him to the trap, where they laid him on the floor with a roll of paperbark under his head. The waterbags reappeared, full and hooked on the hand rails. As she turned for home the young man who had come to get help ran along beside the trap. Trim, the dog, was not happy when Lily urged him up into the trap. He sat on the floor with Steve Lockyer's legs across his lap, gently cradled in his big black hands to prevent them dangling over the back.

With the good sense of a bush girl Lily maintained a gentle pace, walking where the track was rough and then an easy trot between. As she crossed the road past the mail box she saw fresh wagon tracks and the empty mailbox and knew there were visitors at home. Anxious about Steve she never thought about who might have chosen to call. She became aware of a dreadful smell and realised the old man had fouled his moleskin trousers, which were already soaked with urine when she first saw him.

On her own track now she urged the sweating pony to greater speed and with tears rolling down her face she wished Josh could be with her. The native holding Steve's legs across his lap glanced up and saw the distress on Lily's face and he muttered an encouraging word or two. She didn't know what he said but put her hand on his shoulder to thank him for being there.

In front of the forge a great wagon with four big horses was parked and loaded high with a green canvas cover over the load. Then she saw her father running towards her with his arms in the air and just behind him Fungus Firner hurried along, eager to see the happy reunion. People were crowded on the wide verandas of the house waving to her. She pulled Sixpence to a stop and leapt to the ground and ran into an embrace with her father. The overload of emotions got the better of her as she pulled William Brace to the rear of the little trap where the sight and smell of his old neighbour overwhelmed his joyous homecoming like water on a fire. The father and daughter led the pony up to the house with their pitiful load where Will whispered

"Go meet your mother and sisters Lily, I'll take care of Steve."

Tom Brace took in the situation at a glance and went to help his son and the mailman.

An emotional Lily ran to the embrace of her grandmother and explained through her tears how she had discovered Steve just in time.

"You must have had a message from God to send me there Nanna. That black boy was on his way to tell us and he helped me bring Steve home."

Her new mother stood by, feeling bitter sadness that the homecoming day had been upset by the tragic illness of a loved neighbour. Emma maintained her silent embrace of the shaken girl and kissed the top of her head as she gently rocked her in her arms as one comforts a baby. As she felt the calming influence of her arms around her she pulled apart to look up at Miriam, who said softly to Lily, with her hand cupping the girl's cheek,

"Stay here with Nanna and Anna and Jessie and I'll go help Will with your neighbour. You are a good brave girl Lily and already I love you."

Miriam then sprang into action and ran across to the wagon to access a chest under the green cover. She retrieved a black medical case that she always carried since she was a young girl, helping her Uncle Lorimer, who was the village doctor.

Dr Lorimer Doane was one of the few men on Cape Sable Island who did not go to sea, simply because he could not overcome sea sickness. She had seen numerous medical conditions with him before she married and moved to the United States to the lonely and apprehensive life of a whaler's wife.

Dr Lorimer Doane could not complete his studies in his home province and had to complete his degree in Toronto Ontario. Rejecting the comfort of a city practise he returned to his roots along the grey sand beaches of Cape Sable Island, where his young niece proved to be an able assistant.

The men had carried the slight body of Steve Lockyer to the watering trough near the forge and had already stripped him of his soiled clothes and washed him clean of blood and faeces. The water had revived him a little and he was trying to apologise for causing trouble. His words were barely discernible as his face was distorted and partially paralysed, but Tom understood him to say "Iwillome yet."

"Yes Steve, here's Will."

It seemed the bush telegraph had alerted Steve that Will was coming home.

Will cradled him in his arms and stroked his wet white beard gently.

"Its me Steve, Will Brace, your little mate."

The exhausted eyes rose to look at Will and his features relaxed into the beginning of a smile and his right hand squeezed the strong hand stroking his beard, as one would a pet cat.

Miriam stood beside her husband with her bag and said clearly, "Will, this man has had a stroke. His bleeding nose may have saved his life. From the state of his nose and forehead it looks like he had a heavy fall."

Will had great respect for Miriam in such situations and as she threw the soiled clothes into a large bucket to wash the filth out of them the men carried Lockyer to the bathroom for a proper bath with soap and warm water.

Gradually Lily overcame her churning emotions in the calming embrace of her grandmother and was introduced to her new step sisters, who were watching her closely. Her spirits rose as she embraced the two pretty girls, struggling to find words of greeting for them.

"It's not a very pleasant thing for you to arrive just when our kind old neighbour is so ill. I'm so excited to have a new mother and sisters. I have been rushing down to meet the mailman every week since my father's letter told us all about you. How pretty and grown up you are."

"Thank you Lily," said Anna. "You are everything we expected from all the stories Will told us about you. It sure is exciting to be here at last and to attend your wedding. Your father said he must be here for that. When will you be married?"

Lily laughed at last, with the joyous realisation that all her wishes had come true.

"Oh not for a while yet Anna, we planned for when Josh turns twenty and I'll be seventeen. But father had been away so long and I feared he would be gone for more years and might even be shipwrecked and I would never see him again. God has answered my prayers at last."

Then she remembered both girls had lost their fathers at sea and she began to cry at her thoughtless excitement. All she could do was hug them again but could find no words of apology. Anna and Jessie loved her for those tears. Young as they were they understood the love and excitement that had made her so passionate.

She was saved from further embarrassment by the arrival of Jack and Edith Pringle, who had noted all the activity down at the Brace household and like good country neighbours had walked down to find out what was going on. Jack Pringle was not famous for the warmth of his nature but he couldn't hide his joy that Will Brace had come home. After brief introductions to the American girls he hurried off to the forge to see Will.

"There's some bad news too Edith," said Emma Brace to cool Edith's gushing chatter. "Lily brought poor old Steve Lockyer home and he's in a bad way. They've got him in the bathroom cleaning him up. Lily found him collapsed on his veranda covered in blood. It seems it came from his nose. Lily thought at first one of the blacks had speared him, there was so much blood. Those people have lived beside him for thirty years. They are probably scared someone else will move in and make life hard for them again."

"Oh my lord! Poor old feller, and on such a marvellous day for your family Emma. I must go and see him."

"Hold your horses Edith. He's being bathed and he won't like you blundering in on his nakedness. You know how shy he is. Lily, go fetch your blue flannel nightie and give it to your father. Steve can wear that till he's a bit better."

As she ran off Lily was glad her nanna had not mentioned the awful state she found Steve in. After she delivered the garment she switched into her usual busy mode and lit a fire under the laundry copper and shaved off some soap into the water to wash Steve's shirt and trousers. Soon after, they carried the sick man out and laid him down on a couch on the veranda. His dogs arrived at the same time and quietly flopped down beside his bed. Lily's dog Trim was wary of them and slunk away with his tail down, suppressing the low growl he felt struggling to emerge and let them know they were on his territory.

Edith Pringle went over to the couch and knelt beside it. She kissed the newly shaven cheek of her old friend. He touched her face with his right hand but the left lay helpless on the blanket. When she came back to Emma and the girls there was deep sorrow in her expression.

"Emma you can't care for Steve at this time. Your house is full and so much to do. This is your blessed moment. Let him rest tonight and tomorrow we'll come and fetch him and I'll nurse him up home. I'm only busy when the boys come back. It will be easy for me and I love him dearly."

"Thank you Edith. My hands are so crook that I can't be much help and all the load would fall on Lily. Let's see how he pulls up in the morning and we'll decide then. Maybe he'll soon get well; he's a tough old bird."

Fungus Firner stumped up on the veranda in his hobnail boots and sat on the couch holding Steve Lockyer's hand. "Take a spell old horse," he said softly, as he squeezed the helpless hand. He had to leave on his work and despite all the joy of his reunion with William Brace, Lily saw the head down misery on his face at the condition of Steve. She held his hand as he walked over to his team. "Bless you Lily" he said as he stepped up on the wagon. Fungus Firner was uncomfortable showing emotion; he appreciated her comforting gesture. "That's life girl, all good one minute and bad the next. Edie Pringle will take care of the old feller, you enjoy your dad's return and love your new mum." Then he flicked his whip and left at a trot. He was proud of being on time with the mail and already he had lost some time.

Chapter Thirteen

As Lily walked back up the steps onto the veranda her dog touched her hand with his nose to remind her he was still there and a little nervous about all the new people and dogs around the place. She caressed his silky scalp and cupped his chin in her hand. "Its all good Trim" she said, as if picking up on his unease. Then she remembered that Sixpence was still standing patiently in the shafts of the trap so she ran indoors to put on her work clothes before putting the harness away and sponging off his sweaty neck and back while he ate a handful of oats and chaff.

Miriam had seen her walk to the mail wagon with Firner and then comfort her dog and tend to the pony. She took a deep breath of joy that her girls had such a fine sister.

Emma carried a mug of black tea out to the veranda and sat it on a three legged stool next to the bed and then brought a pillow to prop Steve up to drink it. He was able to pick it up with his right hand and at the familiar taste his features softened as he tried to say thank you. She sat beside him and held his hand in her crooked fingers as Miriam returned and sat on the veranda beside them. Both women watched as Lily came back from releasing her pony, holding hands with the two girls.

"Emma its both a sad and joyous day for us but I know that I have joined a heavenly family. Will told us lovely stories about you but nothing could verify them more than your love for your neighbour and each other."

"Yes Miriam, and you and Anna and Jesse are a further blessing. It gives me confidence that my dear old friend here will soon be well again."

Steve nodded his head and mumbled and she thought she detected a slight pressure from his useless left hand, maybe he was already getting better.

The dramatic events of the past few hours were most unusual in such a quiet rustic setting but Emma remained as calm as if such were her daily lot. She had in fact been thinking and planning for many months about how they would cope with more people. Such things as how much ground to plant in the vegetable garden, the new building required for the marriage of Josh and Lily, the increased demand for killer sheep and how their water supply would cope with a doubling of numbers.

Over the next few days they sorted out all the stuff on the wagon, unloading beds and coconut fibre mattresses and trunks of personal possessions and modern tools and books. Will had swung back into work with his father and chores and duties were being gradually devolved among Miriam and her daughters. Emma Brace said barely a word as it all unfolded but every night in bed she whispered to Tom how lucky they were and related how someone had done something especially rewarding.

On Sunday morning Josh Pringle and his older brothers came down after travelling through the night from their camp. Hop Sing was with them and they brought the news that they had all been laid off temporarily as the work was complete. Everyone was crowded on the veranda with mugs of tea and piles of biscuits. Now and then someone would embrace Will and slap his back and look embarrassed for feeling so emotional about his return.

Anna and Jessie were used to strong burly men but the Pringles seemed especially so because of their huge callused hands and dark, sun tanned faces. Joshua fascinated them with his gentle smile and comfortable closeness to Lily as she stood behind his chair with her hand on his brown neck whenever she wasn't serving tea or helping Miriam in the kitchen. Hop Sing tried to help them but they shooed him away to sit on the veranda.

It wasn't a noisy occasion as the only chatterbox among the Pringles was Edith and she had stayed home with Steve and her husband. This soon changed when Selwyn Lloyd and his wife Fiona drove up in a shiny black buggy. Lily ran out in her best blue dress to meet them and gave a small curtsey to Fiona as she stepped down. It was so rare to see Fiona that Lily acted almost by instinct but she felt genuine respect and affection for Mrs Lloyd. They embraced and Fiona held her at arms length. "Lily you are positively beaming with joy. Bring me to your new mother immediately while Selwyn cares for the horses."

Tom Brace was already beside them. "Yes Fiona go on up and meet your new neighbours, you too Selwyn, I'll tend the team."

"We won't stay long Tom" said Selwyn. "This is just a courtesy visit. I can't wait though; just put the rig in the shade and join us."

Fiona hurried along beside Lily who was eager to make the introductions to her new mother and sisters. She was impressed with the perfect manners of Fiona who first embraced and kissed her grandmother before turning to look with delight at the three new women in her district. The Pringle brothers were a bit in awe of Fiona as the wife of the most important man in the area so they all rose and remained standing while the ladies became acquainted. Miriam was a little uncomfortable that it took so long for Fiona to acknowledge the men, standing so respectfully and shy, in the background as it were. She didn't realise at that moment that Fiona had known them since they were babies and felt no urgency to turn her attention to them. As Tom and Selwyn came up the broad veranda steps she at last turned around and addressed all the men.

"We are blessed by the return of William and his beautiful wife and girls. What a lovely community we will be. Please, everyone sit down while I get to know these ladies with some good old female chatter."

With that, in the same 'take charge' manner as Selwyn, she ushered the ladies off the veranda into the kitchen and left the men to their own business, in the usual pattern of bush gatherings where the sexes typically congregate in separate areas.

Emma had never invited Fiona further than the kitchen on her rare visits but this time she gently ushered the women through into what she called 'the other room'. She couldn't be so grand as to call it the 'best' room. People higher on the social scale might call it a library or drawing room but Emma kept things simple.

On the south wall a great stone fireplace with a rough, adze hewn log for a mantelpiece took up a third of the space. Heavy wooden chairs covered in red leather were arranged around the fireplace. Jack Pringle had built them years earlier and Emma had upholstered them long before her fingers were frozen by arthritis. Under a deep window lay a couch that Tom Brace frequently used to take a noon hour nap or where he read his books and newspapers in the good light. Several red roan hides covered some of the stone floor and in a well in the centre of a sturdy table a magnificent glass lamp rested securely, with its shining glass chimney rising two feet from the base. This lamp was used on special occasions because of the beautiful white light it cast from the expensive whale oil fuel.

Several paintings adorned the stone walls, the work of Lily's late mother Rebecca who loved to paint gum trees and aboriginal children. Miriam was surprised to note that Fiona was seeing them for the first time.

After admiring the paintings Fiona turned her attention to Miriam. The girls kept quiet and Emma sat ready to intervene if Fiona became too inquisitive in her interrogation. She was bursting with questions and already saw herself in the grand homes of her friends in Sydney telling all about the American woman residing on the home station.

She quickly dispelled Emma's concern, with the careful way in which she drew information from Miriam and her daughters. She began by asking if they had any homesickness for America and worked her way around to questions about Miriam's first husband and Anna's father. She was so skilful in the way she put her questions that she didn't seem intrusive. She compared the anxiety of a whaler's wife with that of soldiers and sailors who go away into danger for long periods and invited them to respond. Soon they were eagerly relating the anxieties they had lived with for years and the toll the seagoing life took on the communities in which they were born. Miriam finally brought the subject to a halt by telling how Will Brace had come into their lives and brought them to a safe home far away from the hazards of the Atlantic shore. Then she boldly took the initiative and asked questions of equally personal nature about Fiona's life, friends and family.

Emma smiled inwardly, delighted with the wit and confidence Miriam showed, completely at ease with someone to who most people responded with some deference. Fiona seemed to enjoy the experience too before turning her attention to Anna and Jessie.

On the veranda Selwyn was eagerly debating the new situation facing their small community. He was inwardly alarmed that the Pringle boys had run out of work and may be forced to move further afield and be lost to his carefully nurtured community.

In some ways Selwyn's motives resembled a Russian count whose wealth depended on the peasant serfs in the villages on his estate. He had built a successful rural community by encouraging initiative and rewarding the people he valued. He was trying to think of a way to find out their plans without revealing his self interest in their future. Selwyn felt a little ashamed of his manipulative ways but they all knew his motives from long experience and he enjoyed their respect and affection. Before he could ask a question Brian Pringle observed that they had run out of work at just the right time.

"The return of Will and his family and Steve Lockyer's illness seem to have pointed us in a new direction" he said. "Steve can't live alone now, although he's getting better by the day. He wants us to take over Springbrook Station and run it properly. He hasn't done much the past few years. Will wants to train Josh to the blacksmith trade to take some load off Tom so it looks like we are all sorted out for awhile."

"Wonderful!" exclaimed Selwyn. "Springbrook has never been run to its potential but Steve has been a marvellous member of our community, poor old chap. I'm glad to hear he's getting better. I must stop on the way home for a visit and to thank your mother for her kindness. If I can help you in any way Brian be sure to come my way.

"There is a bit of a boom on at the moment so you should do well. But beware the bust that follows a boom and don't borrow money if you can avoid it.

'And you William, do you have any plans other than to help your father?"

"As you know Selwyn, dad is pretty busy so of course our focus will be on getting through the work. Josh is joining us as an apprentice. There is potential for change now so I hope to move forward on some things I saw in America. Steam power, windmill deep well water pumps, corrugated iron tanks and roofing are all in Australia. A British steam traction engine can be bought for two and half thousand pounds and it can be used for well drilling, threshing and chaff cutting as well as driving sawmills and workshop machinery from a line shaft.

'This district is growing fast and if we can move quick without the debt you warn of we can be at the front of the mob on all this."

Tom Brace was well up to date on all these developments from his technical books and pamphlets and he agreed with his son on the business potential. He said nothing though and sat quietly by while Selwyn explored all the topics further while calculating how he could participate in the visions of the younger men. He could feel his position as patron of a rural community becoming less important to the people in it as the district became closely settled and new business opportunities emerged. He was a wise and prudent businessman and genuinely believed he had a role to play in the lives of those he regarded as 'his people'.

He could see that he would have to be patient in getting Fiona to leave so he went inside and whispered to Emma, "I'm just going to slip up to see Steve. It looks like these girls are as thick as thieves just now."

His intention was that she would keep Fiona occupied till he came back but she stood up and held his arm. "I'll come with you Selwyn, I never was one for chatter."

Tom Brace watched them as Selwyn handed Emma up into the buggy and stepped up beside her. Suddenly he felt a surge of warmth for the man as he recalled the countless small instances of his kindness and loyalty to everyone in the district. How lucky I was to cross the path of such a man all those years ago, he thought. William was sitting beside him, also watching his mother drive off up the road to the Pringle's.

"There goes a good man Will. They don't come much better."

Will nodded without comment. He could sense that Selwyn Lloyd was eager to join in some new enterprise and felt encouraged that his hefty financial backing might be available.

In the black buggy Emma looked with pleasure along the glossy backs of the matched team, though she had no desire to own one. Selwyn Lloyd kept them at a walk for the short distance as he said to Emma. "All my life I have tried to surround myself with good people Emma and now, in the last few days, no better reward could I have earned. William has come home with a magnificent family; the Pringles have shown their true qualities in taking in Steve Lockyer in his distress and Steve has turned over his property to the boys just as they run out of work. God himself couldn't arrange things any better."

"Well he might have a hand in there somewhere Selwyn but you are the one who tried to attract good people. You did and we love you for it."

Steve Lockyer stood up on wobbly legs and a stick as Selwyn embraced him and then gently helped him to sit down again. "Easy does it old chap. Its good to see you on your feet so quick but there's no rush. Love and perseverance will pull you through and there's heaps of that around here."

Chapter Fourteen

THE NAUGHTY BOY OF CRIPPLETHORNE VILLAGE

Long ago in Lincolnshire England a boy named Timothy Atkins lived in the tiny village of Cripplethorne. His father was Tommy Atkins and his mother was Rosemary. Timothy's nanna also lived with them but his grandad was killed in the Great War.

Until he was ten years old Timmy was a very good boy and everyone in the village loved him. His teacher in the little school was pleased with everything he did, although he was an outdoor boy. He loved to be with his dad training farm horses to pull ploughs and wagons. They bought young horses and sold them when they were fully trained. The other things they did were catching eels in the fen and making them into jars of jellied eels. Tim and his dad caught them in a funnel shaped net and his mum and nanna cooked and bottled them.

They also did lots of other fun things. They used to catch wild rabbits using snares and ferrets. A snare is a wire noose that catches the rabbit as it hops through a path in the hedge. A ferret is a little yellow creature that is very fierce, with sharp teeth. They used to put nets over all the rabbit holes and then let the ferret go down the burrow. The rabbits would flee at full speed into the nets and that was how they caught them. Then they had to wait for the ferret to come out of the burrow, sometimes he was lazy and took ages to emerge. People loved to have rabbit stew or casserole so they sold them for five shillings a pair. They sold the skins to the hat maker in Ely. They also hunted ducks and geese and wood pigeons and fished for trout in the river. Even the feathers of the birds were valuable for making pillows and doonas.

Any boy you could think of would be proud of a dad like that. The other thing they did was help Farmer Robinson at busy times when he was harvesting barley and potatoes and carrots. Rosemary Atkins was an especially hard worker at these jobs and Farmer Robinson was a great friend of the Atkins family. In fact he had loved Rosemary since he was fifteen years old. She was the most resourceful woman he had ever met and on their tiny farm she produced pickled eggs, jellied eels, smoked chicken as well as red and black currant jam and other things. Ninety per cent of her produce was sold to Mr Bennet at The Wheatsheaf pub and when the war came he did a roaring trade with the airman from bases in the shire.

Rosemary was doing so well at that time that she had guilty feelings that she was a war profiteer. John Robinson did her banking for her in Ely and he too was astonished at her success. On one occasion he found himself hoping that Tommy Atkins would not come home. This caused him such tremendous shame that he tried to join the army himself. His application was of course refused because of his profession but he never recovered fully his pride in his name and estate.

Their happy life had ended one day when the Vicar of the church, the Reverend Dinsdale Pitt told everyone at church that they all had to come to a meeting the next day because a war had started and someone from the government would talk to them about it. Timothy's nana started to cry straight away because she knew people get killed in a war. His mum was very upset too so the fun had gone out of their Sunday.

On Monday the government person told everyone that new rules would apply to everything they did and soon a recruiting sergeant would come to Cripplethorne to see if anyone could be a soldier for the British Army.

And then, just to prove that he was an idiot, he told them not to worry.

Tommy Atkins carried on doing all the normal work he usually did and he thought the village was forgotten. It was so small, with one church, one little school and one ancient pub called 'The Wheatsheaf.' But sure enough a couple of months later the recruiting sergeant and a corporal came to the village, to interview all the men who might want to join the army. Nobody wanted to go. The cenotaph in the village had seven names on it and none of those men had been found and buried. MIA beside their name meant missing in action, probably blown to bits.

Most of the men were needed to grow food for the country anyway. The sergeant was interested in Tommy Atkins. He said the army needed men who could look after and train horses and mules and he looked at Tommy fiercely and told him it was his duty to join the army. Poor Tommy was afraid to be a soldier, he knew of so many men from his father's time who didn't come home. Under the fierce frown of the recruiting sergeant he agreed to join and then went home and told Rosemary and nana. Everyone was crying and it was hard for Tim not to join in, until it became clear his dad was going away. Then he too cried along with his mum and nana. A couple of weeks later Farmer Robinson came to take Tim's father to the railway station.

Before he went away Tommy Atkins said to Timothy, "You are the man of the family now Tim. You must take care of your mum and nana until I come home again. Just do all the things we usually do but be extra careful when you are in the boat on the fen by yourself catching eels. Be a good honest boy and pay attention to Farmer Robinson and don't be shy to ask him for help if you need it." Then he ruffled Tim's blonde curls and left.

Timothy tried hard to do what his dad said. Every night he sat with his mum and listened to the wireless that Farmer Robinson gave them so they could hear the news. Then they got a letter that told them his dad was in India. They didn't know where that was so Tim asked his teacher, Mrs Blackmore. When she read the letter from Tim's father she laughed when she came to his description of India as being hot and teeming with dark people who were thin and poor. He said a boy about Tim's age wanted to be his servant.

"Imagine that" he said, "Tommy Atkins from Cripplethorne with his own manservant to clean his boots. I gave the boy half a crown and told him to buy a present for his mum."

Mrs Blackmore put her arms around Tim's shoulders and said, "Your father is a good man Tim. I hope he comes home soon." Her husband was in the air force, also in India but she said nothing about him. Everything was so tense at the time and she didn't want to be a subject for gossip or nosy questions.

One day in late summer Tim was walking home past Vicar Dinsdale-Pitts house and he saw that his plum tree was full of lovely ripe Victoria plums. The Vicar was in the garden so Tim asked him politely, over the fence.

"Please sir, can I taste one of your plums?"

The Vicar looked at him angrily and said, "Certainly not. If you taste one you will probably steal a dozen."

This astonished Tim. He had never stolen anything in his life. Also he remembered many times when his mum had told him to drop off a dozen eggs for the Vicar on his way to school. Or sometimes she would give him a jar of jellied eels for the Vicar because she knew he loved them. These were gifts, like many he received from other villagers.

The Vicar could see that Tim was angry. Foolishly he added to the insult, "If you try to steal my plums my dog, Monster, will bite you."

Tim almost laughed when he heard this. He wasn't afraid of Monster, who was a big, black, hairy, friendly Newfoundland dog. He had a fearsome bark, like a lion roar, but he wasn't a nasty dog and Tim knew him since he was a clumsy pup.

As he walked home he thought bitterly that the Vicar was a greedy man and he made up his mind to steal some plums. Tim had been christened in church and had known Dinsdale-Pitt all his life. He felt sick with hatred for the Vicar. That evening when his mum was cutting up some meat for dinner he put a couple of pieces in his handkerchief. After everyone was asleep he crept out of the house and ran down the lane to the Vicar's house and threw a piece of meat to Monster. The big dog rushed over wagging his tail and ate the meat. Then Tim opened the gate and gave the dog another piece before he slipped through the gate and closed it. Monster found, to his delight, that he was free and he raced off to the village to meet some other dogs. Then Tim climbed the plum tree and had a good feed of plums.

He laughed all the way home, but he had a bellyache from too many plums. Monster galloped around raising hell in the village and making all the other dogs bark in frustration because they were chained up and he was free. The tremendous din woke everyone and next day they complained to the Vicar that his dog had caused a commotion in the village.

He was furious. He suspected it was Timmy Atkins that let his dog out.

Tim told his friend Bob Eckholm about the trick and Bob wanted to try it too. That night they found that Monster was on a chain near the plum tree. Tim threw him a piece of chicken and Monster wagged his tail, so he went in and undid the chain clip and they let Monster loose again. While the boys were stealing plums Monster bounded around like a big puppy, stirring up all the village dogs and chasing cats through flower beds. Everyone was cursing the Vicar's dog.

The Vicar was so angry he almost swore and committed a sin. The first thing he did was pick all his plums and take them indoors. That Sunday he gave a sermon in church about the evils of being dishonest. He said people started off pinching plums and ended up in jail for robbing banks. He looked fiercely down at Tim, sitting with his mum and nana, but every boy in the village thought it was a great joke. The Vicar's face was red with anger and his fat cheeks were so busy shaking that he stuttered with frustration. He hadn't stuttered since he was fifteen years old, back when a boy was severely caned if he stuttered. He took Tim's mum and nana into his house and told them that Tim was an evil boy who would be a criminal one day if they didn't punish him. He did this in front of his housekeeper Mrs Warrington, who was a notorious gossip and the terror of her little husband. When they came home they were crying with shame at what the Vicar said about Tim being the naughtiest boy in Cripplethorne.

Granny Atkins was usually a quiet, gentle woman but she was very upset with what the Vicar said about Tim. She shook her finger at the Vicar and said strongly, "You might know all about the devil Mister but that boy comes from better stock than you."

This shocked the Vicar. In forty years in the village no one ever spoke back to him. It shocked Mrs Warrington too and soon it was all over the village.

Tim was furious that the Vicar had been so unpleasant to his nana and he was eager to punish him back. The next day, after he had milked the cow and fed the pigs and chickens, he had his breakfast and got ready for school. His mum gave him a box of eggs and a jar of jellied eels to drop in to the Vicarage, which was the Vicar's house. Tim said nothing: he scorned his mother's attempt to placate the vicar. Instead he gave the eggs and eels to his teacher, Mrs Blackmore.

By this time the Vicar was spreading the story that Timothy Atkins was becoming a bad boy because he didn't have a father at home to punish him when he did wrong. When he heard this story Tim hated the Vicar even more. His father had never punished him for anything. His father loved him. Tim made up his mind to be really, really bad.

He explained his anger to his mate Bob Eckholm. In fact he even cried a little bit. Then they came up with a plan. The next Sunday Tim told a lie to his mum that he had to help dairyman Johnson with his hay because it might rain, so she excused him from going to church. Now Mr Johnson had old barns and inside the barns all the wooden doors had holes about knee high from the ground so that the half wild barn cats could move around catching rats and mice. He always poured half a bucket of milk into a pan for the cats after milking and then went home for breakfast.

Tim said to Bob, "I'll hold a sack over the hole in the door of the dairy and you go round the other side where the cats are drinking the milk. You clap your hands and yell SCOOT. All the cats will dash through the door hole and I'll catch them in the sack. Then we'll go over to the church and wait out the back till the service starts. I'll give the sack a good shake to make the cats good and fierce and then I'll let them out inside the door of the belfry up the back. Then we'll run away."

Bob liked the plan, even though he knew his dad would spank him when he found out about it. They did it. When the church bells had stopped ringing the changes and only the toll bell rang, to let everyone know the service would start in five minutes, Tim and Bob hid behind a great buttress in the church wall until the bell ringers could be seen heading off across the fields to "The Wheatsheaf" pub. After five more minutes they crept into the door of the belfry at the back of the church. Tim gave the sack a shake. Tumult began in the sack, claws came through the jute material which heaved amid the turmoil. Savage paws with claws extended waved furiously through small holes in the sack. Then he let the cats out into the nave. That is the main hall of the church.

The cats dashed out in a fury to escape into the open. They leapt off peoples heads trying to reach the windows and raced round the walls like trick motorbike riders. They knocked the candles down on the altar and tried to scramble up the pipes of the organ. Everyone screamed and the Vicar ducked down in his pulpit, quaking in fear; until someone opened the great oak door and the cats flew out into the vestibule like someone being fired out of a canon at the circus.

Boys were laughing, men were swearing (in church) and girls were crying; all except Susan Blackmore the teacher's daughter. Susan was laughing so hard she thought she would wet her pants. She guessed straight away who had pulled this crazy trick. She knew that Timothy Atkins hated the vicar and she thought Tim had good reason to.

The two boys ran away to the fen and rowed Tim's boat into a little side creek to wait until all the yelling in the village had subsided. Tim felt bad because he had told his mum a lie about helping Mr Thompson with the hay. Bob had used the same excuse and he too felt bad for telling a lie to his mum. Bob said,

"Well Tim, old Thompson is carting hay today. If we go and help him it won't be a lie, will it?"

So they rowed ashore and went to Dairyman Thompson and said they would help with the hay. He gave both boys a pitchfork each and they helped him until afternoon milking time. They worked hard in the hot sun loading wagons from piles of hay pushed up by a buck rake. Mr Thompson invited them in for tea and fruit cake before he and his wife did the milking. He said they were both very good boys. He hadn't heard yet about their mischief in the church. Thompson wasn't a church goer. He preferred to visit The Wheatsheaf.

As he plodded wearily home Tim knew in his heart that he had told a lie to his mum, even though he did what he said he would do with the hay, and he had also promised his dad he would be honest, and he wasn't.

Tim's mum was so ashamed of him. He cuddled her and promised he wouldn't do anymore bad things. He told her then that the vicar had insulted him by saying he was a potential thief just because he asked for a plumb. She knew about that but also that when Timothy promised something he would keep his promise, so she gave him a kiss and said "I know you are a good boy Tim. I know too that you don't like the Vicar, but revenge is a sinful emotion. Your father wouldn't like it."

Later that week she was walking home from work on the Robinson farm. He didn't give her a ride home for fear of starting rumours. A red Post Office van went by. The van hit a young magpie that was too silly to get out of the way. The poor thing was still alive but its wing was hurt. She thought, I'll take it home for Tim to look after. It will keep him out of mischief.

Tim loved all creatures and birds, even the rabbits and ducks that he caught, so he made a little cage for the magpie and fed it everyday. He gathered worms and snails and grasshoppers and he gave it bread soaked in milk. Soon the magpie started to get better and by the time he could fly again he was devoted to Tim and made a lot of noise when he saw him because he knew he would get fed.

Now magpies are naughty birds. They love any bright and shiny thing and they collect them and hide them in a tree or a shelf in a hay loft. Tim's magpie started off collecting the silver tops of milk bottles or bits of red paper or silver candy wrappers. Then he flew in the window and picked up some silver coins on the desk. Mrs Atkins couldn't remember where she put those coins.

Later on as Tim walked to school the magpie would sit on his shoulder and then fly home after he went in the classroom. Sometimes the magpie would see something bright in a house, like a shiny teaspoon and he would swoop down and pinch it. This tricky bird did this mischief for a year or two and everyone that lost things always noticed that Timothy Atkins wasn't far away when they lost their stuff, even wedding rings and jewellery. People began to remember what the Vicar said about Timothy Atkins and the rumour spread that Tim was growing up to be a thief. Boys were forbidden to play with him and so his only friends were Susan Blackmore and Bob Eckholm. The three of them couldn't figure out why everyone thought Timmy was a thief.

Then one day Susan actually saw the magpie swoop into her room and pick up a gold hair clip that her mum bought for her birthday. She watched it fly away. Straight away she knew it was the answer to the puzzle because she could see Tim fishing down by the river near her house and that's why the magpie was around. She raced down to the river and breathlessly told Tim that his magpie was the thief and that's why people suspected him.

This was mighty good news for Tim. "Susan, all we have to do is find out where he's putting all this stuff and we can give it back to everyone. Then they won't say I'm going to grow up to be a murderer or something."

They walked back to Tim's house with the fish he had caught, just a couple of pike that he would feed to his ferrets. The magpie flew down and landed on his shoulder so he cut off some pieces of the fish with his jack knife and fed it.

"Susan you go in and ask nana for a couple of bright buttons and we'll see where this crazy bird hides things."

As soon as the magpie saw the buttons he picked them up and flew into the hayloft above the stable. Tim and Susan climbed the ladder and saw him fooling around in a dark nook where the roof beams join the top plate of the wall. Tim climbed up on the hay and sure enough there was a treasure trove of spoons and rings and bits of bright paper and nuts and bolts and hair clips and jewellery, enough to fill a shoebox.

That Sunday in church Rosemary Atkins went to the lectern to read the first lesson from the bible, marked by a silk tape by the vicar. She paused before reading the lesson to address the village and she spoke boldly, with a hint of anger in her voice.

"Many people have said bad things about my son Timothy, that he was the naughtiest boy in Cripplethorne and a wicked thief. But Tim and Susan Blackmore have discovered that Tim's magpie is the villain. Today, after church we will display all the things the magpie picked up and the owners can reclaim their property and apologise in public for suspecting Tim.

'Here beginneth the first lesson, from Matthew five."

Then she read the passage from the bible that the Vicar had selected for the first lesson. He had been bothered by his feelings for revenge.

When the Vicar heard about the thieving magpie he felt ashamed of all the bad things he had said about Timothy Atkins. He couldn't sleep all night and he got out of bed to get on his knees to pray for guidance. He began to remember all the kindness and generosity the village had always shown him, especially the Atkins family. He realised he had been greedy and unkind and was ashamed of himself. The next morning he took his walking stick and his dog and hobbled up the lane for a mile to the Atkins farm. Tim was at school and Rosemary was away working for Farmer Robinson. Granny Atkins was doing the laundry, dunking clothes in the foaming copper with her copper stick. She was nervous when she saw him. Usually he only visited people when someone was sick.

"Mrs Atkins I come to you in shame and remorse for upsetting you about Timothy. God has shown me that I am a sinful, greedy and unforgiving man. If I had been kind enough to give Tim one of my plums a couple of years ago he would not have been angry enough to get up to all the mischief at that time. Please forgive me and accept my apology for being a sinful man."

Granny Atkins was astonished and speechless that one so high should apologise to her. She made a fresh pot of tea and gave the minister some oatmeal biscuits and then he hobbled away home, thinking he would write a sermon on forgiveness for next Sunday.

From that day life got better for the Atkins family. Tim's father Tommy came home from the war, but he had only one leg. The other had been lost in a battle in Burma. It wasn't a bad wound but by the time it could be treated it was too late and he lost his foot halfway up to the knee. He had a wooden leg but he was home safe and that was what mattered.

Very quickly life got back to normal for them. Tim was bigger and stronger now and could help his father more when his wooden leg was a problem, like pulling the dory up out of the fen mud. Farmers were using tractors sent over from America so horses weren't needed so much. Farmer Robinson paid for Tim and his dad to go to tractor school so they could learn how to fix tractors and machinery. It was a way to earn a living but they missed the horses and the old ways.

Rosemary Atkins didn't go to work on the farm now that her husband was home. Her cousin Elizabeth came down from Hull for awhile. She had lost her two brothers in France and she was alone at home. This sad woman eventually became friends with and then married Farmer Robinson; just in time to hide a scandal that had miraculously survived undetected in an English village.

Chapter Fifteen

WHERE'S GRANDAD?

The countryside had a pleasant aspect after recent rain and the arrival of summer. All the way from her school in Sydney to her home on a farm near Parkes in New South Wales the fields and forests were all shades of green as new leaves grew on the trees and crops grew in vast paddocks. Anna Keyworth could identify everything she saw from the train window. She knew the names of all the trees. She could tell which crops were growing in the fields and how well they were doing and she mentally ticked off the names of the various breeds of cattle and sheep she saw grazing behind the railway line fences.

High in the clear blue sky wedge tail eagles and kites soared, their keen eyes searching for small animals or a wallaby or snake, killed by a truck on the highway, not far away through the tall, white gum trees. She admired graceful white egrets, balancing on the backs of red brown cows before hopping down to catch a cricket or a frog disturbed by the feet of the cattle. Sometimes white cockatoos flew by, or flocks of pink and grey galahs, or bright red lorikeets, which fly at lightning speed.

She knew all this because since she was little she was always out with her grandad and he was never lost for an answer to the endless questions she had asked him since she learned to talk.

People used to see Tom Keyworth, along with Anna, riding by on horseback and they would grin and say, 'Why old Tom has a shadow, even on a cloudy day.'

Anna was his shadow.

She had cried bitterly when she went to school in Sydney. Her parents thought she should go to boarding school because the local high school was so far away and her mum was so busy on the farm she didn't have time to do home school. Anna missed her little brother Jonathon as well and her black and white border collie and her brown Welsh pony and helping her nanna bake pies and biscuits and bottling preserves.

Now her tears rolled down her cheeks as she realised how homesick she was. A lady sitting nearby said, "What's the matter dear? Are you ok?" Anna was embarrassed by her tears; she was supposed to be grown up now and would soon be thirteen. She smiled weakly at the kind lady and said simply, "Yes I'm fine, thank you. I just realised how much I missed home now that I'm nearly there. At school I'm always so busy with friends and study that I don't have time to feel sad."

The lady smiled and gave Anna a biscuit from a pack of Oreo cookies in her bag. Anna didn't really want the biscuit, she wasn't a cookie monster like she used to be but she didn't want to disappoint the nice lady by seeming indifferent to her concern.

As the train pulled into the station she saw her mum and Jonathon standing on the platform with her dog Butch, on a lead. She gave a little squeal of delight and was almost 100% happy until a little voice inside her asked 'Where's grandad?' She expected him to be there on her first return from school.

She would have asked her mum where grandad was and a dozen other questions about nanna and her pony, Beach Boy, and if there were new kittens or puppies on the farm. Anna's true nature was always bursting with excitement and curiosity but she had to force herself to be quiet when her mum was around because she hated it when her mum said in an irritated snap, "Oh be quiet, you little chatterbox." She knew she was a chatterbox; it was the impatient and annoyed tone that hurt her.

It's hard to be different from your true nature and Anna was a very inventive girl. Her brown pony was called Beach Boy, because she had once seen a boy on a beach who was tanned very brown, so it seemed natural to name the pony after him. And her dog Butch was such a pretty and clean black and white and so neat in his movements that she named him after the black and white butcher bird. She kissed and hugged her mum and squirming Jonathon and the velvety smooth ears of Butch. It was so good to be home. She decided that as she was on holiday she would forget about all the rules in her life, except about being a chatterbox.

Life was full of rules. Don't eat biscuits because they will ruin your teeth. Don't eat ice cream because it will make you fat. Don't get dirty because it's unhygienic. Wear your hat to avoid skin damage, blah blah blah. Don't rip your clothes off and swim naked in the creek; you are too old for that. Anna was so determined to break all the rules she could that she would have stamped her foot, except she was in the car. She couldn't wait to get out of her school uniform and put on her jeans and riding boots and a raggedy old drill shirt. It was a rule that you had to travel home in uniform, probably as publicity for the school, which charged big fees.

As they drove over the cattle grid onto the farm driveway her mum seemed to guess her thoughts. "Run over and see your nanna and grandad dear, while you still have your school uniform on."

Anna was going to do that anyway, so it wasn't another rule.

Her nanna was on the veranda of her cottage, waving as the car pulled up by the fence around the big house. As she dashed across, her school hat blew off and silly Butch snatched it up in his jaws and scampered around in circles and figure eights trying to get her to chase him and get it back. "To hell with the hat" thought Anna, "Butch will probably chew it up and I'll have to get a new one."

As she wrapped her arms around the broad hips of her nanna she could feel kisses pouring down on her head and she could smell fresh baked bread and coconut biscuits on her apron and then she reached up and kissed the soft pink cheeks as she was lifted off the ground in a bear hug. She was just about to rush in the cottage and find grandad when nanna sat down on a chair and pulled her close and whispered in her ear. "Grandad isn't well Anna. He has lost his memory so he may not know who you are. Sometimes he's just fine and normal and other times he can't remember which boot to put on his right foot. He had a fever just after you went to school and it seems to have hurt his memory. Just go steady with him darling until he gets used to you again."

This news shocked Anna so much that her face went white as a sheet and her knees felt as though they were trembling. Anger welled up in her that no one had sent her a letter or told her on the phone any hint that grandad had been ill. At that moment she didn't realise that the family had agreed to keep the news from her so that she could settle down at school. Her true nature welled up and she rushed into the cottage to find him. He wasn't there and as she dashed out again she saw him, down at the stables, brushing Beach Boy beside the saddle shed. She jumped down the four steps in one leap and ran across to the stables with her dog almost getting tangled up in her feet. She didn't notice her mum holding hands with nanna as they watched her anxiously as she ran up to grandad. He was ok and held out his arms for her as she jumped, sobbing with relief into his arms. They cuddled for a long time and then she took the body brush and carried on brushing Beach Boy as though everything was normal. But it wasn't.

Old Tom felt a warm glow in his chest as he watched his grand daughter brush the pony like old times. But he couldn't figure out why she had on those funny clothes; he had forgotten that she had been at school in Sydney for three months. He was brushing the pony because he thought she would come over. It must have been some sixth sense that told him she was coming back. He hadn't really missed her as each day blurred into the next. Now he felt uneasy as he watched her in strange clothes and taller than his shaggy memory could recall.

It was a good homecoming for Anna despite her shock at hearing her grandad had lost his memory. He was ok that day and almost normal except for being confused about her school clothes. She was a very intelligent girl as well as being full of passion and energy so she decided to act as though everything was as it always had been. She had an uncanny secret feeling that she could cure grandad's memory loss.

Soon she had unpacked her suitcase and had changed into her old blue jeans and red shirt with all the tears in it. Her mum wanted to throw that shirt away but Anna made such a fuss that she was allowed to keep it.

They all piled in the old, grey, Fargo truck to take some sandwiches and tea down to where her dad was planting fodder sorghum with his planting machine and a big red tractor. He was so happy to see her he jumped down from the tractor and ran over to hug her and give her a kiss and look down at her in delight with his big brown smile and stubbly chin and the smell of diesel on his overalls. They all sat down beside the truck and had a little picnic together, as they had done hundreds of times before. Then she got in the tractor and did a couple of trips around the paddock with him before going home with Jonnie and her mum. Dad didn't mind her being a chatterbox and she told him everything on her mind in two rounds of the paddock.

They all had supper together that night and then she went to bed, tired out after the long journey. As she drifted off to sleep she was thinking out a way to get her grandad's memory back.

The next day she got up at daylight and went outside to greet the day. The men had run the stock horses into the yard from the horse paddock and were selecting the horse they would use that day for mustering sheep. Dogs were barking, eager to go to work and down by the yards she saw grandad milking the house cows, like he always did. Anna was eager to run down to help carry the milk bucket but she stopped to say hello to the stockmen, Glenn Knight and Andy Rogers. As they led their horses out to the saddle shed Andy said, "Will you help us with the drenching Anna? No one is as fast as you."

"Not today Andy, I have to pay attention to grandad."

"That's good," said Glenn, "the poor old feller has had a rough time since you went away. Probably missed you Anna and couldn't remember why you weren't here."

Grandad seemed quite ok so she had breakfast with him and nanna and then asked if they could go for a ride. He looked a bit vague and forgetful but later on as they went across to the horse yard he brightened up and soon they were riding away, Anna on Beach Boy at a brisk walk and grandad on Blazo, his favourite chestnut horse with a white face and black mane and tail. They rode a long way without talking much and she realised he was just following her without really paying attention to the country and animals, as he usually did. Soon they came to the little house of an old aboriginal lady named Sarah, who had lived all her life on the station. She said this was her home country.

They always stopped for a cup of tea with Sarah so Anna got down from her pony and had another cuddle from her old white haired friend. While her grandad tied the horses to a timber fence she whispered to Sarah that he had lost his memory. Sarah nodded and said she knew about it and then she cupped her hands around Anna's ear and whispered, "I can cure it."

No one on the station knew, that years before their birth, Sarah and Tom Keyworth had been teenage lovers. Tom's father, great grandad George Keyworth had bought the land from the government and found living on it a small tribe of aboriginals. He didn't know what to do about them but they were a quiet peaceful clan so he just let them be. George was a God fearing man but quiet about it except for banning grog from his property and forbidding his workmen from contact with the blacks. It was rarely an issue except when shearing crews were on the place and he became renowned for enforcing his rules with fist and stockwhip. He sometimes had trouble getting shearers because of his iron discipline.

He had threatened to sack a man who was rumoured to be always on the lookout for gins along the creek. George surmised that such contacts would shatter the long and peaceful co-existence with the blacks. The man resented discipline, especially relating to his time off and the ban on rum. He was therefore delighted to find young Tom Keyworth copulating with a girl in the creek bed when he was out mustering bulls.

He couldn't wait to canter away to find George and tell him his son was 'dog locked' to a gin in the creek.

George was shocked to the liver and took off at a gallop to find his fourteen year old son. He was still in the creek, swimming in a billabong with Sarah as his father skidded down the bank in a fury and started cracking his stockwhip over his head. Tom fled up the other bank to find his horse but his father was on him and whipping him home with vicious cuts with the horsehair cracker of the whip on his bare back. The scars of that flogging stayed with him for life. He stumbled along for the two miles home, his bare feet becoming loaded with goat head burrs and his back streaming blood from the steady whipping.

Three days later he was banished from home for five years and sent off on an old horse to learn his lesson. "If you want the blacks and the grog boy you go find em, but don't come back here till you're a man," growled George mercilessly.

Later he regretted being so hard, especially when his wife fled and went back to England with his infant daughter. He tried many times to find Tom, without success. He had gone north to Queensland where he worked in sugar cane till the kanakas were hired then he went mining for awhile before becoming an overseer on a remote western cattle station. Here he worked for several years with black stockmen but he avoided native women and despised those who didn't. Seven years after being sent away he went home and was welcomed, like the prodigal son, by his ailing, sad and lonely father.

Sarah had married a man of her tribe and had two small children when Tom came home. Her husband was a good stockman on the place and a fine cheerful man. No one seemed to remember the circumstances under which he had left home and a few years later he married himself, before his father died. Families grew up, children left for the city and Sarah's husband died in a fight in town. She stayed on alone but cared for by Tom whenever she needed something. She became the last, much loved remnant of her clan. Her children came to visit from time to time but she never left her home country.

Sarah had a reputation for doing unusual things, like curing sick birds and knowing secret things. Anna believed her claim that she could cure grandad but restrained her impulsive eagerness to ask how she would do it. The old lady gave them some buttered damper and peach jam before she went outside to pick some leaves to 'flavour' the black tea. Before they rode away Sarah told Anna to come back every day for four days, at the same time each day.

On the way home grandad felt pains in his tummy and had to get down from Blazo because he thought he would be sick. After a while he came good and they rode on home. The next day they again rode back to Sarah and had tea and again grandad felt sick on the way home. Anna was sure that Sarah had put some mysterious ingredients in his tea. She said nothing but suspected Oleander leaves, which grew in her garden..

On the third morning grandad looked a bit hesitant and wanted to ride in a different direction. When Anna asked him why, she was thrilled to hear him say he didn't like Sarah's tea. "Aha" she thought, "Now he remembers that Sarah's tea makes him sick."

The discomfort from the tea never lasted until they got home but grandfather was becoming wary and wanted to ride in a different direction. To avoid suspicion Anna agreed so they went along down to the creek where they stopped to give the horses a drink. Sitting in the shade along the bank, while the horses cropped green grass along the waters edge Anna felt the peace and silence and remembered the many times she had stripped off and dived in at this spot. She had the urge to do it now but didn't want to embarrass her grandad. A flash of iridescent blue and gold caught their attention as a kingfisher alighted on a twig and bounced cheekily up and down a few feet away, admiring his own reflection in the water like the beautiful youth Narcissus.

"How I love this place grandad. So many times I have been swimming here with mum and Jonathon and climbing up the rocks to the falls. How blessed we are that it's been ours for four generations."

Grandfather nodded in a thoughtful, even sad way before he said. "Many generations of other folk loved it before us Anna. Sarah is the last one, poor old love."

It was in this very spot that he had come across Sarah and a toddler when he was a boy. He knew them both and Sarah dared him to swim. She was naked already so he tied his horse to a bush and stripped off to swim. They were frolicking around in the water, keeping an eye on the little one. When they came up the bank Sarah was as black and glossy as a seal, full of fun and laughing as he became aroused. She had seen adults having sex but Tom knew nothing except curiosity. On a log she coached him to her. He could recall his confused sensations and the electrifying culmination. They were soon playing in the billabong again until mounting desire brought them ashore, where the child was playing happily in the mud. It was the second copulation that the station hand observed and reported to Tom's father.

As he sat in the shade looking across the black water it was as if a veil had been lifted from his memory of that tragic day. Anna was concerned at the sadness in his eyes. She got up and pulled him to his feet to continue their ride.

He didn't seem reluctant as they rode on along to the south and approached Sarah's cottage. She was watering her flowers when she noticed them coming from the direction of the creek. She stood, tall and slender in her pale blue cotton dress and hugged Anna when she dismounted from Beach Boy.

"I thought you'd be all wet coming up from the creek on a hot day."

Then she gave Tom a hug and a kiss on his cheek and said with a cackle of laughter.

"You too Tom, you used to be as slippery as a platypus duck when you was a boy."

"People used to say you were as black as an eel in those days Sarah, and more slippery too." Tom was grinning at ancient memories and Sarah was giggling too, knowing he was sharing the same recollections.

As they sat on the little veranda he growled, "I don't know what you're putting in this tea Sarah but its givin' me a bloody bellyache."

"Well you get it down yuh old feller, this tea will smarten you up and stop you forgettin everything." She winked at Anna, who was grinning at the banter between them and feeling a deep contentment, like at the creek, because of this ancient friendship between people she loved.

Maybe it was Sarah that cured Tom Keyworth's memory loss. Maybe it was just time, the great healer. People claim all kinds of miraculous cures, from olive leaf extract to pawpaw leaf tea for cancer and sure enough some people do get well. Anna didn't care how it happened, she was just glad to have her grandad back again. She told him he'd better be at the railway station next time she came home from school or he would have an unforgettable memory to deal with.

She shared the secret of Sarah's tea with her mum and she was so pleased about it that she drove Anna all the way to Parkes where they bought the most fancy teapot they could find for Sarah and some new enamel camp mugs. Sarah didn't care for fancy tea cups but they knew she would love the pot.

So many happy things happened on that first holiday from boarding school but none of them could be shared with anyone else, especially that her mum quit calling her a chatterbox.

Printed in Australia
AUOC01n1550090816
278035AU00001B/1/P

9 781504 302838